I0614823

Devil's Dominion

by

Virginia Barlow

This is a work of fiction. Names, characters, places, and incidents are either the product of the author's imagination or are used fictitiously, and any resemblance to actual persons living or dead, business establishments, events, or locales, is entirely coincidental.

Devil's Dominion

COPYRIGHT © 2022 by Virginia Barlow

All rights reserved. No part of this book may be used or reproduced in any manner whatsoever without written permission of the author or The Wild Rose Press, Inc. except in the case of brief quotations embodied in critical articles or reviews.
Contact Information: info@thewildrosepress.com

Cover Art by *Jennifer Greeff*

The Wild Rose Press, Inc.
PO Box 708
Adams Basin, NY 14410-0708
Visit us at www.thewildrosepress.com

Publishing History
First Edition, 2022
Trade Paperback ISBN 978-1-5092-4448-5
Digital ISBN 978-1-5092-4449-2

Published in the United States of America

When he lifted his head, she protested. "Dragos."

His lids dropped over his eyes. "So, you know who holds you." He set her on her feet. Slowly, he unwrapped her arms from his neck and placed her hands on his chest.

She stood mesmerized by the rippling bronze of his skin wanting to run her hands over his body as he did hers.

"Does your rebel make you feel the way I do?"

Oh my God, Rauf! What am I doing? Rolayna stiffened and backed away from him. Without his heat, cold seeped into her bones, and she realized Dragos wore only his breeches. His tunic lay on the ground at their feet.

Her gaze roamed his chest and stopped on the spot where she stabbed him with her hatpin. There should be a wound or a mark, something to herald her attack, but neither were there. Confusion filled her mind. How could he be healed so quickly? She stabbed him yesterday. She glanced up at his dark eyes and the hunger within their depths, suddenly remembering her near nakedness. Rolayna shivered, trying desperately to cover herself with her arms.

"I…he…we…do…not…" she stammered.

He smiled. "I saw you together last night, and he wore only his breeches. He desires to have you."

Her chin lifted, and she stared up at him. "So, you admit he wants me for more than my gold?"

Dragos' lids dropped over his eyes. "I did not say so." He picked up his tunic. "Here, put this on." His gaze flicked over her one more time, lingering on her breasts before he tossed it at her…

Praise for Virginia Barlow

"The Witch of Rathborne Castle is a historical, paranormal romance… I was pulled in the by synopsis of the book but I was hooked by page one. The author created a magical, mystical world and I was enthralled as I read along."

~ *Reviews by Saph*

"This was a new author for me. The plot and storyline were very well done. Such a wonderful story. I would definitely try another book by this author."

~ *Net Galley Review The Wicked Sister*

"A Fallacious Seduction" is a must read for romance readers who love a good western!"

~ *In D'tale Magazine*

"If you're a historical western romance reader, you're going to love Wylder Bachelor. If you're a fan of feisty, independent heroines, pick up Wylder Bachelor. Highly recommend!"

~ *N. N. Light's Book Heaven*

Dedication

For Norma, our beautiful princess. Your smile makes the world a magical place.

Chapter One

Europe, Early Spring, 1702

She never saw it coming.

Lady Rolayna Seville rode through the forest in Papa's new carriage, humming as she went over the details of her forthcoming wedding. Her delicate silk dress came from France, as did her heavy lace veil. She would carry a knot of lavender wildflowers in her hand as she stood beside Baron Rauf Oliveander and took her vows. A sumptuous dinner would follow the ceremony accompanied by musicians and dancing. After which, an elegant cream cake would be served to celebrate their union. Everything would be perfect. She smiled and gazed up at the green canopy overhead. With her marriage, she gave her father the titled son-in-law he yearned for and atoned for her past sins. The unfortunate episode would be behind her, and she could forget it ever happened.

The carriage jolted, and Rolayna bounced off the red velvet seat. She righted her hat and glanced at her father.

In his early fifties, The Duke of Seville was a distinguished man with gray hair and blue eyes. Skilled with a sword and an excellent shot, he possessed a fit body, for he trained regularly with his men. Today he wore his best gray traveling suit in honor of the occasion. He did not appear to notice the interruption in their otherwise uneventful ride.

Frowning, she peered out the carriage window. Trees blurred past with the same serenity as before. Sunlight filtered through the branches, and birds called. The scent of rich dark earth and pine trees filled her senses. Nothing appeared amiss, so Rolayna returned to her musing, smoothing the skirt of her new rose satin traveling gown and ignoring the drumming in her chest.

Her fiancé possessed land, wealth, and titles and could keep her in the manner befitting her station. He commanded a large number of vassals and sat on the king's counsel. His blond hair, muscular physique, and startling blue eyes made him the most sought-after lord in the kingdom, as did his rakish air and knowing eyes.

Her heart fluttered, and warmth radiated through her body when he told her of his love and determination to make her his. Although theirs was a brief courtship, her answer flew from her lips. Nothing could be more perfect than being his baroness. For he possessed every quality Rolayna dreamed about and was the first man she met at court following her exile. The air crackled with excitement whenever he stood near, and anticipation of their union affected her appetite and made sleeping impossible.

The carriage bounced again, and her head hit the padded roof. "For heaven's sake! Horace must slow down, or I shall be a mess for our meeting with the baron." With every bump, her stays cut into her ribs and pinched the last remaining air from her lungs. Whatever man invented them did not design them with breathing in mind. A woman would be more creative and allow for such situations.

The duke frowned. "You make too much out of nothing, daughter. The road is rough from the recent rains. I dare say you will survive." Papa's top hat slipped to the side, and he righted it without further comment, gripped the head of his cane, and resumed staring at the opposite wall.

Rolayna gazed down at her hands. She hoped after today things would improve between them, for she missed Papa's smile of approval and yearned for the easy affection they once shared.

The carriage made a sudden turn, and she slid sideways across her seat, catching the handle mounted next to the window for support. Her head hit the roof again, and her hands went to the ostrich feather situated among the rose-colored blooms atop her new silk hat. She removed it and inspected the feather. It remained intact. Rolayna blew out a breath of relief. The hat arrived the day before from Paris, and she could not afford for anything to go wrong. They must slow down, but she knew better than to comment after her recent rebuke.

Peering out, she caught a glimpse of several black horsemen in pursuit of their carriage and jerked back out of view. Her heart leaped into her throat, and a rock settled in her stomach. Bandits! It *would* happen when she had to leave her sword home and dress like a lady.

The carriage wrenched forward, picking up speed, and her anxiety rose along with it.

They rounded another corner sending her sliding in the opposite direction.

Papa braced against the violent bolting but said nothing.

"Lavender wildflowers and cream cake," she

whispered flattening against the seat. Thoughts of her wedding eased the stone in her chest and calmed her racing heart.

Rolayna gazed at her father. "May I take the sword you have hidden beneath the seat? There are several men on horseback chasing us, and I refuse to be taken hostage or killed on such an important day."

Papa frowned. "Your imagination runs away with you. If there are bandits chasing us, the baron's outriders will vanquish them. There is no need to be concerned. Leave the battle to the men."

She stiffened her back and locked her knees, bracing against the violent jostling. Many a good woman died to the sound of those six words, and she had no intention of joining their ranks.

The carriage jerked as if the horses were whipped.

Horace's voice rang out. "Get along there!"

"Papa! This is serious. Bandits are upon us, and I need a weapon! Think of my dowry! They shall find it and take it if they succeed in stopping us."

He grunted. "I am confident in the baron's soldiers. They will protect us from any unpleasantness. They were *trained* for this sort of thing."

"Damn, damn, damn." She mumbled the words and bit the inside of her lip. The carriage rumbled and bounced at an alarming rate. *I am glad I removed my hat,* she thought and put a satin slipper on the seat opposite to brace against being thrown off. Her hand turned white where she gripped the handle, and tension tightened her jaw. She would never leave her fate to the men. If Papa would not retrieve his sword, she would improvise. Picking up her new hat, she plucked the ornate hatpin from the band and slipped it into the curls on top of her head. Such an item could do damage if wielded in the proper fashion. Captain Jameson, of the household guard, suggested it one day after blade lessons at Seville Castle during her exile and showed her how to hold it.

With a quick glance out the window, she noted the bandits closing in around them.

Papa leaned toward her. "I know you are frightened, but you need not be. The men with us know what they are about." He gave a deep sigh. "I would have your word you will not reveal your foolish fascination with swords and fighting to the baron before the marriage vows are spoken. I had to offer a larger dowry, as it is. This may well be your last chance to wed, and I will not tolerate failure. I hoped after a year of solitude at Seville, you would rethink your view on the duties of being a woman and put this unladylike behavior behind you. Your request for a weapon dashes my optimism."

His denial dashed hers, too. "It will not matter if I am ladylike or not if the bandits overtake us. We will be robbed and left dead beside the road." Rolayna pressed her lips together and crossed her arms, staring with unseeing eyes at the velvet curtains. She could help if he would let her.

Papa removed his hat and set it on the seat beside him before glancing at her in reproof. "You overreact, and I disapprove of any woman wielding a sharp object. Should there be bandits and the soldiers overpowered, I shall protect us."

She held the velvet curtain back from the window. "Take a look, Papa."

He leaned out for several long minutes.

The sharp crack of a whip shot through the rumble of the carriage wheels. The conveyance jolted, picking up speed.

The duke turned sharply to search the area behind them. Then, he jerked his head inside, reaching for the flintlock he kept mounted inside the carriage. "For once, you are correct. Keep down."

She lay flat against the velvet seat, gripping her hat to her chest. "Can you tell who they are?" Her pulse sped up.

The duke peered out the window again. "Men in black. I see nothing more except the baron's soldiers."

Shots sounded out on both sides of them. The duke leaned away from the window. The carriage careened to the left and then to the right.

Rolayna slid across the seat, bracing with her other foot. She held her hat in front of her to protect it, but the carriage threw her against the side, crushing it. Her muscles tensed.

"We have twenty soldiers riding escort, and I count six bandits in pursuit. All will be well." The duke held tight to his flintlock, his eyes on the window.

She wondered if Papa made the comment to comfort her or him, but his reassurance came too late.

The carriage careened again and hit a bump. The duke flew from his seat and landed on the floor with a thud as the carriage tilted precariously to the left, then righted.

Rolayna screamed.

A pair of heavy feet landed atop the carriage with a thud.

Dizziness washed over her, and black spots appeared.

The feet thumped to the front and stopped.

Papa stared at the roof of the carriage, lifting his flintlock in the air.

Her breath came fast, and a cold sweat dampened her brow. What if they were robbed? Murdered? Or both? Somehow, she must survive, protect her gold, and get to Rauf. She searched for her hat having lost track of it when the carriage tilted, and spied it a moment later, lying on the floor of the carriage, smashed beyond recognition. She bent to retrieve the article with a shaky hand as the carriage hit another rut and ended up in a heap on the floor.

Scuffling and a loud thump sounded overhead. A body fell from the roof of the carriage with a thud.

Rolayna scrambled to her feet.

The carriage jerked to a stop, and she fell back with a jolt.

The duke rose halfway to his feet and fell forward with the sudden halt of the carriage. His gun hit the floor with a thud.

Dust rolled inside through the little side windows making it difficult to see.

She coughed and sat upright, glancing around, as silence followed. Dabbing the fear from her brow with her kerchief, Rolayna folded it inside out and pressed it against her nose. The dust made breathing impossible.

The Duke of Seville scrambled to his feet and searched for his gun. "You will keep silent and trust me to handle this."

She took a deep breath to calm her racing heart. Objectivity required serenity so she gave Papa a brief nod of acquiescence.

The carriage door popped open, and Rolayna

turned with her handkerchief still pressed against her face. Alas, she did not gaze upon the blue and white uniform of Rauf's soldiers, but a highwayman dressed in black. He was the largest man she had ever seen and bronzed from the sun.

He held the door open with one powerful arm. A dangerous gleam shone from his dark eyes as he swept the interior of the carriage. Full lips lifted in a wicked smile as his gaze brushed over her before resting on her father.

Rolayna's breath left her body, and she swallowed, too terrified to move.

The bandit lifted a sword and pressed the tip against Papa's throat. "Get out."

She shivered to the soles of her slippers. She must do something, or this entire day would end up a disaster. "We shall not move until you tell us who you are and what you want." Her voice quivered from her trembling lips.

"Daughter, be still. I will handle this." Papa risked a glance in her direction.

Panic tightened her chest. She would never concede, never. Desperation filled her as she glanced around with frantic eyes. The flintlock lay on the floor at her feet, and she bent to pick it up.

The leader inclined his head at someone behind her, and Rolayna realized another bandit stood in the open door on the other side of the carriage.

A muscular arm appeared and pulled her out before she realized his intent.

She swung her arms wide and hit the unseen man in the head with the flintlock. Leaning back, she fumbled with the hammer of the gun with trembling hands. She knew how to do this, dammit. Why would her fingers not work? Her heart beat loud in her ears, and everything happened in slow motion.

Her attacker chuckled and pried the flintlock from her. He held her with one arm and tucked the weapon into his breeches.

Rolayna beat against her attacker's black-covered chest, bucking and scratching. She yelled every profane word she knew, but to no avail.

He carried her around to the other side of the carriage and set her loose.

She stumbled, furious her attempts to rescue them failed, and then stilled.

The new bandit matched his leader in size. He folded his huge arms over his chest and glared at her. Two more men dressed in black approached from the trees. They were six feet tall and as fit as the other two.

Rolayna dropped her gaze in terror. Good God! Who were they, and what did they want? Wiping the perspiration from her brow with trembling fingers, she stared at the ground and fought the panic. Even her sword would not be enough to face these giants.

Her gaze focused on an object at her feet. Realization pumped through her, and she fought the urge to be sick all over the ground.

The bodies of Baron Oliveander's soldiers littered the forest road around them. These few men defeated twenty of the baron's seasoned soldiers, and not a one sported a scratch.

Rolayna wilted against the carriage, gulping in air as tremors racked her body. She turned her head to stare up at the leader. Did he plan to kill them, too?

The bandit's lips turned up in a small smile before

he nudged the duke with his sword. "I said get out." His deep voice brooked no argument.

Papa climbed from the carriage and stood beside her, straightening to his full height. "How dare you stop me and hold us at swordpoint. What do you want of me?"

The leader resembled a demon from hell. Death and danger pulsed from his large frame, and an ungodly light shone from his dark gaze. He wore his midnight black hair tied behind his head with a thin strip of leather, and a black tunic fell open to the waist, revealing a tan, well-muscled chest.

"Let my father go." Rolayna squared her shoulders as she faced him.

His eyes, cold as the grave, terrified her. The glare he threw her way sent fear skittering down her spine. "I have questions and shall not release you until I get the answers I seek."

She opened her mouth to tell the leader what she thought, but Papa took her hand and squeezed her fingers, reminding her she gave her word to trust him. Her mouth snapped shut.

Rubbing her sweaty palms down the side of her new gown, she took a breath to clear her mind.

The bandit's expression gave no sign of his thoughts. "Where do you travel at such speed?" His deep voice rumbled from his chest as he narrowed his gaze on Papa's face. His manner said he would not hesitate to cut them down.

Rolayna stepped closer to Papa.

"What I do is none of your concern." Papa's chin rose in defiance.

The highwayman topped him by a head, yet her

father remained calm.

The demon pressed his sword deeper into her father's neck, drawing blood. "I will not ask again. Tell me the answer or die." His voice turned silky soft.

The duke's chin rose higher. "I am the Duke of Seville. I control the valley leading to the royal city of Evania. I—"

The devil smiled, pressing the tip of his sword a little deeper. "I know who you are." His metallic gaze flickered over his captive, unimpressed with Papa's importance.

Rolayna squeezed her knees together to keep them from shaking. Her father's pride would never allow him to back down or answer the bandit's question. If she did not speak for him, Papa would die.

Clenching her hands at her side, she stepped forward with her chin high. "We journey to Whitehall Abbey to meet with Baron Oliveander to sign my marriage contract." She ignored the quiver in her voice and the quaking of her knees.

Papa squeezed her fingers in reproof once more.

The leader glanced at her. "You carry a dowry, then?" His grin flashed white. "Check the carriage."

"You know who I am, and yet you dare rob us and threaten our lives? I am under the king's protection. Any act of violence toward me will be considered treason against the crown."

"There is a chest in the boot, Master," one of the men called as he carried the gilded chest around to the front and dropped it at the leader's feet.

They opened the lid, revealing a cache of jewels and gold coins.

The leader whistled softly. "This is quite a sum you

pay the rebel to take your daughter off your hands. Is she such a prize?"

Fury lit her blood, and Rolayna let loose her mouth. "Do not touch my gold. If you take one coin, I swear on every virgin saint I know, I will make you—"

"Hush, Daughter." Papa kept his gaze on the demons. "Let the devils have what they want. It is not worth our lives."

Bile rose in her throat as she forced back hysteria. "Not yours, perhaps, but it means everything to me." She turned to the bandits. "Baron Oliveander is not a man to anger. When he hears of this, he shall exact revenge, and you do not want him as your enemy. Leave the gold, and go your way. If you do, Rauf might overlook your insolence and let you live."

The leader gave a shrug of unconcern and turned to his men. "Take the gold and secure it."

She glanced at the leader's sword as blood trickled down the side of Papa's neck. What if he killed them? The bandit was the size of a barn. Her gaze slid to her father. He appeared old and frail compared to the giant in front of them. She would not stand here and allow this demon to rob her of her dreams and hurt Papa. She must do something. But what?

Rolayna glanced up at the devil who mocked her with knowing eyes, and she swallowed tightly. There must be a way out of this mess.

The duke drew the devil's attention. "My daughter speaks the truth. We meet with the baron to form an alliance. Once he realizes we have been delayed, he will search for us. He is a powerful man and will kill you for this."

"It is not your daughter he wants." The devil's lids

dropped over his eyes. "But the coins."

Rage filled her. Did the demon know what they said about her? "Rauf *does* want me. I am his heart's desire. He told me so." She lifted her chin and met the devil's wicked gaze. She had value, dammit, if not as a lady, as a person.

"I do not doubt he wants you, lady. You heat a man's blood with one glance. But you are mistaken about his intentions. Baron Oliveander loves your gold more than you. He will take your dowry and your virtue. Then, he will kill you."

She shook her head. "Rauf would never hurt me. He is a man of honor."

"He will not get the chance," the bandit promised, sheathing his sword. He turned to his men ignoring her. "Fetch the horses."

Rolayna did not think; she moved. A sword lay inches from her feet beside the fallen body of one of Rauf's soldiers. She grasped the hilt and straightened bringing the long blade in front of her. Wielding the sword with both hands, she faced the monster with her legs braced for attack. "Get back, or I will cut you to ribbons. Leave the chest and go before I change my mind."

"Daughter!" Her father's sharp cry sliced through the air. "For the love of God, child, let me deal with this before you get us both killed."

The devil turned and with one quick kick to the handle of her sword, sent it flying straight up in the air. He caught it with his other hand before tossing it to one of his men.

Captain Jameson's lessons did not include such a scenario.

Her lips twisted with anger and frustration.

The demon bandit leaned toward her. "Do not make such a mistake again. I do not fight women, children, or old men." His black gaze roamed over her, dismissing her. He gave an ear-piercing whistle, and two more men dressed in black appeared with two horses. They were as large as the first ones. "Tie the duke to his saddle. I shall take the girl. We go before the rebels realize we stole their prize."

Rolayna gazed in horror as one of the men picked her father up as if he were a child and set him on a black horse, tying him to the saddle.

"You make a terrible mistake," Papa said.

The leader walked toward a massive stallion, black as midnight. "I think not. I keep you from making one." He swung onto the stallion's back and turned to his men. "Azazel, Ramiel, take the duke's carriage two miles up the road and leave it. Create a trail in the opposite direction and meet us back at camp."

"Tell me who you are, or by the gods, I will hunt you down and kill you for the insult you heap upon my daughter and me this day. The king shall hear of this atrocity!" Papa stared at the bandit as he yelled his challenge.

The giant made a mock bow. "Allow me to introduce myself. I am Dragos, fifth Duke of Dragonthorne, Earl of Whitewater, and keeper of the north." His dark gaze locked with Papa's.

Her father grunted. "You lead a lawless bunch of cutthroats. I know of your evil deeds. The king shall look upon this as treason."

Rolayna's blood froze. Dragos! The devil stood before them with five of his disciples. Tales of their battles were legend. They were merciless, brutal, evil, and cunning. The mightiest, deadliest warrior in the kingdom held them hostage and robbed her of her dowry. Known for his ruthlessness and aggression, Dragos resembled a lethal arrow, skittering out of control. No one knew where his loyalties lay. Branded as a vigilante and loyal to his own code of ethics, he held the title as the most feared man on the continent, and his disciples a close second.

The demon grinned. "Allow me to introduce my disciples. The man beside me is Azazel, first-in-command and my explosive expert."

She glanced at the disciple he indicated. The man stood over six feet with dark hair and resembled a Greek God. He possessed a square jaw, straight nose, eyes the color of melted chocolate, and a perfect, sculpted body. He gazed at the scene with a watchful expression.

"The man beside you is Malphas, my second-in-command and a master archer. He can hit a moving target at three hundred yards with perfect accuracy."

Papa glared at the man holding the reins to his mount and grunted. He stood equal height to the devil. Though not as muscular, he was every bit as dark with startling blue eyes.

Rolayna's gaze swiveled to the man beside her.

"Lady, meet Hound, my master tracker. He possesses the unnatural ability to sense things and smells hidden from ordinary men. He can blend into the shadows and disappear without a trace."

Tall and muscular, Hound returned her regard with no expression. His black hair and dark eyes terrified her, as did the intensity of his stare.

"Ramiel goes with Azazel to create a trail for the rebels to find. He is my master blacksmith and forges weapons only a demon can wield. He is the short one." Dragos nudged his chin toward the retreating disciple. A muscular man with hair and eyes black as death disappeared into the trees with Azazel.

She shivered. "At court, they spoke of seven disciples."

"The others wait at camp. Brawn is an Irishman. He uses his fist for battle, possesses the strength of the devil, and keeps us well fed. Scimitar is my master swordsman. He knows every blade and fighting style. He walks with the silent feet of death. And Wolfbane is my master of poison. You shall recognize him by the green glow from his eyes. He came to me from a priest who dabbled in the black arts. He poisoned me for refusing to allow him to train as a disciple and cured me a few hours later. The man has the mind of a demon."

Dragos turned. "Now we are acquainted, we leave."

Rolayna closed her eyes and wished she were back within the secure walls of Seville Castle. Her mind ran rampant with stories told at court about their abductor and his famed disciples.

She brushed a strand of hair from her eyes with trembling fingers. "I am Lady Rolayna Seville." She did not know why she announced it. What did it matter to her what they thought?

Dragos spared her a glance as he spoke in quiet tones to Malphas but did not reply.

Despair filled her soul. How could this day have gone so wrong? Her only chance and that of her father would be to escape. She must get to Rauf!

Frantic, Rolayna gazed around. The urge to flee overtook her. If she could make it around the carriage, she would run through the trees and find her way to Whitehall Abbey. She stared at Dragos' back. She might have a chance if she were quick enough. She glanced at her father.

Papa shook his head, but she ignored him.

Inch by inch, she crept around the carriage, her gaze glued to the devil's massive back. She would find Rauf and tell him what happened. He would know what to do. She would be safe at the abbey with the priests, and Rauf would rescue her father. He would make the devils pay for what they did.

Rolayna made it two more steps before a giant arm caught her about the waist and lifted her high in the air.

Dragos slapped her down on his lap as he rode past her.

A scream rose to her lips. No one took her against her will. Her fingers found her hatpin, and she turned, aiming for the side of his neck. She stabbed down and discovered too late; her aim hit low. In her panic, she misjudged her target. The pin stuck in his chest and not as deep as she hoped. One inch would have to do.

He jerked back, and his great horse reared, throwing them both from the saddle.

She flew high, but the devil caught her and tucked her against his chest as his back hit the ground, protecting her from the fall.

Stunned, she sprawled across his giant body. The impact knocked the breath from her lungs. She stared into his impassive face, gasping for air.

"Master?" Hound towered over them.

Dragos rolled to his feet and brought her up with

him. Placing her on her feet, he glared. His eyes widened and focused on the front of her gown. "You are injured?"

Rolayna glanced down. Blood stained an area as large as her hand across the front of her bodice. She glanced back at him. "I feel nothing."

Fear flashed across his face as he grabbed the neckline of her gown and ripped it to her waist.

She screamed, her arms coming up to fend him off. Every terrible scenario of rape and violation she heard tearing through her mind in an instant.

Dragos gazed back at her. His eyes were the color of the midnight sky, but he did none of the things she feared. Instead, he pinned her arms and inspected the front of her.

Leaning back as far as she could, she searched with wild eyes for another weapon.

He ran his hands over her chest and tugged down the neck of her chemise to inspect her shoulders.

"What are you doing? Take your hands off me!" She struggled to get away, but he held her fast.

"Making sure you are not injured."

Hound appeared at his side. "She is unharmed, Master. Your blood has not mingled."

Relief crossed Dragos' face as he exchanged glances with his disciple.

Rolayna wondered about their silent communication as she glanced down to ascertain the damage. Her undergarments remained white, as did her chest. The blood soaked her dress and nothing else. Filled with concern for her immediate future, she stared into his eyes. "As you can see, I remain intact. No mingling of any sort occurred. Now unhand me." To her surprise, he did.

He let go of her shoulders and maintaining eye contact, he pulled out the offending pin, holding it up for inspection. "Hound, are you aware ladies carry little swords in their hair?" Blood ran down his chest, and anger glowed in his eyes.

"Nay, Master." A chuckle came from him as sunlight sparkled on the jeweled head of the pin.

Dragos tossed it behind him and laced his tunic, covering the wound. His gaze roamed over her.

Rolayna swallowed and took a step back. What other offenses did he have in mind?

He stared at her. "We go."

She wiped the sheen of terror from her forehead and gazed down at her ripped gown. "Do you plan to violate me or not?" The question burst from her lips without warning. She must know; the suspense made her anxiety over the near future unbearable.

They both stared at her as if she were crazed and then at each other in horror and disbelief.

"Nay, lady." Dragos' mouth twitched. "You should not believe every wild tale you hear in court."

Hound turned away and nuzzled his mount. But not before she caught sight of his smile.

Confused, she gazed from one to the other. "So, I am to be abducted and robbed but not violated. How reassuring." They thought the situation amusing while she hyperventilated with worry. She glanced down at the bodice of her new gown hanging in ribbons around her waist. "This will never do. How can I be taken prisoner without proper dress?" She must have spoken the words aloud for Dragos gave a snort.

"Ramiel carries your valise from the carriage with

him."

Rolayna glanced at him. "How convenient and thoughtful. I did not see him do it."

The horse behind them tossed his head and pawed the ground. "You were intent on stabbing me with your tiny sword." The demon patted the horse. "Stand." His soft word calmed the animal.

Her lips twisted with derision. Even the horse dare not disobey.

"Have you more trickery?" Her abductor gazed down at her with an expression as dark as the evening sky. He studied her intently. "We must make haste, or the rebels will be upon us. My horse runs like the wind, and any sudden movement on your part will mean your death."

She swallowed with her heart lodged in her throat. "Not at the moment." Her chin lifted. "But I shall."

He mounted the horse and caught Rolayna with one arm, settling her on his lap. "I do not doubt it, lady, not for one moment." He nudged the great horse to a full gallop. She caught the edge of the saddle in a death grip. Her captor's giant thighs bulged beneath her backside. One massive arm held the reins; the other held her against him. His heat warmed her through. The trees blurred past, and nausea rose in her throat. She leaned forward to put as much space between them as she could, but his arm tightened about her waist, dragging her back. He smelled of the forest and danger. He was all around her. Her breath hitched. Dragos. His arm burned her waist. Where did he take her, and what were his plans?

"Lavender wildflowers and cream cake..." She whispered the words over and over to calm her racing heart. She must keep her mind on the goal.

The demon nudged his horse faster. They raced up the side of the mountain, dodging trees and bushes. What a nightmare this day turned out to be. And where did Papa go?

Rolayna turned, hoping to see her father but could not. Her gaze met a broad expanse of black-covered chest and the bulge of muscle as he guided the giant stallion through the trees.

Ducking her head, she fought to control her wayward thoughts. What did he want with them? Dragos said he kept her father from making a mistake. The only mistake she could see he now committed. She shifted against him and slipped a little to the side.

He clamped her to him. "Have you a death wish? I warned you of the danger. Make no more movement, or I will leave you where you fall. You would not survive at this speed."

Icy fear trailed down her spine. What if he killed them in the woods somewhere? She forgot to ask if he planned to murder them. No one would know where they went. Rolayna trembled in terror. There must be something she could do. She searched the area around her again. There were only trees, and she did not know where they were. She thought of Rauf's smile and the way he teased her. She wanted to be in his arms, not the arms of this devil. She pictured Rauf's face to calm her racing heart. His wavy blond hair and warm blue eyes strengthened her determination to escape. All she wanted in life was to be by his side, be his wife, and make her father proud one more time.

The wind stung her eyes and nipped at her cheeks. She would not give in to the fear. She must keep her wits about her so she could escape. "Lavender wildflowers and cream cake…" she chanted. Rolayna stared at the trees as they rushed past. The stallion slowed as the slope grew steeper. The arm about her waist tightened. The horse leaned into the incline. Soon they were high on the side of the mountain.

At last, Dragos slowed his horse and guided it toward a small clearing. They trotted into the opening and stopped. She gazed about her with dismay. Three more giants stepped from the trees. One of them had red hair. They acknowledged their leader and glared at her.

"So you caught them." The red-haired giant stepped to the mount and gazed at Rolayna with disgust. "What are we going to do with her?"

"What we planned. Make sure she is well guarded. The hell-cat bites."

Chapter Two

Rolayna sat beside Papa on a large log until dinner. She changed into one of her clean gowns when Dragos indicated her valise sitting beside the tent behind her.

"You will sleep in there, lady." He turned to the duke. "You sleep beside the fire."

"I will stay in the tent with my daughter." Papa rose to his feet as he made his challenge.

Dragos shot a glance at Rolayna and nodded. "I will allow your insolence this once. Your daughter fears me and my men. Even though I gave my word, she would not be harmed." His dark gaze flashed over her.

Her face grew hot, and her chin came up. Frustration over her inability to think of a way out ruled her more than fear.

"Do not give me reason to regret my leniency." Dragos stared at her for a long minute before he returned to his meal.

The duke stood silent. "You have not said what you plan to do with us."

The men quieted, and the air thickened. Lean, muscular, and stealthy as apex predators resting before a hunt, they lounged about sharpening their weapons, watching the scene with interest.

Rolayna swallowed hard as her father stood proudly before the warrior, stubborn and demanding answers. He cared not the devil held the advantage in height, weight, and age.

Dragos straightened from his position beside the fire. "What difference would it make?"

"You could have killed us, and you have not." Her father did not flinch.

The demon sauntered toward them. "The night has just begun. Many things happen in the dark."

She resolved then and there she would not sleep but remain alert and defensive.

"I do not believe you intend to harm us, even though you killed twenty good men to capture us." Papa's gaze never faltered.

"Perhaps I wait for nightfall." Dragos stood a foot away from Papa and flexed his wide shoulders. His gaze shifted to Rolayna, wandering from her hair to her breasts and back up to her lips. Desire glittered in his eyes.

She dropped her gaze and shivered. Everything would be fine because Rauf would rescue her. Soon, this would all be a nightmare she forgot.

"I demand an answer. The act you do by keeping me here smacks of treason." Anger turned Papa's face red.

Dragos' eyes glinted. "Be careful what you say to me, old man. I am not the traitor. I come to end the rebellion, not fund it. I took your gold to keep it from falling into rebel hands. You rode with rebel soldiers and admitted you traveled to meet Oliveander."

"We spoke the truth." Rolayna's chin lifted defiantly as she met the devil's gaze. "Rauf is not part of the rebellion, and neither are we. We will accept your apology with the return of our gold." She held his gaze in challenge.

He studied them both for several heart-pounding seconds. "Come with me."

Papa stared at the devil and then nodded his head. They followed Dragos through the trees. Dusk fell, dimming the light filtering through the branches. The forest twittered with the sound of the birds. The smell of the earth and trees floated around her as she hurried to keep up.

Then, the foliage ended abruptly. They stood on the edge of a cliff, towering high above the valley below. Rolayna stopped quickly and stepped away from the edge. She pulled her father with her in case the devils meant to toss them to their deaths.

The demon's eyes flashed at her. He knew of her fear, and it amused him. "Look there." He pointed in the distance. A large army camped around Whitehall Abbey. The light of a hundred fires glowed in the semi-darkness.

"Oliveander and his rebels wait for you." The devil mocked them. "This is no casual meeting for the signing of a marriage contract. Tell me your true purpose here, and do not deceive me. The weight of your treasure is twice a normal dowry. Does your gold fund the traitor's cause?"

The Duke of Seville did not answer. He stared at the army in dismay. "We were unaware of any army. Why would the baron lie to me?" His words were low and thoughtful.

Dragos studied the older man. "Oliveander seeks the throne. With your gold, he can buy mercenaries. With your daughter as his wife, upon your death, he commands your armies and the entrance to the royal city. He will challenge the king once he has what is yours. Look to the east. The smoke you see is the remains of Chandler Castle. Mark the carnage the rebels wreak in their path."

Rolayna peered in the distance. It could not be. The fields and cottages surrounding the castle blazed with fire, and thick black smoke rose to the sky. Her eyes grew wide at the destruction. Everything lay in ruin.

"There must be a reasonable explanation. I know the baron. He is kind, gentle and would never do such a thing. He does not need my gold or Papa's men. And he would never challenge the king. Someone else did this. Rauf did not." She searched the distance. Her fiancé possessed wonderful qualities and a great amount of power. He could not be involved in the destruction before her.

She turned away, sickened. Whoever led the army could not be Rauf. Dragos deceived them, as devils do. Perhaps the army surprised her fiancé. He could be a prisoner in the abbey. Perhaps he fought to escape as she did. One thing she knew: Rauf would come for her because she held his heart. Rolayna marked the army's location in her head. If she escaped and made it to the abbey, she would be safe. The priests would take her to Rauf. She glanced at the demons beside her. They were too large for her to handle. Tonight, she would slip away while everyone slept.

"Try it, and I will rescind my word to your father." The words warmed the inside of her ear. She swung around to face Dragos.

"What word?" She kept her voice even to mask her fear. He stood too close. The heat of his body burned her. Rolayna took a quick step back. He frightened her more than she cared to admit. If he touched her, she did not know what she would do. Swallowing, she took another step back.

"The promise not to bind you. I admit, the thought bears consideration."

His words sent cold chills through her, and she glanced at him sharply. Did he jest? The hoods of his eyes shielded his thoughts from her view.

"This army is a day's ride from Seville Castle. They will be there on the morrow, and I must get to Seville before the rebels do." Papa turned to Dragos. "I demand you release us. We have nothing to do with this rebel army, and my people are in danger. I must protect my castle and those who rely on me."

"I cannot. The risk is too great."

"If I cannot leave, let my daughter go. She can see to the people. This is nothing to do with her."

"It has everything to do with her. She is in greater danger than you. Oliveander cannot leave either one of you alive."

Rolayna stiffened and put her hands over her ears. "I will not listen to more of this. I love Rauf and cannot entertain further defamation of his character. I wish to go back to the clearing." She turned to go.

Dragos' eyes turned metallic. "Heed my warning, or you shall rue the day. Baron Oliveander is evil. He will kill you both and challenge the king. Many will die, and you shall have no one else to blame." He turned away.

She angered him with her defense of Rauf, but did not care. Her marriage mattered most.

The disciples led them back to the clearing.

Papa remained quiet most of the evening.

Rolayna sat beside him, staring into the fire, her

thoughts wild. She wished they were back at Seville instead of here, dining with the devil. The gods must still be punishing her for the unfortunate episode. What else could it be?

The disciples caught several rabbits, and Brawn cooked them.

She had no appetite and picked at the meat when he placed it before her.

"How long do you plan to hold us hostage?" Papa asked.

"Until the danger is passed." Dragos did not glance up. He sharpened a blade before the fire. The metallic scrape of his blade stretched Rolayna's nerves to the breaking point.

"I wish to lie down." Jumping to her feet, she hurried toward the tent to get away from the demons so she could think. Everything hinged on her wedding to Rauf, her relationship with Papa, her good name, and her position in society. Once she regained them, she could go where she pleased and make new friends. This marriage must take place.

She closed the flaps to the tent and changed into her split gown. Papa would be furious when he discovered she did not burn it as he commanded. Made like a regular gown, her split gown had a seam up the middle of the skirt, resembling a pair of men's breeches with the fullness of a gown. With them on she could straddle horses, fight, and run without the encumbrance of all her skirts. Once she finished changing, she stuffed her petticoats and skirts back into her valise and climbed beneath the furs.

Papa came later and lay down with a sigh. He thrashed around for some time, and Rolayna wished she could comfort him but did not dare. He would be furious if he saw her split gown.

The night grew long and cold. Rolayna fought sleep and jumped every time a twig snapped or a creature scuttled past. Eventually, exhaustion overtook her, and she fell into a deep slumber.

She awoke with a start in the wee hours, sensing something wrong. The wind whistled around her and chilled her to her core. Groggy with sleep, she pulled her covers higher and tucked her head beneath their softness. She shivered. Did the fire go out? Where were the servants? A branch snapped near her head, and her eyes popped open.

"Lady."

The soft word drifted toward her through the wall of her tent.

Rolayna sat up. She glanced at the pile of furs on the other side of the tent where her father slept and discovered them empty.

"Lady. You must hurry before we are discovered."

Rising to her feet, she crept toward the voice. "Rauf?" Hope fluttered in her chest like a butterfly preparing for flight.

"He sent me. I am to escort you to him."

She did not wait for further invitation. She knew he would come for her! Gratitude and relief filled her trembling body. "Is my father with you? We must take him with us."

A knife slit the fabric of the tent, and Rolayna faced a thin soldier dressed in Rauf's colors. He held a hand toward her and helped her through the narrow opening.

She smiled her thanks. "Where is my father?"

The soldier shrugged. "My orders were to fetch you."

She shook her head. "My father must come, too. His life is in danger. He is not inside the tent, so we must search for him." She turned to walk away, but the soldier stopped her.

He took hold of her arm. "The baron sent someone else for your father. Come this way, lady."

A shrill whistle split the silence of the night, and men scurried to obey.

"Hurry. They know we are here."

The noise in the camp increased as battle ensued.

Rolayna stood torn between the hope of rescue and loyalty to her father. "What about my father?"

"He left before us, lady, and is safe. Come, we could be discovered any minute."

She hurried after the thin soldier as he disappeared into the dark forest toward his waiting mount.

****

An hour later, they rode into a clearing before a little wooden hut. Candlelight fell from the windows onto the grass beside the hut.

The door opened when the soldier knocked, and Rolayna followed him inside.

The cottage contained a rough-hewn table with four wooden chairs, a bed made of the same material as the table covered with a bright patchwork quilt, an old man with gray hair and a long nose, and a gray-haired woman stirring a large pot over a crackling fire. Two more soldiers wearing Rauf's colors sat at the table eating a thick stew and drinking ale. They looked up from their dinner. "You have her. The baron will be pleased."

Rolayna'a gaze swung to her rescuer. "Papa is not here. We must go back."

The men exchanged glances. "The baron is taking care of him. Do not worry. You are to remain here until the baron comes." They indicated the large bed. "Get some rest. You will need it." Snickering, the men returned to their meal.

Rolayna glanced at the bed and then at the old couple. Neither one met her gaze, and tension filled the air. Were they unwilling hosts? She searched the old couple's faces but found no answer.

"Fetch us some more ale." The soldiers commanded the old woman before turning to question her escort. "Were you followed?"

The soldier shook his head. "The demons were busy with their swords. They will not survive the night. The baron sent a platoon to finish them off."

Her heart beat fast. She warned them not to trifle with Rauf, but they chose to ignore her and paid with their lives. With a shrug, she wandered over to the bed and sat down. Dragos and his band of demons would no longer plague Evania. Relief filled her chest, and the horror of yesterday disappeared. As soon as her father and the baron arrived, they could finalize the details of the contract and go home. Papa would appease the baron over the loss of her dowry, and her plans of redemption would come to fruition. Rolayna lay down and closed her eyes. Within minutes, she drifted off to sleep.

"Lady." Someone shook her arm.

She turned her head.

The old woman crouched beside her. "You must leave while they sleep." She indicated the soldiers, frowing with concern.

Rolayna sat up and glanced toward the soldiers. The men lay sprawled across the table and on the floor. The old man slept on the floor beside the fire, which no longer burned bright but glowed with embers. Several hours passed while she slept. She glanced at the old woman. "I will wait for the baron. He will see me to safety." Lying back, she closed her eyes.

"Lady, you should go. The soldiers said—"

She did not get the chance to finish for the door opened, and Rauf stepped into the small hut followed by three more of his men. "Tell the others to keep guard." He spoke to someone behind him as he entered and removed his cloak. He hung it on a hook beside the door and advanced, dwarfing the hut with his size.

Rolayna's heart sped up. Lord, his handsome face made her stomach flutter with excitement. She rose to her feet. "I knew you would come."

Her voice drifted across the space between them, and Rauf turned in her direction. His gaze searched her face and form. "My dear, I am glad to see you unharmed." His smile faltered when he gazed at her gown. "What manner of dress is this?" He caught her skirt and pulled it sideways, revealing the seam in the middle. "The demons force you to wear wide breeches as if you were a man?" Anger and disgust deepened his frown. "Have they touched you? Tell me you are yet a virgin."

Rolayna gave him her best smile to get his mind off her gown. "They did not. I am pure still."

Rauf's face relaxed. "We shall find you something decent to wear as soon as we are able. For now, come my sweet, and kiss me."

She gazed past him. "Is Papa with you?"

He shook his head. "Do not worry about your father. He is where he should be, and everything will be all right. For now, let us focus on being together."

He turned to his second. "Get out, and take the men with you. I want to speak with Lady Rolayna alone. Do not bother me unless it is urgent."

His second roused the men and ushered them from the room.

The old woman gave her a worried look and hurried to wake her husband.

The baron strolled to the fire and held his hands to the heat. "You there." He motioned at the old woman. "Get me some ale, and then get out. Take your husband with you."

Rolayna took a step toward him, concerned the soldiers would add more bruises to the ones visible on the old woman's wrists. "She should stay. We must not be alone until after the contract is signed. My reputation is at stake."

Rauf turned to face her with a smile of tenderness. His hot gaze roamed her body from head to toe. "I have missed you."

Heat filled her face at his lengthy inspection. "I missed you, as well."

He stared at her breasts and then her lips. Desire and determination darkened his face. "We are to be married, my darling, and have your father's blessing. There is nothing wrong with being alone."

He motioned for the old lady to stay. "But you are right, of course. I have been crazed worrying over you. I yearn to hold you in my arms and ensure you are recovered from your ordeal. Come to me, my love. I hunger for your kiss."

Rolayna hesitated. His manner and urgency surprised her. They shared one chaste kiss before this, and the intensity of his gaze frightened her. Dragos' words played across her mind.

He loves your gold more than you. He shall take your dowry and your virtue. Then, he shall kill you.

"I am relieved you found me. For a time, I worried I would never see you again." Her gaze dropped to his tunic, and she froze.

Blood splatters covered the front of him.

"You were in battle? Are you injured?" His men came without him to fetch her. Where had he crossed swords, and with whom?

The baron frowned. "If my tunic upsets you, I can remove it." He loosed the tie and slipped the offending cloth over his head.

Rolayna's gaze roved the expanse of naked chest before her. His golden hair curled in the flickering light of the fire. The muscles of his chest and upper arms gleamed and rippled. She swallowed a tight breath as propriety twisted her stomach. Her gaze rose to his, and she took a step backward when she read his determination. First Dragos, now this.

He strolled toward her. "There is no need to be afraid. I shall not hurt you."

His arms closed around her and turned her in his embrace.

Before she realized his intent, his full lips descended and covered her own. She opened her mouth to protest, and Rauf took advantage of her hesitation, slipping his tongue between her lips. He stroked her tongue with his while his hands roamed her body. Heat flooded her veins. Her stomach tightened, and her knees grew weak. She wrapped her arms around his neck and held on tight. No man touched her this way, and warmth filled her belly. The baron's proposal came after two weeks of escorting her to various functions. He remained attentive and pleasant throughout their brief courtship, exhibiting none of the passion consuming him now.

Rolayna floated on a sea of unreality. After such a trying day, she should be ecstatic to be in his arms, but something in his manner made her hesitate.

His hand cupped her breast and squeezed. The other hand tugged on the laces at the back of her gown. "I want to see you and taste you."

Panic closed over her like a dunking in a frozen pond. She stiffened and removed his hand. "You must not take liberties until after we wed. What if Papa comes in? I made one mistake which cost me his approval. I have no intention of making a second one."

Rauf's flushed face darkened. "Approval and honor are a man's concern. You are a mere woman. No one will think less of you."

She stepped out of his arms, staring at him. "A *mere* woman?" The urge to strangle him tightened her hands to fists as she backed away, shaking her head in disbelief. Anger stiffened her spine. "I will not lie with you until after the wedding." And even then, not until he changed his mind about her worth. Her knees knocked together as she met the intensity of his frown.

"I did not mean to offend you, Rolayna. Your father assured me you had a delicate nature and to avoid discussing your marital duties until after the ceremony." His gaze swept over her. "You must know the effect you have on me. Since I first laid eyes on you, my desire for you has been difficult to control. But do not fear. I will be gentle when I make you mine."

She dared not speak, for her delicate nature would no doubt burn his ears with her thoughts. "And what shall these duties entail?"

He studied her face for long moments. Then, his demeanor changed, and his voice softened. In a flash, he became the charming man she met at court as he stroked her cheek with gentle fingers. "I apologize if I frightened you. Such is not my intention. I love you, my darling, and yearn to make you mine in word and deed. You cannot imagine how I felt when I learned of your abduction. Rage filled me as never before. No one takes what is mine and lives. Visions of you in the arms of the demon as he ravaged you filled my mind. I made the decision to marry the second I had you back, and this is what I shall do. I will not rest until I possess every part of you."

A disturbance by the door caught her attention.

Men shouted, and horse hooves pounded the ground outside the little hut as the clash of metal rent the air.

The door burst open, and Dragos entered the room, breathing fire.

Azazel followed him inside, holding a broad sword, dripping with blood.

The devil's gaze swept the interior of the hut before falling on Rauf and Rolayna, facing each other in front of the fire. His eyes narrowed on Rauf's naked chest before sweeping her face. He swung his sword and advanced as he stared at Rauf. "Azazel, see the lady to safety."

"No! No! No!" She cast her frantic gaze around the barren room for a weapon vowing she would never be a captive again and spied the poker beside the fire. Grabbing it, she swung it around in front of her as if it were a sword. "Stay away!"

The battle outside burst through the door, filling the small space with men swinging swords and swearing. Chaos reigned.

Rolayna ducked when a sword swung toward her head and dropped to her knees. The tip of another sword sliced her upper arm. With a cry, she crawled beneath the table to get away from the fighting.

Boots stamped, and men cursed. A body fell and then another.

She held the poker with a death grip, kneeling on the dirt floor and waiting for an opportunity to escape. Her breathing accelerated while her heart beat in her ears.

Her opportunity came sooner than she supposed.

Dragos caught her arm and dragged her from beneath the table.

Rolayna screamed in protest. She brought the poker up to strike him, but he knocked it away with his sword. She turned to run, but he caught her to him and fought his way to the door. Tossing her on his great black horse, he mounted behind her, sheathing his sword.

She beat him with her hands and bucked against the iron band of his arm. "Let me go!" Rage filled her, and she cared not where she struck him.

"Nay. This is for your protection and the good of Evania." Catching her hands in one of his, he urged his mount into a gallop.

They raced through the forest for what seemed like hours. Her battle with the devil had but begun, and what became of her father?

As the first rays of light lit the dark forest, they cantered into an open field. A magnificent castle stood before them, glistening in the early morning sun. Dewdrops clung like diamonds to the emerald leaves of the trees, and birds chirped high above her. The scent of fresh grass and the heavy perfume of wildflowers filled the air. The breeze warmed as the sun rose.

"Where are we?"

Dragos trotted to the deep moat surrounding the castle and whistled up at the guards in the tower. "Chattam Castle."

Rolayna sighed and dropped her head. The Earl of Chattam hated her father because the king favored him. Envy and greed made him their enemy. She would find no sympathy within these walls.

The metal portcullis rose, and the drawbridge lowered. "Do you know where my father is?" she asked in despondence, not expecting an answer. If Drago recaptured her, maybe he held her father, also.

"Nay."

She shivered. "Is he alive?"

"I know not."

They rode into the inner court where the Chattam soldiers stood at attention.

The earl stood on the door stoop with a frown of disapproval.

Rolayna slipped to the ground as soon as Dragos dismounted. She would escape this mess and right her life. Her chin tilted up as she followed her captor to greet the earl.

"Is this the girl?" The earl's old gray eyes swept over her and returned to Dragos. "She is Seville's daughter and bears the haughty gaze of her father." Contempt laced his words.

"You shall keep your agreement." A threat of steel lay beneath the words.

The earl recognized it and nodded with a twist of his thin lips. "This way."

They showed her to a sparse chamber with nothing but a bed, a chamber pot, and a water basin. Rolayna kicked the bedpost. Nothing here would serve as a weapon.

"Rest, lady." Dragos' eyes mocked her. "I told them to remove everything but what is before you. I sent Hound to find your father. I will return when I have news." He bowed from the waist and walked away to speak with the guards outside her door in quiet tones.

They glanced at her, nodded, and took up their positions.

Weariness filled her soul, and worry tightened her brow. Where would her father be? Rolayna wandered to the window and gazed out over the acres of greenery. She went over every detail of the previous night. Rauf would come for her again if he lived. She brushed a hand over her lips. He kissed her with surprising passion and determination. If Dragos had not interrupted, she did not doubt she would be married by now and bedded. So much for her detailed wedding. She loved Rauf for wanting her so much, but his aggression concerned her. Perhaps fear of losing her made him so. Not greed, as Dragos suggested.

Dragos. Once again, he held her captive.

She climbed on the bed and closed her eyes. She

must have dozed off for suddenly the door to her chamber swung open, frightening her. Rolayna jumped to her feet.

Dragos stood there, staring at her and frowning.

"What do you want? Have you found Papa?" She did not care if she sounded ungracious and cold.

He entered the room and closed the door behind him. "The duke left in the night before the fighting started. I sent Ramiel to see to your safety when Oliveander's men attacked. He followed you to the hut in the woods and reported back to me. Hound found your father's tracks going toward Seville. He and Azazel will escort him back." He strolled toward her and stopped a foot away.

Rolayna stared at him. "You lie—"

He caught her chin and pulled her face to his. "You will trust my word. I have no use for liars." The glint in his eyes told her he spoke of her past, and she dropped her gaze.

He knew of her folly. She took a step back, bumping into the bed. "I only meant—"

"Your father is in danger. Whatever befalls him is on his head, not mine. I warned him of the peril, and he chose to ignore my words. Know this. If I find he joined forces with the rebels, I shall kill him." His tone softened as his gaze wandered over her face. "Did Oliveander compromise you as you feared I would?"

Her gaze jumped to his, and anger filled her bosom. His remark hit too close to the truth. How dare he pretend he cared when he threatened to kill her father! "Such a thing is none of your concern."

A smile touched his full lips. "Ahh, but it is." He rubbed a thumb over her lips. "You are under my protection, and I require the truth."

Heat filled her cheeks. "Not every man thinks as you do."

He dropped his hand. "How would you know what I think?" His metallic gaze met and held hers. "Tell me true."

"No." The words spilled from her mouth as if he compelled her to answer.

"See? It is not so difficult to speak the truth, is it?" He left before she could think up a reply.

Chapter Three

She sank onto the bed as soon as Dragos left the chamber. Her mind returned to her previous worry. Why would Papa leave in the night? She choked on the sudden tightness in her throat. He planned to leave her since yesterday. But why? She thought he refused to leave her side through the night to protect her from the demons but now understood he did it so he could escape. Rolayna stood still. What did he place so much value on, he risked his life to rescue? Her mind sifted through their belongings and the people of Seville Castle and stopped. The child!

Papa spent his leisure time with his ward, Alex, an orphaned five-year-old boy with dark hair and big blue eyes. Did Papa risk his life for the boy? Or something else? If he would but confide in her, she would find a way to help him. But confidences stopped when her exile began. The incident involving the Duke of Emberly was not her fault. Not entirely. Christina DeGant, now the Duchess of Emberly, and the other members of the *Thorns of the Rose* were as much to blame as she. Rolayna paced and rubbed the scar on her wrist. Her oath kept her from explaining the truth.

What if Papa did not come back?

She must come up with a plan. She would not wait to see what her captors planned to do next. If she could get to Rauf, he would take her away from here. Doubt crept along the edge of her mind as she re-lived their last meeting. Rolayna bit her lip. Passion should be part of marriage, and Rauf backed away when she refused him. Another worm of discontent wiggled in her head. His comment on her choice of gown worried her. What if marriage to him turned out to be as restrictive as being Papa's daughter? Would he require her to remain silent and speak only when invited to do so? Would he force her to ask permission to leave the house or have friends?

Rolayna stared out the window at the grassy countryside. Marriage to any nobleman brought stiff rules and requirements. She would be a fool to believe Rauf any different. And Dragos' claim Rauf meant to take her money and kill her? She paced back and forth. She would keep her sword close by and her eyes open for treachery. She knew a woman at court who married an earl. After she produced an heir, the earl granted her a house, a monthly allowance, and servants. The woman did as she pleased. Rauf possessed a pleasant disposition. Perhaps he would allow her the same freedom once they wed. But first, she must escape and find Papa.

Rolayna frowned at the dirt on her hands. She spotted a stream running near the castle on their way through the forest yesterday. If she demanded a dip in the spring, the guards would leave her alone while she did so. She could escape and hide among the trees. A slim chance remained she could be in Rauf's arms by nightfall.

Encouraged, Rolayna stepped toward the door and spoke with the guard.

"We can carry a tub to yer chamber. The lord will

not allow you outside the wall."

Disappointment tightened her chest. On impulse, she pushed up the sleeve of her gown, revealing an angry red wound she received from the tip of a sword in the battle last night. "You are too clever for me. The real reason I request a visit to the stream is this fearsome wound. The herbs I require grow along the banks. I must collect them to prevent infection. If I do not dress it soon, I fear what shall happen to my arm."

The guard glanced at her wound. "Lord Dragos left an hour ago with his men. Ye must wait until he returns."

Hope bloomed for the first time since the carriage ride. "You could escort me. You are such a strong man and so intelligent, I would not dare try to escape with you close by. I promise to be quick. I spotted the herbs I require from my window." She gave him her best smile and waited. Few men could resist her charm. She learned as much from her time at court the previous year.

"All right."

He led her from the castle and across the moat.

Once they reached the edge of the forest, Rolayna spoke. "I see what I require beyond those trees. I do not wish to tire you with my silly errand. If you give me a minute, I shall fetch it."

The guard leaned against a tree to catch his breath. His protruding belly would prevent him from catching her.

With a sweet smile in the guard's direction, she sauntered through the trees until he could no longer see her. Then, she picked up her skirts and ran as fast as her legs would go.

The corset restricted her breathing, and after a few minutes, she stopped to suck in some air. Damn the current fashion in women's undergarments. How could she outrun even an overweight soldier if she could not breathe?

The gurgle of running water caught her attention. She found the stream!

Rolayna hurried toward the sound, making her way through the bushes. Dragos would send Hound to track her once he knew of her escape. If she floated in the stream for a bit, she could mask her trail, giving her time to get her bearings and find a way to Whitehall Abbey. Once she found Rauf, they would find Papa. When she reached the water, she sank to her knees beside a large oak. Her body trembled, and her stomach rolled. Freedom lay at the foot of the mountain, and exhileration lifted her spirit. Leaning forward, Rolayna splashed the cold liquid on her heated face and took a drink to wet her dry mouth.

A cool breeze carried the scent of pine and wildflowers. Gazing about her, she sighed. No one followed her. She took another sip of the crisp cold water and took several deep breaths to calm the racing of her heart. She gazed down at her gown. If she crossed the stream like this, she would be wet and cold all day. Not to mention, the weight of her skirt would drag her down. Rolayna untied the laces at the back of her gown and let it fall to the ground. She removed her slippers and her stockings. Then she undid her corset and dropped it beside her gown. Good riddance. Quickly she stripped off her split skirt and rolled her clothing into a bundle. She wore nothing but her thin silk chemise and drawers. She gazed at the rolled-up clothes. She did not want to be found in her undergarments. At the same time, the weight of the clothing would slow her down. Rolayna pulled the corset free, tossed it into the bushes, and clasped the remainder in her arm.

She stepped into the cold stream and gasped. The icy water cooled the heat of her flesh. Gritting her teeth, she waded deeper. The water hit her stomach, and she sucked in a breath. It was as cold as a witch's teat. She took another step. The pebbles beneath her feet rolled as Rolayna inched forward. Suddenly, the current caught her and pulled her under. She went down with a large splash and got a mouthful of icy water. Her bundle of clothing slipped from her grasp and disappeared. She kicked frantically as the water closed over her head. The frigid temperature made breathing near impossible. As water filled her mouth and nose, panic set in. She clawed and kicked to get her head above water. The freezing water paralyzed her lungs, and she could not get the air she needed. Her feet touched the bottom, and she kicked with all her strength. Her head came up, and she sucked in a much-needed breath of air before the current tugged her under again. Several times she came up for air until the stream widened, and the swiftness of the water slowed.

Rolayana rolled to her back and gazed up at the sky, breathing deep with relief No sign of Chattam Castle, Dragos, or the guard appeared. Satisfaction settled in her chest. She floated for some time, happy with her success and content to enjoy the serenity of the stream and the blue of the sky. After a while she grew curious about the distance she came and searched for a place to climb out.

The banks of the stream towered over her, and the roar of a waterfall pounded in the distance. The current picked up speed, and terror tightened her stomach. She must get out before she fell to her death. Catching sight of a long tree limb hanging over the water she angled her body to catch it. The current caught her and pulled her under before she could grasp it. Frantic, Rolayna clawed in every direction for help. She got one breath before the water closed over her head again. Throwing her arms wide, she hoped to catch the tree. As her head came above water, she realized the current carried her beneath the limb, and her chance to escape disappeared.

She cried out in terror when a large warm arm caught her and lifted her up. As her head broke the surface of the water she came up gulping mouthfuls of air. Her freezing body collided with a large male chest. Warm arms pulled her against his heat, and she knew who held her.

Dragos!

She had never been so glad and so mad to meet someone in her life. How did he know where she went and how to catch her so fast? She resisted the urge to wrap her arms around his neck and cling to him as the current tugged her legs sideways. She sucked in a breath as her freezing breasts pressed against the heat of his chest, and every nerve in her body sprang to life. Rolayna closed her eyes. If he let go, she would be carried away. At the same time, being this close to him terrified her.

"Trying to sneak away?"

She jerked her head back and met his metallic gaze. "Let me go." Her teeth chattered as she said the words.

His eyes bored into hers. "I will not. You will drown. So, you try to escape me again. I came for you this time. Next time I might decide to leave you to your fate."

Rolayna gasped out loud. "I…was…not—"

"You were." He walked out of the stream with her in his arms. She realized her predicament when the air hit her near-naked body and resisted the urge to flatten against him. Instead, she crossed her arms over her chest to hide her stiff nipples straining against the wet, transparent fabric of her chemise.

"My clothes…I do not have—"

His gaze fell to her breasts, and he stared with hooded eyes.

Too late, Rolayna gripped her arms tighter, but he saw all of her.

"Put me down! Turn…your…head. Do…not look at…me!" Her teeth chattered together.

Dragos looked his fill. His heated gaze roamed up and down her body. "You are my prisoner. I shall do whatever I please with you. When you strip off your clothes, you ask for a man's attention."

"A…gentleman…would…not." Her body trembled against him.

"As you mentioned before, I am not a gentleman." He moved her arms aside and caught her breast, squeezing it gently as he bent his head.

She quit breathing and went hot all over. "What are you doing?"

He gazed deep into her eyes. "I desire to taste you."

Her mouth dried. She opened her lips to tell him to stop, but no sound came out. His finger traced a circle around one straining nipple, and she shivered to the end of her toes.

He tugged the neck of her chemise down and stared at her. "So beautiful," he murmured as his hot mouth settled over one of her nipples. He suckled, and Rolayna cried out. She never felt anything so indecent and exciting in her life. Her mind rebelled, but her body wanted more. Sensual fire licked at her, and the cold stream was forgotten. Only the seductive heat of his lips and tongue remained. A wicked, sensuous lethargy stole over her. She closed her eyes and reveled in the feel of his mouth tugging at her again and again.

How could he be so terrifying and at the same time so intoxicating? The things he did to her were sinful, lascivious, and so satisfying.

Were his sinful lips the reason they called him a devil?

His hands wandered her body, touching, caressing, and feeling every inch of her. Rolayna's blood heated while she shivered with desire. Tremors racked her body as his hands explored every dip and curve.

Then, Dragos lifted his head and pulled her other nipple into his mouth.

Oh, God! Rolayna arched against him. The touch of his mouth filled her stomach with liquid heat. She squirmed in his arms as a deep ache settled between her legs. She panted, wanting more.

He lifted his head and stared at her.

She trembled when she met his slumberous gaze. His wicked, knowing eyes promised all kinds of evil delight.

Shivering with equal amounts of fear and anticipation, she studied him. With his size and strength, he could do anything, and she would not be able to stop him. She held her breath and waited to see what would happen next.

"We could lie in the grass, and I would warm you."

"I am not cold," she lied.

He pulled her close against him. "Then why do you tremble?"

The hair on his chest tickled her sensitive nipples. Rolayna gasped as his mouth came down on hers. He licked at her lips. When she opened them, he slipped his tongue between them to mate with hers, tasting the nectar of her mouth. She could no longer think. Rauf's kisses were nothing like this. Dragos' hand found her breast as his lips slid against hers, and Rolayna drowned in a sea of temptation, floundering on the waves of desire, so overcome with pleasure she could hardly think. Wrapping her arms around his neck, she gave into temptation. His hands were everywhere, touching and caressing her heated flesh. She quivered with excitement, and the air around them pulsed with sexual energy.

When he lifted his head, she protested. "Dragos."

His lids dropped over his eyes. "So, you know who holds you." He set her on her feet, unwrapping her arms from his neck and placing her hands on his chest.

She stood mesmerized by the rippling bronze of his skin, resisting the urge to run her hands over his body like he did hers. She stared at him and licked her lips.

"Does your rebel make you feel the way I do?"

Oh my God, Rauf! What am I doing? Rolayna stiffened and backed away. Without the heat of his body, cold seeped into her bones, and she realized Dragos wore only his breeches. His tunic lay on the ground at their feet.

Her gaze roamed his chest and stopped on the spot where she stabbed him with her hatpin. There should be a wound or a mark, something to herald her attack, but neither were there. Confusion filled her mind. How could he be healed so quick? She stabbed him yesterday. Glancing up at his dark eyes and the hunger within their depths, she remembered her near nakedness. Rolayna shivered, trying desperately to cover herself with her arms.

"I...he...we...do...not..." she stammered.

He smiled. "I saw you together last night, and he wore only his breeches. He desires to have you."

Her chin lifted, and she stared up at him. "So, you admit he wants me for more than my gold?"

Dragos' lids dropped over his eyes. "I did not say so." He picked up his tunic. "Here, put this on." His gaze flicked over her one more time, lingering on her breasts before he tossed it at her and leaned against a nearby tree with folded arms.

"How did you know where to find me?" The question begged an answer. She calculated her time in the stream at least an hour from the sun's position. She slipped her arms into the gigantic sleeves and waited for his answer. Her thoughts swirled around her current situation. *How could I allow such intimacy?* She pushed Rauf away and yet forgot everything with one touch of the devil's lips.

Dragos gazed at her. His dark slumberous eyes gleamed with wicked knowledge. "Your scent intoxicates me. I breathe and know which direction to find you. I cannot resist your sweet fragrance. So, I follow because I can do nothing else."

Rolayna blinked and turned her back, shaking violently. How did one answer such a statement? Her trembling increased. She must be mad to allow him near and would keep her distance in future. Now she knew the effect of his touch, this kiss must never be repeated. She fumbled with the laces until they were tied. Her hands were blue with cold. His tunic dropped past her knees, and the sleeves well past her fingers. She rolled the fabric up until her hands appeared and turned toward Dragos. "I do not have slippers." Her feet rubbed against each other in the grass.

Dragos whistled, and his horse approached. He took her corset from his saddlebag. "I found this, but no slippers. What would you do if I were not here to pull you from the water?" He nodded toward the deepening stream. "This river drops to a hundred-foot waterfall a few feet from here. You would have died."

Rolayna stared at him. "It is my duty as a prisoner to escape. How did you find my clothes? I hid them."

Dragos shrugged again. "As I said, your fragrance draws me like a moth to the flame." He studied her face. "It is my duty to keep you safe. In order to do so, you must trust me. I do not hold you prisoner to hurt you but to protect you. Hound will find your father and lead him to me. For now, let us return. We have a long ride ahead of us." He mounted his great black steed and held his arm down to her.

She stared at it. Were she not so cold, she would put him in his place for the liberties he took. Yet, he saved her life, as well. "You are the only man of my acquaintance I want to hit and thank at the same time."

A quick grin split his face. "And you are the only woman of my acquaintance I want to kiss and throttle at the same time." He settled her, wrapping his arms around her and hugging her shivering body to his warmth. His heat drew her until she gave in and sank against him, thankful for the comfort his body offered.

The ride back went on forever. The sun dipped low when they arrived back at the castle. Dragos whistled as they drew near, and the guards lowered the drawbridge.

He stopped inside the courtyard and helped Rolayna down.

The long ride and the cold water made her knees buckle the second he set her on her feet. With an oath, he swung her into his arms and strode through the castle.

"You owe the guard an apology. Lord Chattam ordered fifteen lashes when they discovered you gone."

She gasped. "He is not to blame. I tricked him."

Dragos glanced at her as he approached the door to her chamber. "I do not doubt it for one second."

A different guard opened her door, his expression hostile.

Rolayna blinked rapidly. "I would like an audience with Lord Chattam once I am warm and dressed. I shall explain what happened."

"It will not erase the pain of the lash."

A sigh escaped her. He spoke the truth. "I would explain all the same."

Brawn appeared with a clay dish and placed it on the small table in her chamber. "Here. The hot soup will warm yer insides."

Dragos' gaze met hers. "Do not run from me again. Next time, I might not be there to save you."

Rolayna dropped her head and nodded her acquiescence. She would not run...until next time. Of this, she promised. And once she paid a maid to create a new split skirt, it would happen.

Chapter Four

Rolayna screamed long and loud when a massive shadow loomed over her in the night, scaring the life out of her.

A hand came out of the darkness and clapped over her mouth. "It is I. I have not come to harm you."

She pinched her lips together. *Dragos.* She could feel his heat and smell the warm musky scent of his skin. "Then why?" she whispered. Did he come to finish what he started by the stream?

"Come. Your father has returned, and he is wounded."

Rolayna froze. *Papa came back.* Relief flooded her. She rolled from her warm bed and got carefully to her feet. They were raw from kicking the stones on the stream bed. "Where is he?" Silence followed her question, for Dragos disappeared, leaving her alone.

Throwing on a borrowed robe over her night rail, she limped to the door.

The guard pointed to a room down the corridor where male voices spoke. "Ye are to go there."

She nodded her thanks and walked toward it.

Malphas and Ramiel leaned over a figure on a cot in front of the fire, covered with fur.

Dragos stood legs braced wide with his arms folded over his chest.

Scimitar stood beside Dragos, his dark eyes

thoughtful while Wolfbane stirred something over the fire.

"Swear to me, Dragos." Papa's voice came from within the fur. "There is no one else."

Dragos scowled with distaste at the figure on the cot for long seconds. "Do not ask this of me."

"You took the first step when you abducted us. Now swear it. You cannot deny my dying wish." Papa's voice faded as he said the last word.

Rolayna picked her way toward them. "Papa?"

"I swear." Dragos' words stopped her. Anger shot from his dark eyes as he lifted his gaze to her. Fury ticked along his tense jaw.

Her feet shuffled backward, her heart pounding in her chest.

The fur moved, and her father peered out, pale as death. His eyes sought hers. "Rolayna?" His weak voice just reached her ears.

She hurried over and threw herself down beside him, keeping one eye on Dragos. "You came back."

"Rolayna." He spoke in a whisper.

She leaned closer. "I am here, Papa."

"Stand aside. Let Wolfbane near." Dragos' clipped voice spoke above her head.

She slid backward as Wolfbane approached. He held a cup of liquid and spooned it into her father's mouth. Then he pulled the furs away.

Her gaze dropped to the gaping wound in his chest. She gasped and fell backward. Blood dripped everywhere.

Wolfbane picked up a cloth to soak it up.

She gagged.

"Take her away," Dragos commanded.

"Nay!" Rolayna sat upright and swallowed, wiping the perspiration from her brow. "I want to stay." She leaned forward and sucked in a deep breath. She could do this. She would sit beside her father and act as though everything were fine, ignoring his wound and the blood on the floor by her knees.

Dragos' dark gaze rested on her.

She drew a deep breath and glanced down at her father.

"Daughter, come closer." Papa's voice floated up to her ear.

She leaned down.

"Swear to me you will watch over Alex." His voice grew faint.

Rolayna drew back. He lay mortally wounded, and he wanted her to swear to care for his ward? Did he make Dragos swear the same?

"Swear it. He means everything."

She frowned. "I cannot go to Seville when I am prisoner, but as soon as I am able, I will fetch him." She smoothed her hand over her father's gray head.

"He is here. I made it to Seville in time to get him before the rebels arrived. The lad is the reason I left you, Rolayna. Now swear." He groaned aloud in pain.

She gazed about her for the first time, meeting the wide-eyed stare of her father's little ward.

"Alex." The Duke of Seville groaned the name.

"My lord," the child's small voice answered.

"I love you, lad."

Rolayna stared at Papa, begging him with her eyes to say the words to her, too.

He did not. "Swear, Daughter. I must hear the words."

"I swear." She threw her arms around him. "I am sorry, Papa. Please forgive me. I love you."

Her words came too late. The Duke of Seville drew his last breath the second she said, "I swear."

Rolayna sobbed on his neck. She could not lose Papa, not now.

"My lord died?" The childish voice caught her attention.

She sat up, peering at the small boy through puffy eyes. "Aye. He died."

The child nodded his head. His blue eyes stared down at her father's pale face and filled with tears.

Alex loved him, too. Compassion tugged at her heart, and she motioned for the boy to come to her.

The boy shook his head and pulled a locket from his pocket. When he opened the locket and stared at the images within, a single tear rolled down his cheek.

"What happened?" she asked, glancing up at Dragos. "Who wounded my father?"

Dragos' dark eyes flashed in the light of the fire. "He went to Seville to get the boy, despite the warning I gave. Rebels attacked him on the way back. When Azazel and Hound found him, your father had the boy hidden behind a tree while he fought four rebels alone. He received the fatal blow moments later. My disciples carried him back here, but Wolfbane could do nothing for the duke except give him medicine for the pain."

Rolayna stared. "Papa risked his life for Alex?"

Dragos' eyes narrowed. "There are people who care more for others than for their own needs. I would have been there to prevent the duke's death if I were not required to search for you."

She jerked back as if she were slapped. "How can

you say this? You do not know it to be true."

The devil leaned toward her. "I do know. I received the message of your escape right before the attack. My men were close by. If I stayed with the duke, he would now live."

Agony tore at her. Papa's death could not be her fault. She refused to believe it. Her chin rose despite the pain of his accusation. "You know nothing of the person I am."

Dragos' metallic gaze flicked over her, dismissing her. "I know too much about you, lady. More than I care to." With those damning words, he turned to his men, ignoring her. "Get the duke cleaned up so we can bury him."

A small cry broke the silence behind her. She turned to Alex. Large tears rolled unheeded down his fat cheeks, and sobs shook his shoulders.

Her heart twisted in her chest. "Come, Alex." She held her hands out and smiled at him.

He gazed at her for a minute and walked around her father until he stood beside her.

"Would you like to sit on my lap? I will hold you if you are frightened."

"Nay," he said and turned away.

Rolayna did not know what to say. Anguish welled in her chest and tightened her throat. She would not give way to her tears until she lay alone in her bed to grieve in private.

"Come here, lad." Dragos stood watching the exchange between her and the boy.

She took Alex's hand. "Let me show you where you can sleep."

Alex pulled away and marched over to Dragos.

"Nay, Alex. Do not go…"

The warrior bent down and scooped the boy up. The child wrapped his arms around the devil's neck, and the two of them held a quiet conversation.

Rolayna grew faint with emotion. Her father died before her eyes, insisting she swear to keep the boy safe, while her captor blamed her for his death. How did one deal with this kind of guilt? She glanced at Dragos. His harsh words replayed in her mind. Yet he held the boy tenderly. whispering in his ear. Rolayna shook her head. She could not be responsible because Papa left of his own accord, knowing the risks. Rising to to her feet, she walked toward the corridor leading to her chamber.

"Are you forgetting the promise you made your father?" Dragos' deep voice stopped her mid-stride. She turned to face him.

Alex lay asleep in his arms.

"You gave your word to keep the boy safe."

"Alex seems safe enough. I am weary and go to lie down."

Dragos snorted. "You leave the child without any thought for his comfort moments after swearing to care for him. You wander off to go sleep, leaving the boy behind." He carried Alex toward her. His eyes flashed bright with fury. "I am aware of the value your word carries. It is as worthless as teats on a boar pig. Beware, Rolayna, lest you earn a place in hell with the rest of us."

Stalking past her, he deposited the sleeping child on the bed in her chamber.

"I keep my word. You know nothing of me or my life." Rolayna rubbed the scar on her wrist as she followed him.

Dragos straightened. "Did you not agree to wed the rebel?"

She stiffened and gave a slight nod. What had her marriage to do with this?

He stepped toward her and bent his head. His mouth settled over hers, and his tongue swept inside her mouth to mate before she could react. He pulled her against the heat of his body as his hand closed around her breast.

Her arms came up to ward him off and ended up around his neck. She trembled despite her determination not to. He stroked her tongue with his, and heat filled her belly as his hands molded and searched her body. In her night rail and dressing gown, her unrestricted body responded with abandon.

Rolayna whimpered and leaned into his warmth, and he pulled her closer with a growl. Her heart beat loud in her ears as excitement spiraled inside her. She opened her mouth and boldly stroked his tongue with hers. He was an aphrodisiac to her soul, and she could not get close enough. His hands dropped to her buttocks. He squeezed them and pulled her against the hard length of his arousal. Shivering with desire, she rubbed against him and gasped as tingles ran up and down inside her, and her belly jumped with awareness. Closing her eyes, she gave into the ecstasy of his touch. He made her feel alive and wanted.

Dragos lifted his head. "You see how easy it is for you to forget your word? I could take you with little effort. Another minute, and you would beg me to strip you naked and lay you down on this bed. I could touch and taste every inch of your satin skin with my lips and hands. I could bury myself in you so deep you would forget everything but me. I could do it over and over again until we fell into an exhausted sleep, still joined together. When we woke, I could take you again and again. You would scream my name and beg me for more. This after promising your body to another man. I know about you, Rolayna. I know what women like you do. You destroy men with your beautiful faces and luscious bodies."

He indicated Alex. "You would do it with no thought for your father's ward. The boy needs someone to comfort him. He has seen more than a child ought to." Dragos glared at her. "Yet you cannot give him the love he needs because your mind is fixated on the pleasures of the flesh and your own comfort instead." With those damning words, he stalked away and slammed the chamber door behind him.

Rolayna sank down on the soft bed. Her body shook with the images his words created in her mind. Their naked, joined bodies burned her conscience. She wanted him with an urgency that shocked her. His touch affected her in ways she could not control. But why torment her with his kisses and then accuse her of being unfaithful to Rauf? They signed no marriage contract. Without it, she remained single and free to choose a different path.

Rolayna rubbed her hand over her swollen lips. It was true. She enjoyed his kisses more than she should and responded with greater abandon. Rauf's kisses were pleasant, but Dragos' made her burn. A grimace wrinkled her brow. The devil initiated the kisses, not her. How could she be blamed for responding? She resolved he would never touch her again.

He had other things wrong about her, too. Her word meant everything. She lost Papa, her good name, and her place in society because of it. His rebuke said he knew of her fall from grace. She suspected as much but decided she did not care. What did it matter what Dragos thought of her? She gave her word to Papa to care for Alex, and she would keep her vow, whatever it took.

Rolayna glanced over at the sleeping child. None of this was Alex's fault. She would keep him safe and see him grow to be the man Papa wanted. Somehow, she would escape Dragos and forget all about the terror of her abduction. Soon it would be nothing but a memory. With Rauf by her side, she could do anything.

Frowning, she lay back and pulled the covers up to her chin. First, she must find her almost fiancé. Having the boy here complicated her escape. Somehow, she must figure out how to get them both to safety—without Papa. Numbness filled her and too many other emotions to sort through. Exhausted, she closed her eyes. She would figure out what to do once she acquired some sleep.

Morning came too soon. Rolayna awoke and glanced over at the other side of the big bed. Empty! Where did the boy go? Tossing her dressing gown on, she hurried to the door. Pulling it open, she came face to face with the guard she tricked into taking her beyond the wall.

She swallowed when she met the man's angry glare.

"Back inside with ye." He stepped toward her, pulling his sword from the scabbard.

Rolaynae stiffened her spine. "I owe you an

apology, sir. I am sorry you suffered because of my foolishness and ask for your forgiveness." Her chin tilted up as she gazed into his eyes.

The guard stared. "I received fifteen lashes for believing yer lies."

Her head dipped. "I know, and I am sorry."

A moment of silence followed. "If ye want the boy, he left for the stables with Azazel."

Rolayna nodded. "Thank you." She closed her door.

A maid brought in an altered gown borrowed from Lord Chattam's daughter, now married and living in Evania. "Yer other gown is being washed and pressed."

When she finished with dressing, Rolayna went in search of Dragos and discovered the men in the solarium, deep in conversation. They stilled when she entered the room. The disciples stood in front of the fire. Dragos faced them, and Alex sat in a leather armchair, playing with a small wooden horse. Her gaze fell to Papa's body, lying on the cot beside the fire, wrapped in clean cloths and devoid of any sign of blood.

"We bury your father. Lord Chattam will allow the duke to be placed in his small crypt." Dragos' voice filled the room.

"Ramiel and Wolfbane prepared the body earlier. The burial must take place after we leave. It is the best I could do in the circumstances."

Rolayna stared. The icy numbness of loss ate at her heart, and tears threatened to spill out. She swallowed hard to get control of her emotions.

Alex rose to stand beside Dragos. He tucked his hand into the warrior's larger one and gazed at her.

"Papa should be buried in Seville, not here, not like this." Rolayna stared at the cloth-wrapped body before her. "He should be buried in the sepulcher beside all the other Sevilles who passed on before. There should be a ceremony, and Father Bernard should be here commending his soul to heaven. He will not find peace in Lord Chattam's crypt."

"There is no time for anything else. The rebels come. Hound informs me they will arrive within two hours' time. Say goodbye, lady, and let us be gone," Dragos commanded. Anger no longer darkened his features. Regret and compassion shone from his eyes.

Rolayna stared in dismay. "We must say the Lord's prayer at very least. We cannot—"

"I am sorry, Rolayna. I cannot change what is." Dragos dropped to his knee beside Alex. "Tell the duke whatever you wish, boy. Then say goodbye. We must leave before the soldiers arrive."

The boy nodded his head. He held his locket in one chubby hand as he stared down at the body of his benefactor and solemnly said, "Goodbye, my lord." Clutching the locket to his heart with his eyes squeezed shut, he kissed it. He cried for a minute or two and then put the locket back in his pocket before gazing up at Dragos. "I done."

"You have one minute, Rolayna."

She jumped when Dragos spoke. Her eyes were glued on the locket. She did not know it existed before last night when Alex held it as her father died. Glancing up at Dragos and reading the warning in his eyes, she hastily made her way to her father and dropped to her knees beside him. Her whispered goodbye held a sense of finality. Tears slipped down her cheeks, and sobs racked her body.

A minute later, a large arm picked her up and held her against a warm chest.

Rolayna had no desire to resist. His loose embrace comforted her, and she gave in, wrapping both arms around his waist and sobbing. Grief racked her body while tears poured from her eyes and wet the front of his tunic. She cried until she could no longer, and he let her.

A knock came at the door. "The rebels come."

"I am sorry. We have no more time to let you grieve. We must go."

His regretful words touched her heart.

She glanced up, transfixed by the gleam of compassion in his metallic eyes. A few minutes later, they raced away from the castle and disappeared into the trees.

Chapter Five

"Take a minute to get your balance," Scimitar said. He held her elbow until her wobbling ceased.

Yesterday, she rode with Dragos. Today, she rode behind Scimitar.

Rolayna leaned against the side of the disciple's stallion until her legs quit shaking. She knew from whispered conversations soldiers trailed them through the forest.

The road forked, and she waited to see which way Scimitar went before asking for a personal moment. He worked with his mount, and she hurried into the forest to take advantage of the situation. Backtracking to the "v" in the road, she gazed around to be sure she remained unseen before plucking the ribbon from her hair and tying it to a tree branch. Rauf would send soldiers to scout when he reached the fork in the road. With any luck, she would be by his side before the sun set.

Hurrying back the way she came, she smiled up at Scimitar when she rejoined him. Joy filled her bosom, for she found a way to signal Rauf without attracting the devil's attention. Rolayna allowed Scimitar to help her onto his stallion and settled back for the show.

They rode for several hours. Once they arrived at the cave, the disciple helped her to the ground.

Her knees shook, and her backside hurt from the

long ride.

"I hungry." Alex ran around inside the cave while Scimitar lit a fire.

Malphas rubbed the side of his stallion, keeping one eye on the boy. "I have a biscuit in my saddlebag, Alex. When Brawn arrives, he will fix us a proper meal."

The boy acquired a wealth of energy from the long ride. He accepted the biscuit and sat down beside the fire, chewing happily on his food.

Malphas handed her a biscuit and stepped outside to scout around.

Walking to the fire, Rolayna held her hand out to Alex. "Would you like to sit beside me?" Rauf would love the child. He was so full of life.

"Nay." The boy kept eating, ignoring her.

She sat down with a frown. At Seville, Alex lived in the nursery. He never ventured far without her father. The two took walks together, went riding together, and ate together. Papa talked about training his ward to be a page, then a squire, and later a knight. At age seven, the duke planned to send Alex to Emberly to serve as page.

Rolayna rolled her eyes over the news. Knights were born of noble blood. They did not arise from orphans and peasants. Her father considered Alex worthy, but he could never be a knight. She wondered at her father's choice to send the boy to Emberly but kept her thoughts secret. She occupied her time with her own affairs and paid them no mind. Now, she wished she'd spent more time getting to know Alex.

Rolayna took a bite of her biscuit. A noise at the entrance caused her to glance up.

Hound stood there holding the reins to his stallion.

"We go. The rebels cut around to the north. They are almost upon us."

Scimitar mounted his horse and held his arm down.

She gazed up at him with dismay. "The rebels follow us? I thought the baron did."

Malphas kicked dirt on the fire and caught the boy in his arms. They rode out of the cave a minute later.

"Give me your arm, lady. We swore to keep you safe. The soldiers will kill you if they find you."

She opened her mouth to dispute him when he scooped her off her feet. A second later, they raced through the trees.

"If it is the baron, I wish—"

Scimitar's hand covered her mouth. "Be still, my lady. Listen."

Galloping horses thundered in the distance. A shrill scream rent the air, and then another. Rolayna's hair stood on end. Metal struck metal. Men screamed, and horses whinnied.

The disciple wheeled his stallion to the right and spurred him forward through the bushes. They rounded a large oak and galloped forward, leaving the sound of battle behind.

She gaped behind them. Turning sideways for a better view, she almost lost her seat when five horses rode onto the path in front of them.

Scimitar wheeled to the right and then to the left. More men emerged from the trees until they were surrounded. All of them wore rebel uniforms.

Her escort whistled shrilly. "Hold tight to me, my lady. I will protect you."

"If I had my sword, I would not need your protection." She gazed at the soldiers facing them. They all stared back at her with varying degrees of hostility. Rolayna swallowed. "It is me they want."

"Aye, but they shall not get you," Scimitar answered sharply, gripping her waist.

She glanced around, hoping to see Rauf and his men. A few more swords in her defense would be welcomed.

"Give us the lady." The soldier in command walked his horse forward and stopped.

Scimitar pulled his sword from the scabbard and rolled his shoulders. "Hold tight, my lady. I cannot keep you from falling while I introduce these bastards to my blades. My arms will be busy, so you must hold to me."

The soldiers drew their swords.

In another minute, she would be in the middle of battle. Rolayna panicked. "Let me down. There is a sword over there. If I can reach it, I will help with the battle."

"Master would take my head if I did. Which is why you shall remain with me." Scimitar reached for his other sword. "If you want her, come and get her."

And they did.

Squirming against her captor, she tried to get free, but he trapped her between his large arms, swinging his sword to the right, then slicing to the left.

Rolayna quivered. In desperation, she called out, "Let me go!" Why did they not trust her word? If they let her handle a sword, she would show them she had skill.

One of the soldiers bunted his horse into them, and the disciple grabbed her arm.

She cried out in pain. The wound she acquired in the battle at the wooden hut had not healed. Off-balance from the jolt, she slipped to the ground.

Scimitar's horse whinnied and sidestepped.

Rolling from under his hooves, she rose to her knees.

A rebel soldier grabbed her around the waist and stood her up.

She stared into his face and shuddered.

He laughed at her fear while his gaze roamed her body. "I shall get gold for catching ye."

"Do not touch me," Rolayna warned. "If you do, I shall cut your heart out."

Scimitar sliced a sword in their direction.

She screamed when the soldier fell to the ground, dead in front of her.

Another rebel, seeing his opportunity, plucked her from the ground, much the same way Dragos did.

She landed on his lap with a thud.

The soldier's thick arm wrapped around her waist, and his hot breath blew across her cheek

Her stomach churned. The man smelled of sweat and stale ale.

"Looks like I caught ye." One grubby hand grabbed her left breast and squeezed.

Rolayna screamed and hit him with her fists. "Remove your hands this instant or you die for this insult." She caught the soldier in the nose with her fist and took advantage of his pain by slipping to the ground. Grasping a fallen sword by the hilt, she raised the blade and braced for combat. "Climb off your horse and face me like a man."

The soldier wiped the blood from his face and swore. "Lady or not, I'll kill ye."

A streak of darkness flashed past the corner of her

eyes.

Dragos and his disciples emerged from the trees like angels of death. They cut the men down, surrounding them in minutes. Then, the devil turned in her direction. His eyes flashed fire at the scene. His fury froze the blood in her veins as he spurred his horse forward and knocked the soldier to the ground.

The other disciples circled them. The rebels were dead. Only the man in front of Rolayna lived.

Dragos slid to the ground holding his broadsword in one hand. He flicked the man with his sword. "Get up."

The soldier scrambled to his feet, his eyes widening when he spotted the warrior. Reaching for his sword, his hand came away empty. Terror made him stumble.

"Someone toss this fool a sword." The devil's gaze never left the man's face.

Ramiel threw a sword at the soldier's feet. It planted itself in the ground, hilt pointing up.

Dragos turned back to Rolayna. "Widen your stance for stability to withstand a blow."

She gaped at him and widened her legs. She expected him to reprimand her, not instruct her.

Stepping behind her, he wrapped his hands around the hilt of her sword, lifting it waist-high. "Now, turn a little, like so, and flatten the blade." He positioned her arms. "Never take your gaze from the enemy."

She nodded and swallowed. Her gaze returned to the wilting soldier. "You wish to kill me? Come and try."

Dragos stepped back and folded his arms.

The soldier glanced around. "I do not fight

women."

"I heard different a minute ago." The devil shrugged. "I will not interfere for the first three blows."

A slow smile crossed the rebel's face. "I 'ave yer word? The lady will die."

The warrior did not respond.

Rolayna rolled her shoulders and studied her opponent's advancement the way Captain Jameson taught her.

With a cry, the rebel charged.

She blocked his strike and thrust at him.

He blocked and knocked her to the ground with his elbow. Crowing with laughter, he swung around for the kill but met Dragos' broadsword instead of Rolayna.

Surprise and fear chased across his face. "Ye said three blows."

The devil nodded. "Yours, her block and thrust, your block, and then your elbow. I count five."

Rolayna shook her head and rose to her feet frowning at the way the trees swayed around her.

Dragos took her sword and tossed it to Azazel before setting her behind him.

Whatever the soldier read on the warrior's face scared him to death. "I did what they commanded," he whined. "Let me go. You have the girl. No one will know you let me live. There is no reason to kill me."

The devil leaned on his sword. "There is where you are wrong. You touched the lady. For this offense, you shall die."

Her heart jumped to her throat. The demon defended her honor? She glanced at him in surprise. "He did not hurt me. I do not think it necessary to kill him."

"You will trust me," he answered without taking his gaze from the rebel. "Tell me how you found us." His cold voice filled her with dread.

Rolayna's throat tightened. Her ribbon trick must have worked for this man to be here.

The devil inclined his head to Ramiel, who disappeared into the trees with Alex securely on his lap.

The soldier glanced at his sword and then at Dragos. "We followed the captain." A calculating gleam entered his eye. "What if I tell ye where we were 'eaded? Will ye let me go?"

Long minutes passed. "Where are you headed?"

The soldier smiled and licked his thick lips. "We 'eard the servants from Seville is traveling along the coast, to Emberly. We is ter find 'em and kill 'em"

Rolayna gasped. "But they are innocent. Who ordered this slaughter?"

He ignored her question and bowed mockingly to Dragos. "Now, yer lordship, I will leave ye to the girl." He snickered and turned to leave but died a second later. His head fell first, and then the rest of him.

She stared in disbelief at the body on the ground knowing she brought this upon them. If Dragos had not been close when Scimitar whistled, they would both lie here dead, as well. A fine sheen of shock moistened her brow. She wiped it away with shaking hands, resisting the urge to be sick. How could she explain her part in this to Dragos and the disciples?

Rolayna lifted her gaze from the body to the trees in front of her and sucked in a deep breath of the cool mountain air. Stiffening her spine, she gripped her hands together behind her to hide their trembling. She gazed at Dragos as he wiped the blood from his sword on the man's uniform.

A new thought crossed her mind.

"How could you? You gave your word you would not kill him if he told you where the rebels were headed." Her gaze dropped to the blood oozing into the ground, and she gagged as the rusty smell filled her nostrils.

"Nay, I did not." Dragos slid his sword into its scabbard and picked up his reins. Mounting, he held his hand down to Rolayna.

She stared at him. "Aye, you did. He asked if you would spare his life if he told you—" She gazed at him. "You said nothing. The soldier assumed you agreed and told you without first getting your word." Her stomach lurched.

"So, you understand. If I give my word, I keep it. Take my arm, lady. We go."

She sighed. "I suppose I owe you my gratitude. I thought the soldiers following us were Rauf's. I did not know the rebels were so close." She let him help her onto his horse. Her entire body trembled. "You told him he would die because he touched me. Why?"

He nudged his horse forward. "You are under my protection. Anyone who touches you will suffer the same fate."

Rolayna did not know what to think. He knew of her fall from grace and made no secret of his dislike, yet he killed a man for touching her.

"You speak as if you do me a service, yet I am your captive. You have done nothing honorable."

He growled low in his throat. "I do you a great honor by offering my protection. When you realize Oliveander leads the rebels, you shall admit as much."

She shook her head. "It shall be a chilly day in hell when I do."

His deep chuckle rumbled behind her. "Snow falls there as a regular occurrence, so prepare your heart. I am most anxious to hear your speech of gratitude."

She closed her eyes but said nothing further. The cool breeze and change of scenery did much to quiet her rolling stomach.

A long time later, Dragos slowed his stallion, turning to the right, where a small stream appeared. Pulling his mount to a stop, he sat staring into the trees until satisfied they were safe before dismounting.

She slid to the ground beside him, her knees shaking.

"You owe the disciples your gratitude for saving your life." He nodded behind her.

Spinning around, she met the furious gazes of Azazel and Scimitar. Then she faced the cold, hostile gaze of Hound as he made his way to Dragos.

He handed him a scrap of fabric and spoke quietly in his ear.

Dragos' gaze turned toward her. His eyes were the color of a winter sky as he tossed the ribbon at her feet. Outrage shot from his eyes. "You marked the path for the rebels to follow?"

Her chin came up. "What if I did?" She would never ask forgiveness for planning her escape.

A low growl came from his throat, and Rolayna took a quick step back.

"You led them to us and endangered your life as well as the life of the boy." His eyes darkened to stormy gray.

She swallowed. She did not consider Alex's

welfare when she tied her ribbon to the tree branch. "I left it for Rauf. I did not consider the rebels."

The devil's gaze darkened to black. "After all we have done to keep you safe, you betray us and Alex? Why should I expect anything different? The first marriage contract you signed, you broke a week later with no explanation. Tell me. Did Emberly not meet your standards? Did his battle wound disqualify him because he would never be perfect and used a cane to walk? Oliveander should thank me, for I rescued him from a fate worse than death. I rescued him from you."

Dragos turned. The disciples were still there, mounted and waiting for orders.

She glanced at the men, but they refused to meet her gaze.

"Meet me at the appointed place. I cannot ask more of you than I am willing to give. Lady Rolayna is my problem and rides with me." Dragos' dark metallic gaze turned to her. "You owe Scimitar your gratitude for keeping you alive. He bleeds because of you." The command in his quiet voice terrified her.

She dare not disobey. "Thank you, Scimitar." Her voice shook as she glanced at the blood-soaked sleeve of his tunic.

Scimitar gave a slight nod of his head and turned his mount away to follow the others.

"When will you trust what I say? Oliveander killed your father. He will kill you, too, once he has what he wants from you." Dragos swung onto his horse and dropped his hand toward her.

What if she turned and ran? How far would she make it?

"Do not test me further." His furious gaze pinned

her feet to the ground.

"How is it you know my thoughts even as I think them?" She would have to search for another opportunity to escape. Rolayna swallowed as she stared at his hand. Her heart beat rapidly, and her mouth grew dry.

"Your thoughts are there for all to see. You were foolish to suppose I would let you go before I honor my word to your father. Take my hand, Rolayna."

"What word?" She remembered the scene at Chattam Castle right before her father died.

He ignored her question. "Take my hand."

She pushed him too far to displease him further. She placed her hand in his, and he lifted her onto his stallion, sitting her before him, and nudgeing his mount into motion.

"Are you so eager for marriage you give yourself to any fool?" Dragos' voice gentled as if he cared.

Rolayna dropped her head. "I wanted marriage to please my father, but it no longer matters. I do not require a man to be happy and shall make my own way. Men are a nuisance, and I have a deep aversion to being ordered about."

"I know of this weakness." A sigh rumbled through him. "I tell you the truth about Oliveander and his plans for you." He remained silent for a few minutes. "If you do not require marriage, know this. If anyone takes your virtue, it shall be me."

Her head popped up, and her mouth dropped open. "I shall give myself to no man, especially not you. To do so without marriage is a sin."

Dragos chuckled. "I am the devil, lady. Sin is what I do best."

She knew because she tasted sin with him, and like an aphrodisiac, she wanted more. Pinching her lips together, she did not say another word.

They traveled far into the night. When at last they stopped, Rolayna slipped from the horse to her knees, cold, hungry, and exhausted.

She wandered to the fire and sat.

Brawn handed her a vessel of soup. None of the disciples met her gaze, and an awkward silence filled the camp.

Woodenly she spooned the warm soup into her mouth. What could she do? They were honest men, and she betrayed them.

Wolfbane sat beside the fire, cleaning Scimitar's wound. "It requires stitching. The blade cut deep."

Scimitar growled. "I wish my lady were here. Her stitches are tiny and easier to bear than yours."

Wolfbane chuckled. "Mine are the only hands available. Will you cry like a babe?"

Rolayna rose to her feet and approached the men. "I will stitch the wound."

All eyes turned to her, and her face heated. "I want to help. Scimitar received his wound because of me. My stitching is tiny."

Wolfbane handed her a needle.

Dragos studied her from the other side of the fire, saying nothing. The disciples were silent while she worked.

When she finished, Wolfbane bound the wound.

"Thank you, my lady," Scimitar said.

She nodded. "I know you believe you saved me today. For this cause, I helped you. But my life is my own to live as I see fit. I thank you for your concern."

At least his wound would not be on her conscience. She took several steps and stopped. "Where is Alex?"

The devil's gaze met hers. "He is asleep inside our tent."

Rolayna's eyes widened. "Our...tent?" Her weariness left her. He spoke of taking her virtue earlier. Was this his plan? Her heart sped up, and apprehension choked her.

He ignored her comment and continued eating his soup.

Rising to her feet, she walked toward the trees.

Suddenly, he blocked her path. "Where are you going?"

She blinked. For such a large man, he moved with amazing speed. "To find a spot to rest in private. I have no wish to sleep in a tent with you or anyone else. Stand aside."

Dragos studied her face. "I have no liking for it either, but I cannot have you out of my sight. You proved you cannot be trusted. Make your way to the tent, or I shall deposit you there."

Rolayna turned and walked back the way she came. Camp boasted one tent, making it difficult not to miss. She trudged inside and spotted Alex asleep on a pile of furs. She walked toward him, but the demon stopped her. "Over there."

Glancing around, she spotted a large pile of furs on the opposite side and nodded her head, surprised he offered her the larger pile of furs. Gratefully, she stepped out of her slippers and slid between the furs, falling asleep within minutes.

****

Dragos entered the tent sometime later. His gaze

slid to the delicate beauty lying before him. Her golden hair shimmered in the flickering light of the fire as its length spilled in rippling waves across the mountain of furs. Her alabaster complexion glowed softly in the darkness, and a rosy blush kissed her high cheekbones. She enchanted all who gazed upon her and embodied the essence of femininity and innocence.

Until one spent time in her company, he amended. The woman had the temperament of a cat. Soft and cuddly one minute, scratching and clawing the next. No lady as fair as this one maintained innocence or virtue. Experience taught him otherwise. She surprised him tonight when she stitched Scimitar. Did she offer out of guilt?

Dragos growled low in his throat as he pulled the flaps to the tent shut. He hated beautiful women, this one in particular. But he gave his word to her dying father to see her safe, and he would honor his word.

Stepping closer to where she lay, he sat down to remove his boots and placed his sword on the ground in front of him within easy reach.

Lady Rolayna mumbled and rolled to her side, clutching the furs tight against her. Dragos gazed at her as he slid beneath the furs beside her. Her beautiful face lay inches from his, and he could feel her breath on his cheek. Many a nobleman spoke upon the beauty of Lady Rolayna, but none of the tales did her justice. When he gazed upon her for the first time in the carriage, she took his breath away. Her beauty outshone all the stories, and he could not get her out of his head. The first time he kissed her, he did so out of lust, plain and simple. He wanted to taste her and feel the softness of her body. Her beauty drew him like a bee to honey.

The second time had been a mistake. He set out to prove a point, and before he knew what happened, things got out of hand. He wanted to bury himself inside her again and again and drown in her sweetness. Her mouth tasted of nectar, and her scent drove him crazy. His body came alive whenever she drew near, and he wanted her with a fierceness which drove him mad. Something must be done before he broke his own rule and touched something which did not belong to him. The devil's frown darkened. From now on, he kept his distance.

Dragos turned his back to her and stared at the sleeping child on the other side of the tent. Somehow, he must deliver Rolayna and the boy to the king. Only then would he and his disciples be free of this mess.

The lady was daft when it came to Baron Oliveander. He could not trust her, and she nearly cost him Scimitar today. He relived the scene in his mind. When Scimitar whistled, he wheeled his stallion around and rode into the fray. Oliveander's men surrounded Scimitar. When he caught sight of her, standing before the soldier with a sword in her hand, his rage boiled over while his word to her father pounded in his head. Scimitar cut soldiers on both sides, wielding his two blades with deadly precision. His disciple's quick thinking saved her life. Killing the soldier did nothing to alleviate his rage. The traitors were headed to the seashore to kill what remained of Seville Castle. He and his disciples must arrive first and save the servants. Dragos shook his head. He puzzled over Oliveander's ability to sense which route they took through the forest until Hound showed him Rolayna's ribbon. Then, he wanted to throttle her with his bare hands.

Chapter Six

Dragos woke her in the wee hours of the morning. "We leave."

Rolayna rubbed the sleep from her eyes. "The sun has not risen."

He glared at her. "Brawn has food. Get up now, or I shall set you on the first horse saddled. You will wait until we deem it safe to stop before you eat." His eyes flashed in the darkness. "Or anything else."

She stumbled to her feet, but he disappeared.

Alex's childish voice drifted through the walls of the tent, and she smiled at his excitement. Brushing a hand through her hair, she slipped her feet into her slippers. Once she exited the tent, the disciples took it down, rolled it, and strapped it to the back of Hound's mount before Rolayna finished spooning the hot gruel into her mouth.

"We ride." Dragos scooped her onto his lap as he rode past.

Outrage tightened her chest. "Must you manhandle me so? I can mount a horse on my own. I am an experienced rider."

"You have proven I cannot trust you. So, you will ride with me."

She snapped her mouth shut. She did not trust him, either. Nothing Rauf did or said proved he commanded the rebel army or killed her father. Yet Dragos demanded she believe it on his word alone. Did he lie about Rauf for his own benefit? She folded her arms in defiance.

The devil nudged his stallion into a gallop, and she grabbed the saddle with both hands as they flew through the forest. She gazed around her. Rauf correctly guessed which path they took the last time. If she could leave him another bit of fabric or a sign, he would come for her again. She searched for a landmark but seeing only forest, Rolayna leaned forward and nearly lost her seat. She righted herself, remembering his prediction she would not survive a fall from the top of his massive steed as they raced through the trees.

They stopped late in the afternoon. Sliding to the ground, she studied the area. She did not know where they were or where they were going.

"We eat." Dragos walked toward his men, leaving her behind.

Rolayna made her way toward a clump of trees to care for her personal needs. The blood returned to her trembling limbs with pricks of pain. She took a minute to breathe in the scent of the forest to calm her nerves. Lifting her face to the sunlight filtering through the trees. She smiled. She would find a way to escape, one way or another. Dragos may be a mighty warrior, but she was an intelligent woman. She would win, for she held the advantage.

When she returned to the clearing, she spotted the warrior deep in conversation with his disciples a few hundred feet away. So, she inched back into the forest and around to the trees behind the men. If she could figure out their location and where they planned to take her, she could figure out how to let Rauf know. Leaning on the far side of a giant oak, Rolayna peeked around the trunk. She could just make out what they said.

"What about the survivors from the castle? We must see to their safety," Hound said, rising from his seat on a log.

Survivors? Did they speak of Seville Castle?

"They go to Emberly. I sent a squadron of Seville's soldiers to protect them once we rescued the duke from Oliveander. They take the road beside the sea. We must reach them before the rebels do."

"Emberly? Why do you send them so far to the east?" Azazel asked.

"Emberly Castle is the only fortress besides Dragonthorne which cannot be breached by the rebels. The Duke of Emberly will protect them. Oliveander will kill any survivor he finds. He wants to conceal his treachery until he rides against the king." Dragos stood in the center of his men with his hands on his hips.

"What about the lass?" Brawn asked, stretching his legs out before him. "We canna trust her."

Rolayna held her breath and waited for the answer.

"We keep the lady with us until her people are safe. Then we take her to Evania. The king is her guardian now." He shook his head. "She betrayed us because she believes Oliveander will help her."

"Is the lass daft?" Brawn asked. "Dinna she ken the baron means to kill her?"

Dragos shrugged. "She is convinced the baron loves her, despite my warning. We must protect her until we deliver her to the king. Once we do so, my word to the Duke of Seville will be honored."

The disciples grunted.

Her head spun. So, he rescued her because of his

oath.

Scimitar threw a knife into the dirt and bent to retrieve it. None of them were happy with the situation.

"Do we travel over the peak or through the Royal Valley to the sea?" Azazel asked.

Wolfbane glanced up. "I say we take her over the peak. She will slow us down if we go through the Royal Valley. She betrayed us once, and we cannot risk her doing it again."

Dragos nodded his agreement with Wolfbane's comment.

Rolayna pinched her lips together. She *would* betray them again. They could count on it.

"She makes too much noise and draws the enemy's attention," Hound agreed. "When she is frightened, she chants strange things."

Dragos nodded. "Aye."

"What does she chant?" Brawn scratched his beard. "Now ye got me curious about the lass. And just when I decided I dinna like her."

Her breath caught in her throat.

"She says, 'lavender wildflowers and cream cake,' " Dragos answered. "It reminds her of her wedding and calms her."

How does he know?

"Why would a wedding make ye calm? It riles me up. I canna keep food in me stomach and I dinna sleep. The lass is daft fer sure," Brawn said shaking his head.

Rolayna blew out her breath and then slapped a hand over her mouth.

Hound's eyes shifted to the trees.

She took a step back, her heart thudding in her chest.

"I could give her a wee tap on the head, and she would sleep the whole journey," Brawn offered. "Then she woulna' be chanting."

"I could make her a potion," Wolfbane suggested. "A little bit of this and the other and the lady would sleep like a baby for days."

Rolayna frowned. Would Dragos allow the men to do as they suggested? She leaned against the tree.

The men lowered their voices.

"...does not matter. The sooner we get her to the king, the better," Dragos said. "We travel east until we cross the summit. Then we go south until we reach the coast. Once we know the servants of Seville are safe, we will take the lady to the king. I have a ship ready." He stopped speaking for several long seconds. "Come out from behind the tree, Rolayna."

She stepped out.

Dragos' metallic eyes mocked her.

"What do we do with her now?" Azazel looked her up and down. "She knows where we go. She knows there are survivors, and she knows where they are."

Dragos' eyes darkened. "She stays with me. If she betrays us again, it will be on my head."

The disciples grunted and remounted their horses. Azazel gathered Alex up in his arms and nudged his horse forward.

Dragos shoved a crust of bread and a piece of cheese into Rolayna's hands. "Eat."

"They do not like me." She took a bite of the bread.

"You expect smiles and acceptance when you betray them?" he asked, one eyebrow up.

Rolayna took a savage bite of her bread. She meant to return to her former life, nothing more.

He waited until she finished her bread, and then they were off.

They rode east, up and over another pass in the steep mountain peaks. At dusk, Dragos stopped to allow the horses some water.

Rolayna slipped to the ground and hurried into the trees as fast as her shaking legs would go. Once she finished, she walked back toward the others but did not stop to smell the trees or enjoy the cool breeze. She hoped they spoke of their plans again. Any information she could get would help in her escape.

But they did not.

When she exited the trees, the disciples were all mounted and waiting.

Dragos held his arm toward her. Rolayna ignored it and walked toward Ramiel, tired of the devil's company. Ramiel at least smiled on occasion.

"You ride with me," Dragos commanded.

"Nay, I do not," she answered.

He plucked her from the ground before her squeak of protest left her lips. Slapping her onto his lap, he nudged his black mount forward, and the skittish horse bounded into a full gallop.

Her breath hitched when she encountered his bulging thighs, and she ground her teeth together. Dammit, she grew tired of him manhandling her. Her traitorous body responded with a passion that angered her. His scent intoxicated her. Why could he not leave her alone? She could walk on her own and ride on her own. The devil wanted to control everything she did, but he would learn differently. She *would* find Rauf, and she *would* be free. So what if Dragos allowed her to handle a sword and took the time to instruct her on her form? He meant nothing.

They reached the sea as dusk settled around them, lengthening the shadows. Dragos slowed to a canter and stopped at the edge of the forest. The disciples filed in behind him.

Hound trotted forward, blending in with the shadows.

They waited beneath the trees until Hound gave the signal.

"There!" The disciple pointed into the distance.

Dragos stilled, then nodded.

Rolayna strained to see what he and his men stared at. It proved a false hope. The devil and his disciples did indeed see in the dark. Metal struck metal. Screams of the dying filled the night air. She swallowed against a dry throat as the sounds and smells of battle rose around her.

Dragos gave a loud, ear-piercing war cry, dropping her to the ground by her arms.

Azazel dropped Alex beside her. The seashore and the ocean lay before them.

Rolayna turned. A small group of soldiers disappeared in the opposite direction.

The devil swung his horse around. "Stay here where it is safe. I shall return for you and the boy as soon as I can." He nudged his horse to a gallop, raising his sword in challenge and shouting his war cry. His disciples were right at his heels. Their howls of displeasure echoed through the night and disappeared.

Rolayna remained alone in the dark with Alex. Waves crashed against the rocks along the shore, and the salty smell of the ocean filled her nose. A cool breeze tugged at the curls of her hair. Turning toward the water, she tripped over something lying at her feet. Glancing down, she froze as recognition filled her with horror. A body lay twisted on the sand. She glanced around. Bodies were everywhere.

Bending over, she retched as her stomach twisted in painful aching knots. Then she stopped as memories flashed through her mind. She knew the woman at her feet. She was one of the maids who helped in the kitchens. Rolayna covered her mouth in anguish.

Over there lay the butler. In the other direction lay two footmen and the stable master. The horrific scene dropped her to her knees. She knew every one of the people here. Every man, woman, and child worked at Seville Castle. The squadron of soldiers Dragos sent must have lost the battle. All the people of Seville lay here, slaughtered like animals. Terror clawed at her throat, and she fell forward, weeping into the sand. Seconds later, Alex's small hand slid into hers. The child trembled with fear.

Good lord, Alex.

With a sob, Rolayna pulled him into her arms and rocked back and forth. They clung to each other and wept. Their hearts became one, in the dark amidst the terrifying brutality lying around them. The two of them were all that remained of a once magnificent castle and its people. She clutched the boy to her until weariness overtook them. "Come, Alex, we will find a safe place to wait."

Chapter Seven

Dragos and his disciples ran down what remained of the band of soldiers Oliveander sent to slaughter the servants of Seville. The rebel bastards were now in hell facing the real Prince of Darkness. The devil and his disciples returned to the seashore as the first fingers of dawn lit the morning sky. Dragos stared at the scene as rage boiled within him. The rebel sent a portion of his army to the seashore while the main army crossed the summit. Only a handful of Seville's squadrons remained. The soldiers were outnumbered ten to one and could not protect the civilians while waging battle.

Dragos weighed the situation in his mind. His men were valiant warriors and gave whatever he asked of them. The lady and the boy were all that remained of Seville, and the king would demand an accounting. But if they took them to the royal city, would Oliveander follow? The bastard kept nipping at their heels, and he wanted nothing more than to give this bastard the lesson he deserved. But he could not until Rolayna and Alex were safe. They must be protected at any cost. Speaking of the lady, where did she go? Dragos frowned. He signaled to Hound, and together they searched the sand for signs. She could not be too far away.

Hound whistled a few minutes later and led them to the tree where the lady lay sleeping with Alex curled in her lap and her arms about him. She held the boy against her, protecting him in her sleep.

The demon studied her. She loved the child. Her aura told him she would give her life to see him safe. He shook his head in wonder and turned to speak with his men.

****

Rolayna woke sometime later to an empty lap. "Alex!"

She spied the child in Dragos' arms. The devil held him close while they held an intense conversation. The child nodded gravely and wrapped both arms around the demon's neck. Then, he wept.

She took a step forward and stopped.

The demon bent down and whispered something in the boy's ear.

Alex lifted his head and smiled. Tears streaked down his face, and he dashed them away with his hands. A moment later, his childish laughter floated toward Rolayna.

Folding her arms, she studied the two. Who would have guessed this fearsome warrior could be so tender? A sudden longing washed over her. She yearned to feel safe and warm, as she did when he held her after Papa died. The man possessed both passion and compassion. A surprising revelation for such a fearsome reputation.

Dragos would protect Alex with his life. An odd feeling tugged at her heart when she gazed at the child. She, too, would protect the boy at any cost. The thought frightened her and amazed her at the same time, but she knew it to be truth, nonetheless. Something changed inside her last night when she held the boy and came to the realization they were the last of Seville. If anyone threatened Alex again, she would hunt them down and kill them. The ferocity of her emotions took her aback. His chubby little arms around her neck melted a spot in her heart she did not know she possessed. The child belonged to her now, and she would fight to the death to keep him safe.

"What direction do we travel now, master?" Azazel asked. "With Oliveander one step ahead of us, we cannot not risk going to Evania. The bastard will follow us into the palace and up to the throne."

Dragos swung into his saddle and took up his reins. He gazed at her and then the surrounding forest. "I cannot wage a war with a woman and a child. We go to Dragonthorne."

"I have no desire to travel north, nor do I desire to go to Dragonthorne," Rolayna said as she hurried toward the waiting horses.

"I did not ask after your wishes. My duty is to see to your and the lad's safety," the demon returned. His metallic eyes sparked in warning.

Rolayna placed her hands on her hips. "Then I shall stay right here." Her chin lifted in challenge.

He plucked her from the ground once more and set her none too gently before him.

"I give you no choice," Dragos answered, wheeling his horse around and plunging into the forest.

This time, she kept silent. She could do nothing to stop him. Not yet.

They traveled north until sundown when the demon passed Rolayna to Azazel and galloped ahead to scout out a safe location with Hound. He returned a few minutes later.

Alex peeked from behind Ramiel's cloak, where he

rode. "Why did we stop?"

Dragos trotted toward them. "We have a lady with us. She does not have the stamina to travel as men do."

Rolayna glared at him, grateful they stopped, for her legs and back ached. The fact the demon knew it made her furious. "I can ride as long as any man can." She glared in defiance as she met Dragos' gaze.

He chuckled but said nothing more.

She stared at him for several minutes, so he knew of her displeasure.

But the man ignored her. His attention remained on the forest and Hound.

Rolayna could not decide if she were grateful or angry; he dismissed her from his mind so easily. She winced as she shifted in her seat.

Azazel chuckled behind her. "If you did not move about so much, the master would not notice your discomfort."

"Mind your own affairs and not mine," she answered quietly.

"We canna help but notice your pain when ye groan and carry on so," Brawn commented from his position beside Dragos.

Her head snapped up. "I do not groan, nor do I carry on. Why would you suggest such a thing?"

"Aye, you do groan, lady," Azazel said. "I am near deaf from the noise."

The other disciples chuckled.

Rolayna glanced around. A whimper escaped as she turned in her seat, and she froze.

None of the disciples met her gaze as they turned grinning faces away. Before she could think up a retort to let them know how wrong they were about her,

Hound trotted back through the trees with news of a small clearing near the river.

He led them to it. The men hacked branches from the trees for a rough shelter and lit a fire for warmth.

Brawn and Scimitar wandered off toward the river to fish, arguing over which one was the better fisherman.

Dragos helped Alex to the ground and instructed him on the proper care of horses. The child became absorbed in rubbing down the massive stallion while the men attended to their duties.

Rolayna wandered away from camp to find a few minutes of privacy, hoping none of the men noticed her uneven gait and shaking legs.

The sound of the river tempted her to investigate, and Rolayna pushed through the heavy brush beneath the trees until she stood next to the rushing water. Closing her eyes, she let the cool breeze brush across her hot face. The cut on her arm ached, but she ignored it. The ground rolled beneath her feet, and she shook the dizziness away. Sighing, she leaned back against a massive oak tree for support and inhaled the scent of the pine trees, the rich earth, and wildflowers. Her legs wobbled, but she did not care. She enjoyed the freedom to lean back and just breathe.

Her mind whirled. *Dragonthorne!* Rolayna shivered. She must escape before they traveled north. Once there, she would never find her way back. So far, she tried running away or using a weapon, but both methods failed.

Time for a new plan of action.

The guard in Chattam responded to her smile and flirting. The demon might, also. She could use his desire for her against him. With a bit of ale and a lot of luck, it could work. Captain Jameson taught her to change tactics mid-battle to throw her opponent off.

Rolayna did a little jig. Her plan promised to be effective. Turning, she walked right into the solid muscular wall of Dragos with a yelp of surprise. "Oh! I did not see you there!"

"Obviously," he answered dryly. "Brawn has dinner."

Rolayna's mind whirled as they walked. When they emerged from the trees, Brawn handed her a dish containing fish from the river and cooked wild yams.

She thanked him and sat on a log to eat. When Azazel passed, she asked for ale.

He handed her the jug. "Are you well, lady? Your face is flushed."

"Quite. I am thirsty, nothing more." She picked at her fish, having no appetite.

Azazel nodded and returned to his meal.

Once she went to the tent, she took the ale with her and waited. Soon, Dragos brought a sleeping Alex in and laid him on the fur.

"Will you walk with me to the stream? I need a moment, and I do not want to walk alone in the dark.'

He glanced at her and nodded.

She bent and picked up the ale on her way out of the tent.

He said nothing until they stopped beside the stream. "You require ale when you seek privacy in the night?" One eyebrow quirked upward.

She took a deep breath and turned to him. "I do when I want to be alone with you." She gave him her sweetest smile and took a sip from the jug. "Join me, please."

Dragos took the jug, his gaze sharpened when her hands went to the laces at the back of her gown. "What are you doing?"

Rolayna fluttered her eyes. "I should think it were obvious." Her laces came loose, and she tugged her gown from her body, dropping it on the ground at her feet. Stepping free, she untied her skirts.

His gaze heated as he stared at the shadow between her breasts and the rapid rise and fall of her chest.

She stepped out of her gown and turned to him, her hands making quick work of her corset. It dropped on the ground beside her feet.

The cool evening air brushed over her, setting her teeth chattering.

A frown darkened Dragos' face. "You are cold."

"Then share your heat with me." She stepped close and wrapped her arms around his waist, leaning into his warmth.

His arms closed around her, and she shivered.

"Kiss me." Her head felt light, and the trees danced in front of her.

"Why, Rolayna?"

She frowned. "Does it matter? Kiss me."

He searched her face, and then his mouth came down on hers. He kissed her thoroughly, his tongue mating with hers until she whimpered for more. When he felt her response, he turned her head to the side and drank deeply. All her pent-up emotions rushed to the surface. Rage turned to passion, and fear turned to desire. The uncertainty of her future made her bold. Her blood lit with fire, and she burned for more. Her insides quivered with excitement. She wanted to feel needed, she wanted to feel safe, and she wanted to be loved. Throwing her arms around his neck, she opened her mouth to his assault and responded to his kisses with every ounce of fire in her soul.

Dragos growled. His hands rubbed lazy circles over her back and then dropped to her buttocks. He pulled her against his arousal, sending a shiver of desire through her. He tasted so good, felt so good, and smelled so good. She mimicked his every move with a boldness that surprised them both. When he reached between them and cupped her breasts through the fabric of her chemise, Rolayna groaned out loud. His fingers found her hardening nipples and rubbed them back and forth until she cried out and arced against him.

Thusting a knee between her legs, he pulled her tighter against his throbbing shaft, and she grew faint. Heat gathered in her stomach, and her belly tingled with awareness and sin. Rolayna panted, moving restlessly against him. God, he felt good. She rubbed against his knee and shivered as a wave of pleasure coursed through her.

Dragos lifted his mouth.

Her head tilted back, exposing the long line of her throat as she gulped in a breath of air. She burned with yearning and passion. "Dragos," she whispered, pulling his head back to hers.

He stilled. "If I do not stop, I shall not be able to keep myself from taking you here in the grass."

Rolayna meant to tease him and get him drunk with ale so she could escape. But now, she no longer cared. She wanted more. "I do not want you to stop. Please, Dragos," she begged. She reveled in the strength of his embrace and the gentleness of his caresses. Every lonely part of her heart welcomed the touch of his hands and lips. Numb to all else but him and the fire inside her, she kissed along his jaw and pressed closer to his heat.

He tilted her chin up. "Do you want me to take you, Rolayna, like a housemaid here in the dirt?" His dark gaze challenged her.

"I would not care," she muttered.

"You should." He searched her face. "It should matter a great deal to you. Tell me, Rolayna, if I accept your offer and take you here and now, would you persist in finding Oliveander? Would you give yourself to him, as well?"

She stilled.

He studied her face as she digested his question.

She planned to run to Rauf, yet she begged Dragos to lie with her. She had no answer to give him. She embarked on a flirtation, nothing more, nothing less. When Dragos touched her, she lost all reason. Heat rushed to her face as she stepped back. Her arms fell to her side.

"I share with no man. If you give yourself to me, I will kill anyone who comes near you. If I find another touched you, I will kill him and then you." He stared into her soul. "Think hard on it, Rolayna, before you ask again."

She turned to go, but he caught her arm.

"What is this?" He indicated the inflamed wound she acquired the night in the hut.

She shrugged. "It is nothing."

He disagreed with a shake of his head and a shrill whistle. "It is something when it oozes, and fever addles your mind."

Jerking his tunic off over his head, he dropped it over her, covering her to her knees.

Disciples filled the area beside them. "Wolfbane, get your herbs. She fevers, and a wound festers on her arm."

Within minutes, Rolayna lay on the furs in the tent while Wolfbane applied salve to her wound. He instructed Brawn on the right herbs and amounts to make a tea for the fever.

Dragos' gaze caught hers. "Why did you not tell me of the wound?"

She blinked up at him. "I did not think it would matter. We do not have time to wait for me to heal."

"It does not matter, now. After tomorrow, the rebels will no longer seek the prize."

Her feverish mind repeated the words over and over. What did he mean?

The men left the tent.

Rolayna dozed off in an herb-induced slumber and awoke sometime later to the sound of their voices.

****

Dragos sat beside the fire, thinking. His gaze wandered to the tent. He did not doubt she meant to betray them again. Her plan to seduce him and get him drunk failed, and he wondered what she would think up next. Her antics would amuse him if the situation were not so serious.

"The lass is daft," Brawn said.

"The rebel army still follows," Scimitar put in. "They have not come this far north before."

"They have never had a reason before," Dragos answered.

"So, what is your plan, master? How do we get the

lad and the lady to safety? We race the rebel army to Dragonthorne," Hound said.

"The rebel army will turn aside before too long," Dragos announced. His gaze met theirs. "I plan to remove the reason Oliveander chases her."

"How?" Wolfbane broke in. "The rebel will not quit until he gets what he wants."

"He will stop when another takes what he seeks," Dragos said.

Brawn straightened, his gaze on Dragos. "Are ye thinking a wedding, then?"

"Aye," Dragos said in a quiet tone, trying to settle the nausea rising in his stomach. He vowed he would never make the same mistake his uncle made and here he sat, preparing to make the jump. "It will keep Oliveander from coming farther north and allow me to honor the vow I made to the Duke of Seville. Fetch me a quill and paper so I can update the king."

****

Rolayna drifted in and out of the conversation. Her fever broke at midnight, and by morning her head cleared.

Alex wanted to inspect her bandage before climbing onto Azazel's mount. "Did a real sword cut you?" His rounded eyes stared at the strip of white around her arm. At her nod, he continued, "Did Zazel have to sew it?"

A smile tugged at her mouth. "No. Wolfbane put salve on it."

"Oh." He sounded disappointed. "If you get cut again, can I watch? One of the people in the sand got their arm cut off, and I found Cook's head." He made the statement as he walked over to let Azazel lift him up.

Rolayna gaped in shock. The boy spoke of horrors as if they happened every day. He should be learning to ride a pony and playing with wooden swords, not studying decapitated corpses.

They rode for most of the morning.

Her mind returned again and again to Alex's comments, and she vowed to give him the life Papa wanted. "Lavender wildflowers and cream cake—" She did not realize she said the words aloud until Dragos' growl rumbled behind her. She snapped her mouth shut and stared straight ahead, refusing to acknowledge his irritation.

After a minute, she cleared her throat. It would be best to rid his mind of any lingering doubts about her plans for the future. "I would like to apologize for my behavior last eve. I admit, I enjoyed your kisses and asked for more. I experienced a momentary lapse in judgement created by the emotional week and the fever. I miss my father, and your kisses...comforted me. It will not happen again. I belong to Rauf. He is my future, mine and Alex's."

Dragos stared at her. "You respond to me because of your father?" The tick appeared on his jaw. "My kisses...comforted you?"

She nodded, hiding her trembling hands within the folds of her skirt. She would never admit his wicked, knowing touch took her to a place where reason quit. She would never confess he made her come alive in a way she never did before. He was an aphrodisiac to her system, and she must get her head on straight. "What else would it be?" Rolayna closed her eyes and feigned sleep to avoid further conversation.

Dragos stayed silent the rest of the way.

They stopped briefly beside a large bushy area at the foot of the mountain. She gasped in surprise when the demon nudged his horse around the bushes. They entered a long dark cavern that carried them through to the other side of the steeply sloping mountain. She gripped the saddle tightly, her eyes clamped shut. The creepy things inside the dark tunnel frightened her. Stiffly she leaned away from Dragos and recited an old nursery rhyme to distract her mind from what might lurk in the blackness. Sometime later, they emerged beneath a canopy of trees.

Rolayna drew in a shuddering breath of relief and relaxed her shoulders. The fresh air soothed her nerves. They waited while Hound removed all traces of their passage, and then they were off once more.

At two in the afternoon, they rode into the town of Northernfell, gateway to the northern provinces.

Chapter Eight

"Have you lost your mind?" Rolayna screamed in a very unladylike, un-angelic voice. "I will not marry you!" Panic clawed at her stomach. When she agreed to Dragos' bargain, she did not know he meant to wed her today! Her entire body dripped with the fine sheen of hysteria.

"You agreed," Dragos responded mildly.

"I will not do it!"

"Do you break your word, then?" he inquired, one eyebrow climbing upward, as he pinned Rolayna in place with a single flash of his dark eyes.

Her ire dropped like a dead weight. Her head fell forward, and her shoulders slumped. "Nay," she answered quietly. She knew what he thought of her, knew by the way he asked he had knowledge of her past. Her hands fisted at her side, and her gaze rested on the ancient wooden floor of the church. She focused on slowing her ragged breathing. She would do the right thing and keep her word if it killed her. Slowly she turned and faced the priest once more.

The small village of Northernfell contained one quaint little church with an elderly priest and a few dozen village folk crowding each other to see the infamous Duke of Dragonthorne. A wedding presented a treat they could not resist, especially one involving someone as powerful as Dragos.

The devil and his disciples stopped midday at the town's only tavern and booked all three rooms and the stables. A warm bath and a quick meal were provided before they walked to the little church. Rolayna stood stiffly beside Dragos, her mind coming to terms with the fact she bartered herself to the devil instead of Rauf. When she agreed to the bargain, she thought she would have more time, time to think of a way out without compromising Alex's safety, time to get word to Rauf, and time to make her escape.

****

Dragos nodded for the priest to resume the ceremony for the third time. Rolayna proved to be a she-devil when crossed. He had no stomach for the marriage either and never wanted to be tied to this vixen. But like it or nay, without her maidenhead, the lady held no value to Oliveander.

He did not doubt the rebel would follow them to Northernfell. The villagers would no doubt fill him in on today's entertainment. In fact, Dragos counted on it. Once he bedded Rolayna, the marriage linen would be displayed for all to see. Oliveander would realize he pursued them in vain, and the rebellion would be slowed. With the lady and the boy safely inside Dragonthorne, Dragos and his disciples would cut the rest of the rebels down, and the throne would be safe.

He had one choice. Someone must marry Rolayna and bed her. As distasteful as he found the task, he could not ask his men to do something he hesitated to do. With her passionate nature, the bedding would be pleasant enough. But the thought of the marriage itself created a bitter taste in his mouth. Here he stood, tying his life to a woman as beautiful as Dahlia and every bit as deceitful, despite his determination to learn from his uncle's mistakes.

Dragos tightened his hold on Rolayna's hand. She agreed to the union to protect Alex. He glanced at the fair face beside him. Ever since the night on the seashore, the boy followed her around like a pup, seeking approval. She sought the boy out just as often. She enjoyed Alex's company, and a palpable bond grew between the two. She never let the boy stray far from her side, even in her sleep.

He presented the arrangement to her outside of Northernfell. If she agreed to marry, he would take the boy in and raise the child as his own, thus fulfilling Rolayna's promise to her father. Alex would have his protection for the rest of his life, and she need only stay until the end of the rebellion. Afterward, she could leave if she desired to do so. He would provide land, a house, and a monthly income as long as she lived. They need never cross paths again, and Alex would become Dragos' son and heir. He did not plan to produce an heir of his own. Not after what happened with his parents. He would bed Rolayna the one time to ensure her safety from Oliveander. After which, he would not come near her. When the rebellion ended, she could go, and he would return to his life as the king's enforcer. He would not make the mistake of falling in love with his wife as his uncle did. Love produced pain and a host of other evils. Their marriage provided a sound solution that benefitted them all.

Rolayna agreed with the barest hesitation.

"Have you forgotten your promise to protect the boy? What becomes of him if you back out now?" His softly spoken words created the desired effect.

She did not make another sound until Father Jarek asked her if she took Gabriel Michael Dragos as her husband. Then, a giggle escaped, and she shot him an amused glance before she answered.

Once the ceremony concluded, he planted a chaste kiss against the silky-smooth skin of Rolayna's cheek.

She waited until they stepped away from the priest before she spoke. She could not withhold a chuckle when she asked. "Your mother named you after not one but *two* angels? Were you so fearsome, even then?"

A dangerous gleam entered his eye, and the muscle ticked along his jaw. "We will not speak of my parents again. You will address me as husband or Dragos."

She grinned with amusement, and he frowned at her. The names angered him and should be used when appropriate.

The village people cheered and wished them a happy life together. More than one commented on the striking couple they made. They were exact opposites, dark and muscular versus fair and womanly. Dragos paid Father Jarak in gold and motioned for the disciples to keep an eye on the boy. Then, he took Rolayna by the hand and walked toward the door.

"Where are we going?" she wondered. "The women are gathering dishes together for our wedding supper."

He led her down the empty street toward the tavern, not bothering to answer. She would know his plan soon enough, and he could not endure any more of her screaming. His ears still rang from the shrillness of her voice during the wedding ceremony.

****

Rolayna gazed in dismay at the empty tavern.

Everyone gathered at the churchyard to celebrate. Dragos led her up the narrow stairs to the room she bathed in before the ceremony. They must be leaving again, she thought and sighed deeply. She hoped for a little rest before they traveled farther and privacy to send a note to Rauf telling him of her whereabouts. Once they reached Dragonthorne, Alex would be safe. She need only wait for the rebellion to die down. After which, she would be free.

Dragos led her into the small chamber and closed the door. Turning, his metallic eyes assessed her from head to toe.

"Thank you for escorting me to the tavern. You may go now." She waved a dismissive hand in his direction.

A disquieting feeling worked its way around her stomach when he bolted the door.

Her breathing hitched in agitation. She thought Dragos would leave after escorting her safely inside her chamber.

He shook his head as he walked toward her.

She backed away until her knees hit the edge of the cot and stopped, her knees quaking in fear. Surely, he did not think to be intimate with her. Were they not in a hurry to reach Dragonthorne? Her heart pounded in her ears, and her mouth grew dry.

Dragos pulled her stiff form toward him and planted his mouth on hers as her scream tore up her throat. He lost no time taking advantage of her open mouth and swept his tongue inside to taste her.

Rolayna pulled her head back to escape his invasion, but he followed, angling his head to gain deeper access to her mouth. Her eyes widened in alarm at the first stroke of his tongue. No, he could not want to bed her so soon after the ceremony. She needed time. Perhaps a year or two to get used to the idea.

His tongue rubbed along hers while his hands caressed her back. The panic inside her subsided. His tongue explored her mouth softly and then, with boldness, igniting a fire within her. A whimper escaped her throat. Languid heat seeped into her blood. He knew his effect on her. Rolayna rubbed her tongue on his, starved for affection. Whatever the price she paid for allowing his boldness, she accepted. After all, they were married.

Excitement spiraled inside her. He tasted so good. She wanted more. Rolayna rubbed against him as pleasure wound its sensual tentacles around her. Her whimpering increased. She returned kiss for kiss, touch for touch, yearning for the heat of his body.

Dragos pulled her up against his broad chest while his hands found the laces at the back of her gown and untied them. He caressed her slowly, rubbing the tension from her neck and back.

Rolayna trembled against the warmth of his hands and leaned into his embrace. His kisses seared her soul. Wrapping her arms around his neck, she pulled him closer. Dragos' touch created a myriad of emotions inside her. Heat radiated from him and spiraled in her stomach racing through her blood like wildfire catching her ablaze. Thought and reason vanished. Only Dragos existed with his wicked knowing tongue and the wild excitement he created. Her dress pooled at her feet followed by her corset and petticoats. Then she stood there in nothing but her chemise.

His hands found her breasts, and Rolayna gasped in

pleasure. Rubbing his thumbs over her throbbing nipples and sucking on her mouth, he rocked his pelvis against the cradle of her hips. The hard length of him pressed into the hollow of her stomach, and her mouth went dry. Moisture pooled between her legs where an ache grew inside her. Rolayna rubbed against his arousal, her knees buckling.

Dragos caught her against him and ripped her chemise from her shaking body. Cradling her against his hard body, he pulled the coverlet back from the little cot and laid her back on the pillow. His hooded gaze roamed her pale naked beauty laid bare to his view. Quickly he removed his clothing and covered her with his large, naked body. His arousal stood on end, swollen and aching.

Rolayna gasped when her body made contact with the cool sheets of the bed. She did not have time to react before Dragos moved over her, opening her thighs with his knees. Then he kissed her again. His large hands roamed her body, touching and caressing every inch of her silken skin. His lips teased and nipped at her mouth while his tongue stroked inside her. He drank of her sweetness and growled low in his throat.

When his mouth caught one rosy nipple, and he suckled, she cried out. Her hips came off the bed, and a scream rose to her lips. He suckled hard, stroking her other nipple with his fingers. Rolayna thought she would go mad. Her secret place throbbed with every beat of her frantic heart. She moved her legs restlessly against him, stroking his arms with the tips of her fingers.

"Please," she whispered, unsure of what she asked him for.

Sliding his hand between their naked bodies, he stroked her moist, heated center. Rolayna went faint when he penetrated her with a large finger, moving it slowly in and out of her tightness while he dropped his head and pulled her other nipple into his hot mouth, gently tugging on the straining tip. She groaned in pleasure. Dragos worked his fingers in and out of her while he suckled. She bucked against his hand, her head thrashing side to side. When her breathing changed to a pant, he centered the head of his arousal at her narrow opening. Moisture pooled on the sheets beneath her announcing her readiness for his invasion, and Dragos pushed inside.

She gasped and tilted her hips to meet his as he leaned forward and kissed her open, panting mouth.

He knew the tearing of her virginal barrier would be painful and wanted to ease into it as slowly as possible, but her hot tight sheath drove him crazy. It clung and gripped him like a glove, throbbing around him until he gritted his teeth to keep from plunging deep inside her.

When the fullness of his sex penetrated her, she came off the bed. His large, rock-hard member inched deeper. She screamed aloud with delight, panting with anticipation. He pushed inside a little farther. Rolayna shook her head side to side. She wanted all of him, deep inside, stretching her. Tilting her hips again, she grabbed Dragos' buttocks to urge him in farther.

He held back for a second or two, gazing at her tightly closed eyes before pulling her mouth up for a deep kiss. He stroked her tongue with his until she whimpered with need. Then he thrust forward in one powerful surge, tearing her membrane and seating his shaft fully inside her.

Rolayna screamed. Pain ripped her apart. Pleasure and excitement vanished, leaving her shaking with cold and frightened of what came next. "Get off me!" she yelled, shoving his chest with all her might.

He took her mouth again, drinking from her lips in gentle sucking motions as his hands wandered her body caressing, soothing, stroking. When he found her nipples and rubbed them between his thumb and forefinger, the heat returned, and Rolayna stroked his back tentatively. She could not bear the pain again and grew uncertain about what happened next.

He caught her hands with his and held them. "It will not hurt again," Dragos said as if reading her mind. "Now, there will only be pleasure." His husky words were followed by another drugging, open-mouthed kiss. Reaching between their joined bodies, he found her. His knowing fingers stroked her with gentle, delicate motions, and Rolayna cried out in ecstasy. Within minutes she writhed and panted beneath him again.

Dragos rocked his hips forward and back just a little. She clawed at his back, her whimpers escalating to screams as he pumped in and out.

"Please!" she cried out again and again.

He responded, thrusting faster and deeper, and the tension built inside her. Higher and deeper, it surged until wonder and ecstasy rose up and over her, crashing her into a sea of the most exquisite pleasure Rolayna had ever known. She held on to Dragos for dear life, screaming her release into his already deafened ears.

****

Dragos thrust harder. His release crashed over him with the same intensity, leaving him shaking and weak.

He never experienced such a soul-consuming climax like he did just now with Rolayna, and the thought made him frown. Why her? Why now? He withdrew and rolled onto his back beside her, wiping the sweat from his face as he considered what happened between them. He did not like it. No way in hell would he repeat this situation. He did what he set out to do. He married her and took her maidenhead. Now she no longer held the power to command an army. As her husband, the land, title, and property of Seville Castle with all her vassals belonged to him. Lady Rolayna Seville was now well and truly the Duchess of Dragonthorne and a pawn in Oliveander's rebellion no more.

Chapter Nine

Rolayna lay still as tremors of her release still shook her. She gazed over at Dragos, her mind reliving the feeling of him inside her, and she wanted him to do it again. Stacking her hands under her head, she sighed wistfully.

"I did not know lying with a man could be so...pleasurable." Euphoria still pumped wildly through her veins. So, she failed to notice his silence.

Dragos grunted and rolled to his side, away from her.

"Mating is a wonderous activity," Rolayna mused. "Since we have been...intimate...with one another, may I call you Gabriel?"

"Nay. I told you how you should address me." His clipped words penetrated the sensual haze of her mind. When she glanced at him, her gaze met the broad expanse of his back, and she frowned in alarm. Massive angry scars crossed and re-crossed his skin disappearing beneath the bedclothes partially covering him.

She sucked in a breath. "What happened here? Who hurt you so?"

It must have taken a legion of men to hold Dragos down. She gasped in horror as he sat up. Large scars riddled his back from his neck to his hips. Reaching out, she traced a shaking finger over one long, jagged scar.

He jerked away. "Never touch me there again." Nude, he strolled toward the pile of clothing on the floor and sifted through it.

"Are you leaving?" Bewildered, she clasped the bedclothes to her naked chest.

His cold indifference finally made an impression on her. Rolayna tugged the blankets to her chin as fear settled into the pit of her stomach. "Will you tell me what I did wrong?" She levered her body gingerly to a sitting position. Her nether regions were very tender, and a painful blush covered her face. "I know nothing of mating. Perhaps with a little experience, I shall improve." She studied him with growing agitation.

****

Dragos tied the laces on his breeches and tugged his shirt over his head. "There will be no more mating." He picked up his jacket and turned toward her. "Get dressed. We leave as soon as you are proper."

He needed air. He had to leave the chamber before nausea overcame him. Bedding Rolayna brought back painful memories of a different time and place, a different woman, and her betrayal. He acted a fool, and because of it, he paid dearly. Lady Dahlia saw to it. Blonde and beautiful like Rolayna, her slim body and full breasts were a temptation he could not resist. In his innocence, he believed lust and love walked hand in hand until he learned differently. She taught him a savage, brutal lesson.

Dragos had not taken a comely woman to his bed since. Rolayna asked if she did something to displease him. She did everything right, and therein lay the problem. She felt too damn good, tasted too damn good, and made him feel things he never felt before. She scared the hell out of him, and he eyed her with distaste. He stared at her messy blonde hair and swollen lips. If anything, she outshone Lady Dahlia, damn her. Glaring at his wife, he stomped out and slammed the chamber door behind him. He left the tavern through the kitchen and leaned against the outer wall. Sucking in a breath of air, he caught a whiff of wasted food thrown out by the cook and manure from the nearby stables. He preferred the aroma compared to the perfume of Rolayna's satin skin, mingled with the scent of their lovemaking. Dragos took another minute to regain his composure, then he went in search of his disciples. It was time to leave for Dragonthorne.

****

Rolayna stared at the closed door. She must have angered him, although she failed to see how. She knew not what to do when a man bedded her. Somehow, she bungled her first time so badly Dragos stomped off in a fit of rage. She brushed her hair to one side and stared at her hands where they lay in her lap. She had no idea the mating act could make her feel so many things. Mayhap she should have paid more attention when the chambermaids prattled on about their many couplings. Even if the experience were totally disagreeable, should he not at least pat her or something and tell her it would get better? A tear splashed onto her hands. Surprised at her own emotions, she wiped her eyes with her fingertips.

The crisp air of the bedchamber cooled her wet, heated flesh. Climbing to her feet, Rolayna tugged the blanket from the bed and wrapped it around her quaking limbs. She glanced at the bed. Bright red blood stained the linen where she lost her innocence. The offending spot mocked her with its significance. It happened so swiftly she did not have time to prepare her mind.

When she agreed to marry Dragos, her thoughts were on Alex. With Dragos' protection and training, Alex would become a powerful lord. A generous offer for an orphan and one she could not ignore. With her marriage, she kept her vow to her father and gained the thing she valued most—her freedom. The boy would no longer be an orphan or alone, and she could live without bowing to the rules of some man.

Rolayna assumed the wedding would take place at Dragonthorne, giving her time to adjust to the idea. After the wedding, she thought she would prevent the bedding by making excuses and pleading headaches. Her mother would do so, and the Duke of Seville always slept alone at such times. Rolayna frowned. She did not guess Dragos' intentions when he led her from the church. And once his lips touched hers, she floated away in the sensuous spell he wove, unprepared for his impassioned onslaught.

His cold behavior afterward stung. Rolayna considered her situation. She traded her innocence for freedom. Not a bad outcome as long as she kept her heart in check and her expectations realistic. Never again would she let Dragos touch her. Vulnerable and tender, she walked to a small basin and quickly soaked a cloth. She cleaned the blood smears from her thighs and washed herself. With trembling hands, she dressed as best she could.

A timid knock sounded on the door. Surprised, Rolayna stepped toward the door. Had Dragos returned to apologize for being so brusque with her?

Instead, a shy little maid stood outside. She explained she came to help her with her dressing. The brown-haired woman stepped quickly into the chamber and deftly helped Rolayna finish her dress and tidy her hair, keeping her eyes averted from the messy cot.

Rolayna blushed brightly when she noticed the blood spot vividly displayed and quickly threw the discarded blanket over to cover her shame.

A few minutes later, the door banged open, and Dragos entered. He spared Rolayna a quick glance and nodded when he discovered her toilette almost finished. With two quick strides, he reached the bed and yanked the offending sheet off. Turning on his heel, he left the chamber.

Mayhap he sought to hide her shame as well. He must not be as indifferent to her feelings as she supposed.

Encouraged, she descended the stairway and left the tavern to discover the disciples all mounted and waiting in the courtyard. Her husband stood beside his mount, his gaze upon her face.

Rolayna blushed at his stare, remembering the liberties she allowed such a short time ago. Once she mounted, she turned to glance back at the inn. As she did so, she discovered his true purpose in taking the linen, and her jaw dropped open. Red suffused her entire being. The sheet with the telltale stain hung from the upstairs railing of the tavern.

She whirled on Dragos. "You display the linen for all to see? Everyone will know how the spot came to be there." Shooting a glare at Dragos to let him know her thoughts about his actions, she lifted her chin in challenge.

Her husband smiled. "I care not what everyone sees or thinks. The sheet is there for Oliveander. He will know the true meaning." Dragos' lids dropped down over his silver eyes, hiding them from view, as he waited for her reaction.

She choked. "You hung the sheet there for Rauf...er...Baron Oliveander?"

"I did."

"Why?" Rolayna trembled with trepidation as she waited for his answer.

"So he will know his quest is in vain. You belong to me, and so do the men you command. I have taken your maidenhead, so the marriage cannot be annulled. His cause is lost, and soon, I will finish the war he started." His satisfied smile chilled her to her core.

"What about the pact you made with me, Gabriel Michael? Is it a lie?" She said his name to goad him and make him rethink his decision to embarrass her.

Fury lit his eyes to a mercurial onyx. "I do not lie," he gritted out. "Alex is now my son and heir. You shall have your release once the rebellion is over."

"But you took me to your bed. I thought—" She frowned in confusion.

Dragos laughed out loud. "How does mating change the pact we made?" He smiled silkily. "You agreed to wed. The bedding is the usual conclusion. I know you enjoyed it. My ears still ring with your cries of pleasure. Oliveander cannot take what you no longer have."

Rolayna stared at him. It would never happen again. She would make certain.

"Never address me by my first names again unless

you are prepared to accept the consequences." His whispered words shivered down her spine.

Nudging his mount forward, they raced after the disciples.

She made a deal with the devil, and now they must both abide by the terms. Once Alex was safe and the rebellion ended, she would leave without looking back.

Alex tugged at the heartstrings within her. Heartstrings she did not know she possessed, and she would do anything to keep him from harm, even if it meant being incarcerated within Dragonthorne's impregnable walls.

They stopped beside a stream well after dark. The men unsaddled the horses and made camp.

Rolayna avoided Dragos and walked toward Alex, needing to hold him close to her and remind herself why she agreed to the marriage.

The boy ran toward her and hugged her about her knees. "We ran!" he said excitedly. Obviously, the gallop through the woods delighted the child.

"Aye, we did," Rolayna agreed with a smile, wrapping her arms around him and holding him. His small warm body once more calmed her restless spirit.

Alex wiggled to get her to let go. "I want to help." He pointed toward Dragos.

The devil held a soft cloth and rubbed the sweat from his horse.

Rolayna let Alex go.

A sharp pain tore at her chest over the gentle way her husband welcomed the boy and rubbed the large black stallion, patiently answering Alex's many questions. If he only smiled, just once, in her direction the way he smiled at the child.

Rolayna straightened and walked quickly away, stopping beside a stream and staring into the water. She did not want or need the devil's approval nor his tender smiles. She would be fine without them. Wrapping her arms around her waist, she let the rippling sound of the stream wash over her. The evening breeze blew against her face bringing the rich aroma of damp earth and the crisp scent of the mountain stream.

"Come." Dragos stood behind her.

Rolayna jumped in alarm. She listened to the night with her eyes closed and did not know of his presence until he spoke. She stayed still, refusing to answer his command.

A large, warm hand descended on her shoulder. "The men have food prepared. Come to the fire." The hand squeezed her shoulder.

With a sigh, she turned and followed him back to the fire and the men. It would do no good to argue. The devil always got his way.

The delicious stew filled her. The men spoke in quiet tones and were cordial and polite. Rolayna smiled ruefully. She understood the change in their demeanor. With her marriage to Dragos, she became part of them. Her gaze dropped to Alex where he lay curled into her side, sleeping soundly.

"Let us get you to bed, so you can rest." Dragos picked Alex up and strode toward a crude shelter of branches where a bed of furs lay inside.

"Why do we not use the tent?" Rolayna pulled the furs back so he could lay the sleeping child down.

"We do not have the time to put it up or take it down. With a tree shelter, we can leave in a matter of minutes." Her husband studied her face. "We will not risk you or the boy. Once we are at Dragonthorne, you will have privacy, but not here."

Sighing, she climbed under the furs beside Alex and turned her back to Dragos before closing her eyes.

Less than two minutes later, the furs lifted, and he slid in next to her.

She whirled toward him, her earlier anger returning with a vengeance. "Get out! This is my bed. You are not sleeping here!"

He lifted a brow, his face mere inches from hers. "This is *my* bed, and you are *my* wife. You sleep where I see fit. Tonight, I allow you to share my bed and offer you and the boy my protection. Do not tempt me to change my mind." He threw a large arm around her and pulled her against his warm body.

She wiggled away, and he pulled her closer. Rolayna stiffened. She did not want to be so close and opened her mouth to tell him when his snore vibrated above her ear.

Alex rolled over the same moment and snuggled closer. If she moved, she risked waking the boy. Rolayna pinched her mouth shut and closed her eyes. She could stand Dragos' closeness for Alex's sake. She doubted the devil would force her with the child nearby. The combined warmth of their bodies drugged her tired mind, and soon her eyelids drooped heavily. Her husband would never share her bed again, nor would he ever touch her again. She would demand her own chamber once they reached Dragonthorne.

Chapter Ten

They arrived at Dragonthorne three days later. A weary, travel-worn Rolayna eyed the fortress with distaste. She did not know what she expected but certainly not the heavy, desolate picture before her.

Situated in the northernmost part of the country, thick ancient forests surrounded Dragonthorne Castle, making it remote, distant, and impregnable. Embedded in the southern side of the steep slopes known as the Devil's Backbone, the fortress rose from the base. Large, dark, and formidable, the stones forming Dragonthorne were part of the mountain slopes it resided within, making it difficult to determine where the fortress ended and the mountain began. The castle rose from the gray rock in majestic proportion. Pillar and spire alike reached upward in endless darkness. For the southern side of Devil's Backbone rarely, if ever, enjoyed the warmth of the sun. As a result, the fortress lay smothered in darkness, shrouded in mist, aloof, and mysterious. Dragonthorne towered above her as stark and forbidding as the very gates of hell. A fitting castle for the devil and his disciples.

Rolayna shivered. There would be no escape or rescue from within those walls. Heavily protected by staggeringly thick stone walls, only an army ordained in the heavens would be able to penetrate the fortifications of Dragonthorne. Two formidable stone towers equipped with arrow slits cut into the stone from every direction guarded the only entrance. The defensive structure of the towers, with their many secrets, ensured the fortress remained secure from invasion. A deep, thick moat lay before the towers. A large wooden draw bridge straddled the moat allowing entrance to those the devil invited in. Visitors at Seville Castle told tales of Dragonthorne, but nothing prepared her for the gray, stark murkiness before her.

Dragos and his disciples thundered across the wooden drawbridge. Once they passed the stone towers, soldiers raised the drawbridge and lowered a heavy portcullis into place.

She jumped when the portcullis stopped with a sinister thud. The heavy metallic ring shook her to her soul. The gates of hell were closed with her inside as the devil's prisoner, with no way out.

The courtyard filled with men, women, and children. They came from every direction, smiling and calling greetings to Dragos and the disciples. Their cheerfulness at variance with the shadows surrounding them. The women came forward and hugged the men, laughing merrily at their jests. The men thumped the returning warriors on the back and called insults back and forth, while the children crowded around too, eager to be part of the happy crowd.

Rolayna gaped in amazement. The people were genuinely happy to see the demons. How did one enjoy the confines of hell and wait with eagerness for the devil's return? She stared at the scene for some time until her gaze caught on a tall, homely, red-headed woman with a crooked nose and bulging eyes, dressed as a lady. The woman did not smile, nor did she participate in the joy around her. She stood surveying the crowd with a sneer of displeasure. When her gaze rested on Rolayna, she gave a haughty toss of her head and sauntered toward them with swaying hips.

"Welcome home." The woman smiled up at Dragos.

Rolayna gazed upon the scene with interest.

Dragos slid to the ground and turned toward her.

"Rolayna, this is Lady Josa, my mother's younger sister. Josa, this is my wife, Lady Rolayna Dragos, Duchess of Dragonthorne. Any questions or concerns with the household, you will report to her." His tone brooked no argument.

The woman's smile fell as she stared at Dragos in disbelief and turned hate-filled green eyes in Rolayna's direction. "Your…wife, Dragos?" Josa's shrill voice carried across the courtyard.

A hush fell over the crowd. Everyone stopped talking and turned toward the trio.

The woman's fists rested on her well-rounded hips, and anger tightened her face. Her thin red lips drooped in a pout. When the silence of the crowd became deafening, Josa lifted her chin in challenge regarding her new mistress with disdain.

Dragos glanced around the courtyard and repeated his words. "This is my wife, Lady Rolayna Dragos. Treat her with respect." His tone commanded attention and submission.

The crowd assented.

"And what of me?" Josa challenged. Emerald fire shot from her eyes. "I am lady here."

The crowd stilled once more. Ramiel and Azazel strolled toward their master.

Dragos shrugged in response, dismissing her. "Not anymore. My wife will arrange the household according to her wishes. Attend to the duties she assigns or leave."

The disciples stopped on either side and waited, their gazes fixed on Josa.

Rolayna gazed from one to the other. They meant to protect her, she realized with a start, glancing at Dragos.

One eyebrow rose as he met her gaze. "Azazel will see you to the castle." He nodded at the disciples and led his stallion toward the stables without a backward glance.

Rolayna glanced at Lady Josa.

The woman stared at Dragos' retreating form, and with a toss of her red hair, she stomped off toward the back of the fortress.

The crowd dispersed with Josa's retreat, and Rolayna let out a shaky breath. She hated confrontations, and this one contained all the ingredients of a hurricane.

Ramiel bowed and walked away.

"This way, my lady." Azazel held out his arm.

She placed her arm on his and allowed him to escort her toward the keep.

Halfway up the cobblestone path, a small priest stepped in front of them. He wore his modest black frock tied around the waist with a cord. A tuft of brown hair blew gently in the slight breeze. "Allow me to introduce myself." A whimsical smile played with the corners of his thin mouth. "I am the demon's priest, Father Nikolas."

Rolayna chuckled as she took the thin hand he offered. "You have quite a task before you, Father

Nikolas. How do you plan to transform the devil into a god-fearing Christian?"

The priest's eyes danced with amusement. "One day at a time. I plan to wear him down with goodness until he gives up his evil ways."

A laugh burst from her lips. She liked this little priest. Perhaps Dragonthorne had potential, after all.

Azazel smiled and continued with Rolayna toward the keep.

****

Rolayna's tinkling laughter floated across the courtyard, and Dragos stopped mid-stride. Her joy was bliss to his ears, and he hoped to hear more of it. He glanced back as his wife smiled at the priest, and jealousy slammed him in the gut. She never smiled at him in such a manner. Frowning over the direction of his thoughts, he continued walking. Of a truth, he did not give her much reason to smile, but as her husband, she should share her mirth and happiness with him, not some other man.

Her beauty mesmerized him. Long, blonde hair gleamed around her heart-shaped face. Her blue eyes sparkled with joy, and laughter turned up her pink lips in a wide smile. Her thin body cast a silhouette against the dark stone of the castle, drawing his attention to the perfection of her form, and his chest tightened. What would it take to make her smile so at him? Commanding her to do so would bring her rebellious nature and the opposite reaction. He had no wish to see more of her frowns.

"Dragos." Josa stepped from behind the stables. "Why have you brought this woman here?"

He turned toward her, irritated at being interrupted

in his inspection of his wife. His eyes narrowed at the challenge in her voice. "She is my wife and lady of this fortress." By the gods, Josa annoyed him. "Do you question me?"

She pouted. Her thin red lips stuck out past her large nose. "I am the lady of this fortress. I assumed you and I—"

"You thought wrong. Lady Rolayna is my woman and my duchess. You will do as I ask and respect her, or you will leave." He turned his back and walked away. Josa proved to be a jealous, possessive woman. He repented of allowing her to stay when she appeared at his gate begging for shelter. They were not blood relatives. So, he had no real obligation other than fondness for her as his mother's sister.

In her mind, his kindness sanctioned a rise in her status within the household. She abused the servants and lorded her position over them. Several complaints reached his ears about her haughty ways. Lanky, homely, and a pain in the ass, she meant nothing to him as she would soon learn. If she did not obey his command, he would set her outside the gates.

Dragos handed his stallion to the stable master and strode back to the keep. He would see his wife settled before attending to other, more pressing tasks. Her smiling face flashed across his mind. Her sullen, angry behavior of the past four days disappeared with the appearance of the priest. Perhaps she would share her smiles with him, too. Taking the steps two at a time, he entered the long hall where he found Rolayna inside, standing beside his housekeeper, Gretta, laughing. Her mouth turned down, and the laughter ceased the second she caught sight of him, and Dragos' frown deepened.

She shared her joy with everyone but him.

He snarled at his own thoughts and shook his head. He had enough on his mind with the rebels hovering over them. He did not need his wife distracting him from his duties. Women were a nuisance, and Rolayna would do well to stay out of his way. As soon as the rebels were defeated and he released her from their pact, the better.

"Rolayna, I see you have met my housekeeper, Gretta. She will see to your needs." He motioned to his housekeeper. "Gretta, my wife, Lady Rolayna." Dragos turned away from the beauty of his wife's face with a growl. "Take care of her."

Gretta dropped a deep curtsy. "Aye, my lord."

Dragos put her out of his mind as he strode away to find his disciples. Azazel gathered them to his war room, so they could plan their strategy. His wife meant nothing outside his vow to keep her safe. Dragos shrugged his massive shoulders to remove his guilt for leaving her standing there so wide-eyed and alone.

****

Rolayna watched him walk away. Anger rolled her hands into fists at her side. Did he have nothing more to say to her? Three long days on the trail without so much as a kind word, and now they were within the walls of Dragonthorne, he dropped her and forgot her. She grimaced at his back and stiffened her spine. She would survive the next few weeks and gain her freedom if it killed her. Once the rebellion ended, she would leave and forget him as quickly as he did her. Rolayna stared after him for a second and then stepped outside to search the courtyard for Alex. Malphas took him by the hand and led him toward the stables, and she sighed in resignation. The lad would be busy helping with the horses until time to change for dinner.

"Come with me, your grace," Gretta said. "We will get ye a nice warm bath and into some fresh, clean clothes. Then we will see what Helga has cooked for your supper." The housekeeper smiled again.

Rolayna smiled back. She liked the dark-haired, welcoming woman, and a bath sounded heavenly.

A bristling Josa strode past from the direction of the stables shooting daggers in Rolayna's direction.

"Let me introduce you to Ivan," Gretta said as they approached an elderly man resplendent in a crisp black uniform, his snowy white cravat in stark contrast. It framed his old face and graying hair, giving him a very dignified presence.

"Ivan, our master brought us a duchess today. Meet her grace, Lady Rolayna Dragos, Duchess of Dragonthorne." Gretta smiled happily and turned to Rolayna. "This is Ivan. He is our butler and the master's trusted servant. He commands the fortress in the master's absence."

Rolayna raised an eyebrow in surprise. She assumed one of the disciples took command in Dragos' absence. "I am delighted to make your acquaintance."

Ivan bowed in response. "It is my pleasure, your grace."

The old gray eyes peered into hers. Rolayna got the distinct feeling he took her measure. She must have passed inspection, for Ivan's face relaxed a few minutes later, and he winked at her.

"Her grace requires a bath," Gretta informed him. "As will the young master, I am sure, after he finishes in the stables." She wrinkled her nose in distaste as she made the statement.

"Of course," Ivan responded as he walked away to organize the household for the two new occupants.

The housekeeper smiled. "Ivan likes you. This is good." She led the way to the keep and off to the left. A narrow twisting staircase led them to the upper chambers. They stopped outside a heavy oak door on the right side of the corridor.

Rolayna frowned. "The stairs are on the left. The chambers are on the right. How is it possible?"

Every castle or fortress she visited was identical, with the stairs located to the right of the long hall and the bed chambers situated on the right of the corridors.

"Master is an unusual man. You will find he likes things…unusual." Gretta ushered her into a spacious chamber with a magnificent fireplace taking up nearly one whole wall. A massive bed stood in the center of the room, covered in a heavily embroidered red coverlet. Heavy red drapes covered windows containing glass panes.

She gasped in surprise at a heavy trunk sitting against the opposite wall. Inlaid jewels and frolicking cherubs adorned the lid and sides of the wooden box. She traced her fingers over the intricate carvings. "How beautiful."

"The chest belonged to the master's mother," Gretta told her. "It is one of his most precious belongings."

"I can see why." Rolayna stroked the exquisite craftmanship in awe. "How kind of Dragos to let me stay in his mother's room. I shall take every precaution I do not disturb the chest."

Gretta gave her a curious look. "Once, it belonged

to the master's mother. Now it is yours." She busied herself ordering servants around in preparation for the bath.

A freshly pressed gown and undergarments were laid out for her to wear. Tying a sash around her waist to disguise the fact the gown needed altering to fit her slender form, she stared at her reflection in the mirror. The pale blue silk framed her fair beauty and added color to her pale face.

Gretta patted powder beneath her eyes to hide the dark circles gained from sleepless nights and pinched the pale cheeks to add a tinge of pink. Once she arranged Rolayna's hair high on her head, she ushered her new mistress out the door to dinner.

As she descended the narrow stairs, Rolayna smiled over her freshly washed hair and garments.

The housekeeper borrowed the clothing from the chest of the late Duchess of Dragonthorne and had them laundered and pressed. The borrowed stockings were silk and the slippers satin. Rolayna luxuriated in the slide of silk against her delicate skin and smiled blissfully. She enjoyed the swish of the silk gown around her feet and the click of her slippers against the stone floor. A mere fortnight passed since she last enjoyed such luxury, but it seemed a lifetime ago. A few minutes later, she took the last step and walked into the long hall in anticipation. The smell of roast duck floated on the air, making her stomach grumble. The aroma of roasted venison and pigeon followed. Rolayna's mouth watered.

A long table stood at the end of the room. A large fireplace blazed behind it with a hearty fire. The warm room smelled of freshly cooked meat and breads.

Dragos and his disciples were already seated at the long table. Several other tables lined the opposite walls and were filled with soldiers wearing the red and black colors of the Dragonthorne Guard.

Alex sat on the bench beside Dragos, his dark hair combed neatly to the side. His little face shone from its recent scrubbing in the warm bath he received. Sporting a clean red woolen shirt and black woolen trousers, he squealed with delight when Rolayna entered the hall and scrambled from the bench, running toward her.

She caught the boy to her in a quick hug. Then she took his little hand and listened with amusement as he spoke rapidly about the stables and the horses. He told her about his new room and the bath he'd received. Then he puffed out his little chest and asked her if she liked his new clothes.

Rolayna laughed in delight. His face beamed with happiness and merriment, and the sight took her breath away. She made the right choice to marry and bring Alex here. The difference between the boy holding her hand, pulling her toward the long table and Dragos, and the terrified boy gazing anxiously at her across the dying body of her father amazed her. Her own discomfort and humiliation were well worth the change she witnessed in Alex.

She smiled down at him and squeezed his hand. When she glanced back up, she caught Dragos' gaze. His dark, brooding eyes roamed over her from head to toe. Rolayna blushed at his lengthy inspection. What thoughts lurked behind his watchful gaze? She wondered. Did he approve of her appearance? Did he like the delicate blue silk gown she wore? Did he like the way her golden curls were piled high on her head?

****

Dragos nearly choked on his wine when Rolayna stepped into the long hall. The pale blue of her gown echoed the blue of her eyes and highlighted her long golden tresses. The silk of her gown clung to her breasts and hips like a lover's hands, while a pale pink sash emphasized the tininess of her waist. Her figure embodied every man's dream and desire, and he could not tear his eyes away. His gaze roamed hotly over her from head to foot as lust slammed him in the stomach like an opponent's fist. She took his breath away with her perfection. Several ideas and positions danced across his fevered mind as he stared.

The silence of the table broke through his hungry, sensual fantasies. He gazed around at his disciples and realized they all thought the same. Lady Rolayna was the most beautiful woman they had ever seen. She looked every inch as alluring as her reputation spoke of. His disciples stared rudely at her, and not one of them blinked.

Dragos slammed his goblet down on the wooden table. Damn it to hell! Why could he not be drawn to a warted peasant or a witch? Fury burned bright within him, and he turned his anger on his disciples. They should know better than to stare! "Lower your eyes, you damn fools, unless you care to die!"

They immediately dropped their gazes and focused on the food on their trenchers. Not a one looked up when she stopped before them.

****

"Good evening," Rolayna said with a smile as she and Alex reached the table.

The men ignored her. Not one of the disciples

lifted their gaze at her greeting. Dragos stared at her with contempt.

She frowned in response. What had she done?

"Have I displeased you?" she asked with hesitation. The evening had just begun, and already he glowered. The man had a devil of a time being pleasant.

"Aye," Dragos ground out. His dark gaze flashed over her again as he sipped his goblet of wine.

"But how?" Rolayna asked. "Will you make known to me where I have offended you?"

"You walked in," Dragos said as if the statement explained everything. He got to his feet and strode from the room without another word.

Chapter Eleven

Rolayna stared at the crackling fire in her bedchamber. Its merry sound did little to lighten her mood. She anticipated and dreaded her next meeting with Dragos. After his abrupt departure from the long hall, the disciples followed suit. They filed out without a word and did not reappear for the rest of the evening. She ate her supper alone at the high table with Alex for company. He asked endless questions about the fortress and anything else which caught his attention.

She explained where ducks came from and how rabbits were caught. After the hundredth question about animals and their many uses, Rolayna laughingly declared enough.

"If you find out everything tonight, what shall we talk about tomorrow?" she teased the boy.

"I do not know," Alex answered honestly. His ability to enunciate words correctly improved daily.

She suspected it had everything to do with feeling safe and wanted.

"What is her name?" The boy asked suddenly.

Rolayna gazed around and caught Josa glaring at her a few feet away.

"I am Lady Josa," the woman said as if the information explained everything. Her hands were on her hips, and her chin tilted defiantly as she advanced toward them.

The child stared at the redhead. "I do not like you."

Rolayna turned to the boy in surprise. Alex liked everybody.

Before she could reprimand him for his lack of manners, Josa responded. "I do not like you either. You are not welcome here." Venom dripped from her words.

Rolayna swiveled toward the woman. Her lack of manners appalled her as much as Alex's. Although she made allowances for the boy because of his age. Josa was naught but a distant relation relying on Dragos' giving nature.

She rose to her feet and stared into the haughty green eyes before her. Anger tightened her mouth. Perhaps the woman did not know Alex's position. "This is Alex Dragos, son of the Duke of Dragonthorne, and his heir. Perhaps you address him so rudely out of ignorance. Do not do so again. Apologize now, and the matter shall be forgotten. Do not, and you shall be set outside the walls." She would protect the child no matter the cost. If Dragos took her to task for challenging Josa, so be it. She would not be ruled by man or woman.

The woman's chin came up another notch. "You do not speak for Dragos. He has no son. I am the lady who oversees this fortress." She sneered in Rolayna's face. "I will not tolerate your interference. Take the boy and leave. Do it now!" Josa's eyes glowed with hatred, her face a sinister mask of malicious intent.

Alex scooted closer to Rolayna, shaking with fear. He took hold of her hand where she stood facing the depraved woman and hid his face in her side.

Gretta suddenly appeared beside her taking the boy's hand. "I shall take him to the kitchens, m'lady.

He is frightened through."

Rolayna nodded and patted Alex to reassure him as he walked away. Once the boy disappeared from sight, she tossed caution to the winds. Dragos would catch hell once she caught up to him for leaving her alone to face his fiendish relative.

"How dare you address me thus! I will not allow you or anyone else to challenge my position. My place is here, as well as Alex's. I am Dragos' duchess, and Alex is his son. It is done. There is no argument. You have stepped onto dangerous ground when you threaten me or the safety of my son. You will leave immediately and never return! If I see your face again, I shall kill you myself!"

She kept her gaze focused on Josa as she called out, "Ivan, remove this woman from the castle and the grounds! See she is locked outside the gates. Let no one allow her entrance again." As soon as she got the chance, she would ask Dragos for a sword and instruct Gretta to make her a gown with wide legs so she could run and fight. If she had them now, the woman would know of her displeasure.

Josa gazed around the room. The soldiers and other servants in the long hall surveyed the scene with interest. No one stepped forward to aid her cause. Screaming with fury, she lunged at Rolayna, pulling a dagger from her belt.

A large soldier from a nearby table rushed forward, catching the demented woman before she reached her goal and spun her away from her target. "The master will slit your throat if you touch the duchess or the lad. What ails you, lady? Have you gone daft? You best get as far from the castle as you can before nightfall. Once the master hears of this, ye will be dead for sure."

The woman gazed at the soldier. "Dragos would never hurt me. He gave his word I could live here as long as I like. Make her go away! I will not allow her to take my position from me!"

Ivan approached with more soldiers and grabbed Josa by the arms.

She erupted in a fit of rage, kicking and screaming savagely. "You will die for this!" she screeched as the soldiers wrestled her out of the room.

Father Nikolas entered the long hall from the kitchens, licking the food from his fingers as he hurried toward them. "Are you all right, my lady?" His face wrinkled with concern as he stared after the soldiers and then back at Rolayna.

"Aye. Josa threatened Alex. I ordered her escorted outside the gates." Her voice shook as she explained the situation to the priest.

"You are right to remove her before something dreadful happened. If you will excuse me, your grace, I shall see to it your orders are carried out. Oft times, I am the only one Josa will heed." Father Nikolas bowed and hurried after the soldiers.

Rolayna sank onto her chair, staring for several minutes at the uneaten food in front of her. If Dragos or Josa thought for one second she would allow Alex to be bullied or mistreated, a surprise lay in store for them. She rose to her feet, her appetite gone. She did not wait to see what happened next but ran to the kitchens and scooped a shaking Alex up in her arms. Turning, she hurried to her chamber. It took forever to get the boy to calm down. Josa and her threat of death frightened the child, and Rolayna held him close for some time. At long last, he slept. Laying him gently on the high bed within her chamber, she covered Alex with a blanket. She kissed his forehead and brushed his silky hair from his face. Poor mite did not deserve to be frightened. He had enough drama in his young life and did not need more.

Weary from the confrontation with Josa, and her arms aching from holding Alex for such a long time, Rolayna tiptoed to the chamber door and asked the soldier stationed outside to fetch Gretta. Now the boy slept, perhaps she could, too.

The housekeeper appeared some time later with a fresh-faced maid she introduced as Liska. "She is our new nanny. She comes from a large family and is good with children. She will take Alex and care for him."

Rolayna gazed at the dark-haired boy tenderly. "He is very frightened. It took me ages to get him to sleep after what happened with—"

"Shh," Gretta responded, putting a comforting hand on her arm. "Liska will not let him out of her sight. It will be all right, you shall see."

Reluctantly, she stepped back and allowed the two women to carry the boy away.

"If he calls for me—" she broke off.

"We will come and fetch you," Gretta answered. "Get some rest, your grace." She closed the door behind them.

Rolayna stared at the door for long minutes, resisting the urge to run after them and demand they bring Alex back. She liked having the boy close.

"No harm will come to him," a deep voice said behind her.

Rolayna whirled around to find herself nose to

chest with Dragos. He must have entered through the communicating door leading to the duke's chamber. "What are you doing here?" she squeaked in surprise.

"I live here. This is my castle," Dragos answered. His deep voice settled around her like melted butter.

"But why?" she questioned. "What do you want?"

****

Dragos' gaze roamed over her before settling on her breasts. What he wanted and what he would get were two different things. He wanted to be free of the task the king set him on. What he got was a complication he could not afford. He kept his word to the Duke of Seville. Rolayna and the boy were safe from the rebels. His problem? He could not get his wife out of his mind. He still had the taste of her in his mouth, and he wanted more.

"I understand you ordered Ivan to escort Josa outside the walls." He watched her through half-closed eyes so he could judge her response. Ivan claimed her defense of the boy in the long hall rivaled a mother bear defending her cub. Dragos wished he were present to witness such a scene.

Rolayna's chin came up. "I did." She folded her arms over her chest, challenging him with her eyes.

"What reason have you to give such an order? I decide who stays and who goes." He watched her flawless face as he said the words.

"She threatened Alex." Her chin came up. "I will not allow anyone to frighten him."

"And if I say Josa stays?" he asked curiously.

Rage flashed in her eyes. She tilted her head back until her gaze met his. Blue fire shot from their depths. "Then I shall slit her throat right before I slit yours. You promised to protect him, and by God, that is what you are going to do. I made a pact with you and sealed it with my innocence. If Josa stays, you all die." Rolayna stared hard at him with her spine ramrod stiff. She meant every word she said.

Her boldness impressed him. His wife spoke with a fire, which lit his blood. By God, she presented a sight with her head thrown back in challenge drawing his attention to the long line of her delicate white throat. Her eyes sparkled with rage, and her lips parted as she fought to control her anger. Lust clenched his stomach tightly in its closed fist. He vowed to never touch his wife again, but seeing her so alive, so furious, and so full of passion changed his mind.

"Josa goes. She is no longer welcome. If she returns, she dies." His words were silky soft. His heated stare roamed her slender figure. He wanted to rip the silk gown from her luscious body and lay her on the bed behind them. Then he wanted to bury his staff inside her until he lost all reason.

****

"Thank you." Rolayna turned away from him. "You may go now." At least they were amicable about Alex. Her knees shook beneath the intensity of his gaze. She wandered over to the bed and sat down to hide her trembling. Clasping her hands tightly in her lap. She thought of what to say to break the silence.

Suddenly Dragos stood before her naked from the waist up, and his breeches were unlaced.

Her gaze snapped up to his.

His eyes were half-closed, and he studied her intently.

"What…what are you doing?" Rolayna asked in

alarm. She averted her eyes from the muscular chest and focused on his bare feet. Surely, he did not think to be intimate.

Large, gentle hands reached around behind her and tugged at the laces of her gown.

"I should think it obvious." Dragos' amused voice rumbled above her. "I am taking my wife to bed."

Heat gathered in her stomach at his words. She remembered the last time and how he made her feel. She also remembered his withdrawal afterward and her resolve to never let him touch her again.

"I do not think I am up to mating with you, Gabriel Michael." Rolayna licked her lips. "I believe it would be best if you slept in your own bed. I am tired." She hoped her use of his first name angered him like last time. Tremors raced through her at his touch. He was so warm. His hands burnt her skin where he brushed her. Her dress came loose and fell from her shoulders.

Dragos did not reply. He reached for her corset and unlaced it also. His lips caressed the side of her neck while his hands worked.

Warm, languid heat stole through her. She wanted to lie back and open her thighs to him. Her breath hitched as his hands caught a full breast, and his thumb stroked lightly over her swollen nipple.

Memories of his coldness flashed through her, and Rolayna jumped to her feet, angry her body responded so quickly to his touch. "I want to sleep alone. Please leave me and retire to your own chamber, Gabriel Michael." She yelled the words, unsure if her anger were to convince Dragos or herself.

He grinned at her outburst, leaning toward her. His dark eyes gleamed in the light of the fire. "I am in my own chamber, Rolayna," he whispered right before his hot mouth settled against hers.

Chapter Twelve

Rolayna awoke with a smile and glanced through half-closed eyes around the duchess' chamber. She had been at Dragonthorne for two weeks, and already, it felt like home.

The men rode out daily to hunt for rebels. Small bands were in the area, looting and burning local villages and tenant farms. Dragos thought the rebel army traveled south toward the royal city, and he and the disciples planned to follow within the week after they exterminated a few more rebel bands.

She overheard their conversation as she entered the long hall one evening, where they sat with a messenger from the king. The man handed Dragos a scroll bearing the king's seal. He read the missive and invited the king's man to rest before he began his return journey.

She led the messenger to the kitchens for a bite to eat, busy with her own thoughts.

"The king approves of my battle strategy. He can think of no better man to entrust Seville and the royal valley to than me." Dragos' voice followed her down the corridor.

Is this how her husband viewed their marriage? As a battle strategy? Rolayna frowned. She ignored the pain in her chest and lifted her chin. Alex, alone, mattered. Alex, and gaining her release. The incident happened the first week following her arrival at

Dragonthorne.

A tentative peace existed between herself and Dragos. He spent his days caring for his people and planning strategic battle maneuvers to use against the rebels. At night, he came to her bed and showed her pleasures she never dreamed of. The devil knew much when it came to bedding.

Her mind returned to the present. She stretched lazily and winced at the soreness. Dragos no longer lay beside her, and Rolayna frowned. She missed waking to find his slumberous sensual gaze on her face. Where had he gone? Sliding from the bed, she jammed her feet into her slippers. The thought irritated her. Since when did she care about her husband's location?

Shouting came from the courtyard.

Rolayna washed in the little basin and dressed. Donning a pale pink gown with rose-colored embroidery around the neck and hem, she brushed and plaited her hair. She slid her feet into matching satin slippers and hurried from her chamber. Correction, Dragos' chamber. She felt her face grow red as she shoved thoughts of what happened the night before from her mind. Her husband made her feel things she never believed possible. The essence of sin, drugging and addictive laced his touch, while his heat was both sensuous and seductive. His knowing fingers and lips drove her mad. She wanted to lie in the erotic fires of hell with him while he pleasured her as only the devil could. Rolayna stumbled as she remembered the things he did to her.

A large hand caught her elbow. "Dinna fall, my lady. The master wouldna' like it." Brawn hurried past her with a satchel of food over his shoulder.

Scimitar caught her other elbow. "My lady," he greeted as he, too, hurried past her.

"What is happening?"

Servants ran everywhere.

Rolayna followed them out the large front door.

Dragos stood beside his massive black warhorse covered in black armor. He held a black helmet in his hand and spoke with Gretta and Ivan quietly. They nodded their heads in agreement. The disciples were mounted and waiting behind him.

"Dragos?" Rolayna stepped off the stone steps and hurried toward him. "Are you leaving?"

He turned in her direction, and a glimmer of approval lit his gaze. He stood watching her, his face impassive. "You look well this morning, my dear. Your blush becomes you." He caught her with one sweep of his arm and plundered her mouth.

When he released her, she stepped back, her face aflame.

Dragos chuckled over her embarrassment. "After all we do together, I did not think you shy." He climbed into his saddle. "I do not have much time. If you have something to say, say it. We ride."

Rolayna gaped at him. "Where are you going? I thought you planned to leave in a week. What is happening?"

Her husband's eyes darkened. "Oliveander slithered from his hiding place. He burns the village to the east. We ride to give the villagers aid."

She tripped. "It is the rebels who must pay the price for all the killings. They wear the blue and the red. Rauf's colors are blue and white. You have no proof he committed these crimes. Promise me you will not kill him."

His eyes burned into hers. "You ask this of me after the devastation you have seen? After Oliveander killed your father? After the rebels massacred your people? He seeks your life, and you would have me spare him?" He shook his head. "Nay, wife. I have the proof Baron Oliveander is the traitor, and he shall die for what he has done. You must trust me in this matter."

Rolayna opened her mouth to protest, but Dragos turned and rode away without a backward glance.

She stood silent until the dust of their departure settled. Did she truly desire Rauf? Or did she seek freedom? In her mind, one equaled the other. Rolayna walked around the castle courtyard while she worked it out in her mind. Once she dreamed of Rauf and being a baroness to make her father proud. Now, she did not. She wanted Dragos, with the wind blowing through his black hair and desire glittering in his metallic eyes. Rolayna sighed. She found contentment and security in his arms. He was the one she turned to in the night when she woke up frightened, and who she confided in.

She replayed their conversation in her mind. When Rauf appeared at the hut, blood covered his tunic. Her father's blood? When she questioned him, he answered her father was where he should be. Rolayna swallowed. Did he strike the death blow or order it done? She prayed to God for the chance to look into his eyes and ask the question. Only then would she be certain.

The next morning, after breakfast, Rolayna took a walk around the courtyard, empty without Dragos and the disciples. She soon grew bored and came back inside, uncertain of what to do next.

A small hand slid into hers. "Dragos will come

back. He is the best warrior in the world, and he will kill the rebels to make us safe."

Rolayna glanced down at Alex. "Aye, he will." The boy should not be so involved in the war her husband waged with the rebels. "What shall we do to pass the time until Dragos returns?"

"Can we play hide and seek?" The boy asked with excitement. "I found some secret places in the castle, and you will never find me."

She laughed. "Aye, we will play. But you must show me these secret places first, or I shall be at a disadvantage."

Alex nodded and tugged her toward the kitchen, strutting with importance. They walked through the long hall and into the corridor beyond. The boy stopped halfway down the corridor and pushed a heavy tapestry aside, revealing a small space behind it. He inspected the floor carefully. Then he lifted a brass ring and tugged. Nothing happened.

Rolayna frowned. "When did you find this?" Walking toward him, she motioned him out of the way.

"The mean red woman hid here. I watched her lift the floor up." Alex squatted beside the ring as Rolayna pulled up on it. The floor split and a section lifted, revealing a tunnel below.

He squealed in excitement. "See?"

"I see." She glanced around for a lantern and lifted one from the wall. Peering into the tunnel below, she caught sight of a ladder attached to the side of the wall. "Stay behind me, Alex. We shall see where this tunnel leads." Rolayna stepped gingerly onto the ladder holding her lantern high. What did Josa do in the tunnel, and where did it go? Slowly, she took one step down at a time, careful with her footing. When she stepped onto the dirt floor, she glanced up.

Alex climbed down right behind her.

"Did you follow Josa when she came this way?"

He ducked his head and nodded. "Only 'til I got to the bottom. It was dark, and I was scared."

Rolayna squeezed his hand. "I am glad you are such a smart boy. Do not go into dark places again unless you tell me first."

"All right. Can we see where it goes?" He peered excitedly down the dark tunnel in front of them.

"Aye." A mystery would keep her mind occupied for she could not bear to think of what might be happening at this moment. Would Dragos kill Rauf? Would Rauf kill Dragos? Rolayna stumbled. Why did her chest hurt when she thought of Dragos'death? He could be formidable, ruthless, frightening, and terrible. But he could also be gentle and kind. He touched all the aching places in her heart. In his arms, she felt wanted and desired and became a real person with needs and feelings. He met those needs and feelings on every level. Shaking the voices from her head, she walked forward, determined to see where this tunnel went.

Several hundred feet later, they came to a "y" in the tunnel. Rolayna held the lantern high. "Which way?"

Alex pointed to the right. "That way."

"All right." She turned to the right, and together, they walked for some distance until they came to another ladder leaning against the tunnel wall.

She glanced up. "Let us see where this goes. Stay here until I call you." Setting the lantern beside Alex she climbed the ladder. When she reached the top, she pressed hard on the wooden cover, and it gave way. Rolayna peered over the edge into a small empty room.

"Leave the lantern, Alex. You may come up, but I am not certain where we are." She stepped into the little room and investigated every wall. The space contained just enough room for the boy to stand beside her. The last wall slid back, and Rolayna found herself in the keep. They stood beneath the stairs leading to the family's chambers. She shut the door. Had they stumbled into a secret escape? They traversed the length of the kitchens and the long hall in the tunnel below.

Alex peered over her shoulder. "I want to go back down."

"All right. We can see what lies in the other direction." She pulled the trap shut on her way back down the ladder.

They returned to the "y" in the tunnel and followed it for some time. The air became moist, and the ground sloped downward. Sunlight appeared.

"Look, Alex."

They pushed their way through the bushes hiding the entrance to the tunnel until they stood on the grass beneath the dark trees of the forest. They were outside the fortress walls! Rolayna gazed around her as she set the lantern down on the grass. Stones and earth lie in heaps about them. Twisted metal fragments littered the ground. Picking up a handful of dirt, she let the moist, fresh clumps run through her fingers. The metal fragments were once a grate covering the tunnel entrance. The tunnel had been sealed, and someone recently excavated it! She gazed up at the high stone fortress above them. The towers overlooked the valley.

Whoever did this went undetected, leaving Dragonthorne vulnerable.

A sixth sense pricked her conscious mind. Rolayna glanced up and caught a glimpse of blue and red through the trees. The rebels! Soldiers crossed a crude makeshift bridge anchored against the base of Devil's Backbone where Dragonthorne and the mountain became one. They were almost across the moat!

Grabbing Alex and the lantern, she hurried back inside the tunnel. "Someone is coming, and we must warn the soldiers." Rolayna caught Alex's hand. "We are going to play a game of hide and seek. We are going to run and hide in the tunnel from whoever is coming. And you must be still, so we are not found." She whispered the words into his ear.

The boy nodded.

They ran back the way they came. It was difficult for Alex to keep up, and Rolayna stopped after a minute to pick him up. Fear lent her strength, and she flew on winged feet, stopping at the "y" in the tunnel. There, she blew out the lantern, so the soldiers would not know of their presence.

Cool air drifted around her face. Men's voices whispered behind them, and their boots scraped along the floor of the tunnel. Light from their lanterns bounced around on the dirt walls. Their swords clanked as the soldiers advanced. The rebel army was infiltrating Dragonthorne in Dragos' absence. The alarm about the village must have been a ruse to get him out of the fortress.

Terror tightened her chest. She must get Alex to safety. Would the men behind her attack the keep or go to the kitchen? Rolayna made her decision quickly.

There would be only one safe place for them. Turning toward the kitchens, she felt her way along the tunnel wall until her hands found the ladder. Alex remained quiet, and she thanked the gods the boy understood the danger. "We are near the kitchens where you showed me the tunnel entrance. Climb the ladder and stay behind the tapestry until I am there."

"All right." His little voice barely reached her ears. He climbed the ladder and disappeared. Rolayna hurried after him. Once she reached the top, she took his small hand. Peering around the tapestry, she found the corridor empty. "Come." She rounded the corner and ran into Ivan.

"We are under attack. Soldiers are entering Dragonthorne through the tunnel. I must hide Alex." She ran past him, ignoring the surprise on his face.

His roar filled the area behind her as he called soldiers to their posts. Rolayna pulled Alex with her through the kitchens, ran across the courtyard, and entered the little church opposite the keep. She found the priest's hole and climbed inside, taking Alex with her.

"How did you know about this hiding place?" the boy asked in awe.

"Father Nikolas showed me when he gave me a tour of the castle the morning after we arrived." Her body trembled with fear. The rebels must not find Alex. She held him close and rocked him back and forth in her arms.

"I am not scared." He wiggled against her.

"Nay? What a brave boy. You have more courage than I, for I am terrified." She said the words aloud without thinking.

Alex stared at her for long minutes. "You may rock me if it makes you brave."

Rolayna smothered her laugh. "You remember how to play the game? We hide and be quiet, so we are not found."

The child nodded his head. "I remember."

They waited.

Angry shouts filled the silence, followed by the clank of metal striking metal. A swoosh of arrows shot past them, and then came the thud of bodies falling to the ground. Screams of dying men rent the air. The sounds got louder, and Rolayna held her breath. Suddenly, the door to the church burst open, and men's boots thudded toward them. The wooden floor clattered with the sound of their feet and weapons.

"Where are they?"

Rolayna's heart thudded in her ears. She swallowed against the knot of fear as she peeked through a small crack in the wooden wall. The room filled with soldiers wearing red and blue uniforms. Shock rocked her to her core. *Rauf* stood in front of Father Nikolas. She reeled backward. Why did he stand there and not fight the rebels? Surely, he knew the danger, unless— She glanced down at Alex and met his terrified gaze.

His expression froze the blood in her veins. "He killed my lord."

The childish whisper shot to her core. "Who, Alex. Can you tell me which man?" Terror gripped her. She peeked out again. Rauf's soldiers were not in the church, only the rebels. Realization penetrated her mind, and her body trembled with disbelief and outrage. *Rauf stood with the rebels!* Up until now, he appeared with his own men in their white and blue uniforms. *Dragos was right about him.*

Rolayna jumped when the door to the priest's hole yanked open, and a soldier stood there grinning. "We got them both."

Chapter Thirteen

All hell broke loose.

The soldier who opened the door fell back with the force of the arrow penetrating his heart. Dragos and his disciples entered the church from every direction. Their war cries rent the air. Rolayna gathered Alex close as metal struck metal, and men cried out with pain. *Rauf!* She leaned forward to peek out. One question burned in her mind. Did he kill her father? If God were merciful, he would help her get to Rauf for she wanted to stare into his eyes when she asked the question.

Alex tugged at her sleeve. "Papa will come. He will save us."

Rolayna gaped at him. "Who will come? Father Nikolas?"

"Nay, he speaks of me." Dragos stood in the little doorway, a broadsword in one hand and a massive shield in the other. "I am his father. Come to me, son."

The boy ran to the warrior and wrapped his arms around Dragos' knees. "I was not frightened, but Rolayna was. She cried."

Her husband's gaze met hers. "Is that a fact?"

Alex nodded his head. "We played in the tunnel until the soldiers came. We ran in the dark, and then we climbed out and ran here. We played hide and seek from the bad men. Rolayna hugged me and cried when I showed her the bad man who killed my lord."

At his inquiring look, she shook her head. "I did not see who he pointed at. The soldier opened the door before I got a chance."

"Why were you in the tunnel? How did you know about it?" He studied her face intently.

"I showed her." Alex boasted. "We went to play, and I showed her the tunnel. It is a good hiding place."

Dragos dropped down until he reached eye level with the boy. "Who showed you the tunnel?"

"The red lady. After she yelled at me and made Rolayna mad. When I woke up, my tummy hurt, so I went to the kitchen. The red lady lifted the floor up. I followed. She walked in the dark and talked to a man."

"What man?" The warrior's tone gentled. "Tell me what happened, Alex. It is important."

The boy dropped his head. "I could not see anything but the red lady and a black man."

"Did you hear what they said?"

He shook his head. "Just something about the air. The black man said the red lady was wrong."

Dragos nodded. "Did you hear anything else, Alex?"

The boy shook his head. "The red lady got mad, and I ran because I didn't want to see her. She hates me. She told Rolayna to make me go away."

"The red lady will not be allowed inside Dragonthorne or near you ever again. You were a smart lad to run." The warrior lifted Alex's chin until their eyes met. "Do not go into any more tunnels or off on any adventure unless you tell Rolayna or myself where you go, understood? I want your word, Alex."

The child nodded his head gravely.

"Oliveander escaped. We cannot find him." Azazel

stood beside them, frowning ferociously. "Where the hell did he go? We have every entrance guarded."

"Search the castle. Look behind every door and in every chamber. He may be hiding somewhere." Dragos rose to his feet.

Azazel's face darkened. "Who opened the tunnel? Who told him about it? Who helped him get in?"

"Someone betrayed us."

Azazel tilted his head toward Rolayna.

Dragos shook his head. "Not this time. Whoever did this dug the tunnel out and planned today's mischief before Lady Rolayna arrived. Keep this among us. We will find out who the traitor is. When I have them, I will show no mercy." He swooped Alex up in his arms and took Rolayna by the elbow. "Come, sweet lady, let us get you back to the keep. I want you and Alex to remain in my chamber until it is safe."

She raised her eyebrow at his endearment but did not comment because her mind returned to Rauf. Did he hide somewhere as Dragos suspected? She allowed herself to be drawn along while she pondered the question. Rolayna did not blame Azazel for thinking she was the traitor. Up until now, she thought the rebels only meant to capture her. As she stared into the soldier's eyes when he opened the door and found Alex and her, she realized he meant to kill them. She shivered. Thank the gods Dragos returned when he did. She frowned as she remembered Alex's revelations. Who dug the tunnel out? Who led the rebels into the castle? And who did Josa speak with? Rolayna glanced at Alex content in Dragos' arms. He should be terrified by the events of the past hour, but he was not. He asked a million questions as they strolled toward the keep, and her husband answered them all.

She marveled at his patience. He possessed such gentleness and kindness when it came to Alex. With her, too, her mind corrected. She blushed as she remembered the way he loved her the night before. He made every movement slow and deliberate, driving her mad while he gazed deep into her eyes so there could be no doubt about his desire for her. She would never get enough of their coupling if she lived to be sixty. He created a hunger within her only he could satisfy. Heat settled low in her stomach, for she knew he would find her again tonight. A smile lifted her lips, and her insides quivered with excitement at the thought.

They entered the keep and approached the stairs. Rolayna followed her husband, her mind consumed with images of their naked bodies and all the things they did when they were alone in the dark.

But a sound caught her attention, and she stopped at the bottom of the stairs.

Dragos glanced back and arced a brow at her.

"I will be along in a moment." She smiled to put him at ease. A glimmer of metal flickered through the slats of wood from the little room above the tunnel.

Rolayna waited until Dragos disappeared before she caught the panel and pulled it back. *Rauf stared back at her!* He held a hand to his chest. Blood seeped through his fingers and dripped onto the stone floor.

"What are you doing here? If they find you, they will kill you!" Her gaze took in his appearance. Though a big man, he appeared small in comparison to Dragos. His blond hair and blue eyes did little to excite her, she realized with a start. At one time. she considered him handsome. Now, he appeared pale and colorless compared to Dragos. Rauf's shoulders bunched together as he leaned against the wall staring at her. He resembled a snake with thin, shifty eyes. How could this shadow of a man ever appeal to her? Rolayna shook her head in disbelief.

"I came for you, my sweet. Surely you knew I would rescue you from this hellhole. You are my heart's desire." He smiled at her the way he did at court.

This time, he did not enchant her.

"Come with me, darling, and we shall be together. Gather your father's ward and anything else you cannot leave behind but hurry. We must exit through the tunnel before we are discovered." His voice shook as he swayed and reached for her hand.

Rolayna stepped back, frowning. "How do you know about Alex?" Her mind whirred. "Dragos said you killed my father. You would not know about Alex's presence here unless your soldiers were the ones who attacked Papa." She stared at him, seeing him for the first time without the blinders of the fantasy world she created.

Rauf's gaze met hers. His eyes narrowed. "Why would you believe the devil? He lies."

She took another step back, swallowing hard, realizing Dragos spoke the truth about him. He murdered innocent people and meant to kill her, too. "You *did* kill Papa. Why?" She cast her gaze around for a weapon.

Rauf straightened, his eyes glimmering with rage. Suddenly, he lunged and caught her, jerking her toward him, taking her by surprise.

Rolayna opened her mouth to scream, but he

clapped a hand across her face. "Do not make a sound, or it will be your last." He held her tight with his other arm while he brought a knife to her throat. "I killed the Duke of Seville for the same reason I am going to kill you. I want Seville's men. With them, I have everything I desire."

She swallowed. "They belong to Dragos. If you followed us through Northernfell you know I speak the truth."

The baron jerked her around to face him. "What difference does soiled linen make? The men belong to me. At least they shall in short order." A crafty smile tugged at his thin lips. "Your under lords do not know who you married, and I have a signed contract from your father giving you to me."

Rolayna frowned. "We never made it to Whitehall Abbey. How could you have a signed contract?"

Rauf chuckled. "The Duke of Seville and I worked it out the day I asked for your hand. We planned the meeting at Whitehall Abbey to collect your dowry."

Her mind went numb. "Papa would never sign without informing me later. You lie."

He merely shrugged. "Who is to know?"

She made a huge mistake trusting him and an even bigger one being alone with him. She needed Dragos. Rolayna's knee came up hard into Rauf's groin. She throat-punched him at the same time, and then she ran.

He doubled over from the pain, but his long arm caught her before she took two steps. Wheeling her around to face him, he backhanded her across the face.

She dropped like a rock, skittering over the stone floor. Rolayna screamed at the top of her voice as she hit, knowing Dragos would hear her. Her shoulder and side ached, and her head swam.

The baron froze when running footsteps approached. "I will come for you when you least expect it, Rolayna. Like the shadows in the night, I will find you. Then, I will give to you all you deserve." He wheezed and disappeared into the tunnel.

Violent tremors racked her body from the encounter.

Ivan reached her first. "What is it, lass?" He bent to offer her his hand.

"Baron Oliveander. He hid in the room above the tunnel. There." She pointed at the open panel. She could not rise and told him so.

Dragos appeared a moment later at the top of the stairs. "What is it, Rolayna?" He dropped to his feet beside her and took her in his arms in an instant. He growled when he turned her face toward him. "Who did this?" His expression darkened as he inspected her.

"Oliveander." Ivan gave a shrill whistle, and the disciples appeared. "He is in the tunnel."

The disciples dropped one at a time through the opening.

Dragos nodded at Ivan. "Send Ramiel to me." Ivan would command the men while he tended to Rolayna.

Her husband tilted her face toward his. "Where else did he touch you?" His voice dropped whisper soft, but he did not fool her. Dragos would tear Rauf apart.

"Nowhere. He struck me, and I hit my shoulder and side on the floor. Nothing else happened." She gazed into Dragos' amazing granite eyes and drew comfort from the violence of his thoughts. He would seek retribution.

He took the stairs two at a time, whistling shrilly as

he ascended. Kicking the door to the master chamber open, he laid Rolayna gently on the bed.

Gretta appeared at his side.

"Care for my lady until I return."

The housekeeper curtsied and reached for Rolayna's hand.

Ramiel appeared at the door.

"Stand outside. Let no one in."

The disciple nodded and took his spot beside the door. "Who touched the mistress?"

"Oliveander." Dragos disappeared in the blink of an eye.

"Now, my lady, tell me where you hurt and what happened to you to have the master so upset." Gretta ordered a warm bath and a hot cup of tea while she worked.

Rolayna explained the sequence of events.

"Why did you not call for the master when you discovered the rebel behind the panel?" the housekeeper asked as she helped her mistress from the brass tub.

Rolayna dropped her head. "I wanted to learn the truth about my father's death. I did not believe Rauf killed him. I thought if I looked into his eyes when I asked the question, I would know the truth."

"And did you? If the master said it is so, it is," Gretta announced. "You must trust the master. Many call him a devil, but the master is nothing of the kind. There is not a better man anywhere." After this observation, she gathered up the soiled clothing and towels and left the chamber.

Rolayna sighed. She knew the truth, and it frightened her. If Dragos had not abducted her and her father in the woods—she trembled beneath the fine linen—she would be dead, and no one would know where or why. She owed Dragos her life, Alex's, and everything in between. A lifetime would not be enough to show her gratitude.

Easing onto her back, she stared up at the rich plaster ceiling and thought of her father and his insistence she promise to care for Alex. Now, she knew why. Rauf would have slaughtered the boy with no mercy.

Sometime later, the door to their chamber swung open and Dragos strolled inside, a curious expression on his face. He leaned against the wall and stared at her. "Why did you converse with Oliveander below stairs before calling for help?"

Her head came up, and she answered without flinching. "I wanted the truth about my father's death. I asked him if he killed Papa."

Dragos' eyes darkened. "Perhaps you care to explain why you would believe the word of a murderous rebel over mine?"

Chapter Fourteen

"My lord, the Duke of Emberly approaches the drawbridge." Ivan made the announcement at breakfast two weeks later.

Rolayna's hand rose to her throat. "Did you say the...Duke of Emberly?" Her voice dropped to a whisper. It could not be. Just when she thought things could not get any worse, they did. Dragos had not returned to her bed since the night of the attack. He and his disciples chased Oliveander into the forest. His tracks led them to the river, where they disappeared.

The men set up teams on both sides and scouted the banks for a sign. They tracked two miles of riverbank before the rain began. It poured for four days. The riverbank grew so muddy and slippery, it became impossible to track anything. They found no trace of Oliveander. Whatever sign he left got washed away, and he had not been seen since.

Dragos questioned Rolayna about not sounding the alarm the second she knew Rauf hid below the stairs. If she warned them, Oliveander would be dead. With him loose, and God knew where, the fault lay with her.

"What if he killed you? Did you stop to consider what might happen?" He paced back and forth as he lectured her. Then, he stopped. "Why do you doubt my words? I cannot understand your reasoning. I have never lied to you, yet you continue to doubt me. I told you the day I rescued you what Oliveander intended to do with you. I told you who killed your father, and you refuse to believe the truth of it. If you trusted me, Oliveander would be dead, and the rebellion would be over." The lecture went on and on.

Rolayna stared at her hands. She had to admit she agreed with him. The murderous intent in Rauf's eyes told her she'd made a mistake about him. She said as much to Dragos, and it infuriated him further. She must trust him. Lives depended on it.

"I am sorry," she whispered. "You spoke the truth in all you told me."

He carried on as if she had not spoken. "What of Alex? Should I relay the message you are sorry when he weeps for you at night?" When Dragos finished his interrogation, he left the chamber and did not return.

Ramiel approached her the next day with a dagger and leather sheath, curved to fit inside the pocket of her gown.

Dragos accompanied him. "You have not the strength to wield the broadsword. This weapon will be more effective. Ramiel took special care when he crafted it. Scimitar will train you in its use."

And he did.

For the next two weeks, Dragos ignored her and spent his time in the courtyard training with his men. With Oliveander close by, Dragos canceled their plans to leave and spent the time scouring the countryside for the rebel army.

Rolayna gazed down at the table before her. If it were not for Alex and his constant chatter, she would have gone mad.

Things were tense between them, and she knew not

how to make it better. She could not undo the past, and now the Duke of Emberly, her former fiancé, arrived at their gates. Her hands shook beneath the table. She knew what Dragos thought of her and her actions concerning the duke. She did not know how much more of her husband's contempt she could bear. Rising from the table, she excused herself.

"Going somewhere?" Dragos' dark gaze rested on her face. "You will stand by my side, Rolayna, and welcome the duke and duchess."

She met his gaze. "If this is your wish." She would do as he asked to promote peace between them while she remained at Rathborne. Her chin rose. She yearned to see the flash of approval in Dragos' eyes once more when he gazed at her. And she wanted him to return to their bed, so large and cold without him. If dancing in attendance to Miles Emberly paid part of the price to regain Dragos' trust, so be it.

Rolayna rounded the table and gave Dragos her arm. Together, they walked from the long hall and stood outside the large front door, side by side.

A black carriage stopped in front of them, and the carriage door opened. The Duke of Emberly emerged. He ducked his dark head and stepped onto the cobblestone drive. Tall and muscular like Dragos, he flashed a smile to the lady inside the carriage and accepted the cane she handed out.

The Duchess of Emberly stepped from the carriage moments later, a petite lady with long dark hair and brown eyes. She stood beside the duke dressed in the latest fashion. Her elegant traveling gown of peach silk molded her slim figure like a second skin. Her head just reached the duke's shoulders. Laughing, she accepted his arm, and they turned toward Dragos and Rolayna.

"Miles, good to see you." Dragos stepped forward to take his friend's hand.

Rolayna stood stiffly at the top of the stairs. Her gaze darted from her husband, to the duke, and then to Christina.

"Good to see you, too, my friend." The duke shook Dragos' hand and clapped him on the back. When his emerald gaze met hers, a frown crossed his handsome face. "I knew you married. I did not know who—" He turned to his wife in confusion.

"How are you, Rolayna?" The duchess covered the awkward silence with a quick hug. "It is nice to see you. You are looking well."

Rolayna set her personal feelings aside. She smiled at Christina and curtsied at the duke. "Please, come inside." Stepping inside, she motioned for them to follow.

Dragos shot her an assessing glance before ushering their guests into the hall.

The Duke of Emberly hobbled toward the fire with his cane. The duchess followed suit, talking constantly about the drive and the horrors of travel.

Rolayna stood awkwardly beside the door. Now what? Should she follow, or should she see to their dinner?

Dragos caught her gaze and smiled. "Come, wife, our guests are hungry and tired. Make them welcome in our home."

She nodded and hurried to the kitchen to find Ivan. She forgot Dragos and Miles were close friends. They were inseparable before Miles married Christina DeGant, founder of the *Thorns of the Rose* group.

Rolayna shook the heavy feeling from her heart. If she could go back in time, there were many things she would change. Once she ordered dinner and a guest room prepared, she hurried back to the long hall.

Dragos' voice floated toward her.

"Oliveander hid in the tunnel entrance while we walked past. Rolayna knew of his presence and spoke with him. She did not alert any of us to his presence until it suited her. She betrayed me, and I find I cannot forgive her for it." Dragos faced the fire with his back to the door. So, he did not see her standing there.

Rolayna turned to stone. He thought she betrayed him.

"Perhaps she has a good reason," the Duke of Emberly murmured.

The duchess nodded her head. "Rolayna would not do something so foolish. Did she explain why she waited to sound the alarm?"

Dragos turned around. "She said she wanted to look into his eyes when she asked about her father's death. She knew Oliveander killed him."

Miles frowned. "Did she watch it happen?"

"Nay. I told her how it happened. She doubts my word and seeks the truth from my enemy." He ran a hand through his hair. "She swears she is loyal to me. But I do not know what to believe. I cannot trust her or her word."

Rolayna's knees shook.

"What reason would she have to lie?" Miles asked.

Dragos snorted. "Does she need a reason? Remember what she did to you. One week after your engagement announcement, she broke it off. Such a scandal is hard to live down. Everyone stared at you and your injured leg. They assumed you offended the lady in some way and speculated on the cause. All of the drama Rolayna created with her childish actions. She could not marry a scarred man while she was so perfect. You are lucky Christina came along and rescued you. Otherwise, you would still be the headline on the daily scandal sheet."

The Duke of Emberly frowned. "She gave me no explanation at the time. If this is her reasoning, how does she bear her marriage to you? Does she gaze upon the scarring on your back with the same distaste?"

Dragos glanced up and met Rolayna's gaze across the length of the room.

She heard enough and stalked toward them, shaking with fury. "No, I do not. When I look at Dragos, I see so much more than his scars. I see a warrior bound by honor to do the right thing. And despite the manner you gossip behind my back, I will join this conversation and defend my actions. I have kept my word on *every* count, and I would ask a question of each of you. If a man killed someone precious to you, would you not wish to gaze into his eyes as he confessed to the crime? I have not betrayed you, Gabriel Michael Dragos." She stared at him. "Nor you." She indicated the Duke of Emberly. "You know nothing of my reasons and refuse to accept my word, as well." She turned and walked from the hall with her head high.

"Rolayna!" Dragos called out to her, but she did not care.

Their disagreement should remain between them and should not be discussed with their visitors. She needed time to sort through her feelings. Seeing the

Duke and Duchess of Emberly roused many old feelings and emotions she thought she put behind her. She had not come face to face with either one of them since she broke the engagement. Her father whisked her from Evania following the scandal and quarantined her at Seville. She learned of their marriage and Christina's betrayal while in exile. Now they were privy to her private battle with Dragos, as well. Rolayna climbed to the north tower. She did not see Father Nikolas and ran right into him.

"I am sorry, Father," she mumbled.

"Lady, what is wrong?" He peered past her to the open door of the long hall. "Who made you weep?"

Father Nikolas possessed a kind soul, and he always spared the time to talk. She often unburdened herself on him, but this time she would not.

"'Tis nothing, Father. I have something in my eye." She hurried off before the priest could question her further. She must sort through this alone. The dear priest could do nothing about the mess she made of her life.

Rolayna ran across the courtyard. She brushed past Brawn when he stepped in front of her.

"Mistress?" He caught her elbow. "Did someone hurt ye? Point the way, and I shall see they pay for making ye sad."

She could hardly tell him the responsibility lay with his master. "I am fine, Brawn, thank you." She hurried away and ran into Malphas and Azazel. Twice more, she explained she must have something in her eye. They were kind to worry for her welfare, but she must solve this on her own. The mess belonged to her.

At last, she reached the tower steps. Rolayna

climbed to the highest turret to be alone and think of what to do. She did not break her engagement, as Dragos said. Christina knew the reason why, yet she said nothing.

She rubbed the jagged scar on her wrist. How foolish she had been her first year at court. If only she'd considered the havoc her actions would cause, much hurt would have been avoided.

Rolayna closed her eyes and let the cool breeze from the tower dry the tears on her cheeks. It did no good to wallow in self-pity. The past could not be changed. She must face the future and create her own destiny. Staring at the forest surrounding Dragonthorne with unseeing eyes, she wondered if Rauf died trying to escape Dragos and the disciples.

They would not give up until they found him or his body. They left the fortress daily, searching for a trail or clues. Hound resembled a dog with a bone and would not let it go.

A flash of something in the trees caught her gaze, and she leaned forward. A carriage surrounded by a squadron of soldiers approached the castle. More visitors. She sat back. Who came now?

"Hello."

Rolayna turned sharply at the sound of Alex's voice. "Hello yourself. What are you doing up here?" She slid from her seat on the stone ledge and hurried toward him.

Dressed in black and carrying a wooden sword, he announced, "I am training to be a disciple." He waved his wooden sword around, mimicking the actions the disciples used when they trained. "You came up here. So, I came to protect you."

Rolayna smiled. "I am so glad you did. Where did you get your clothing? I do not remember you having black clothing."

Alex grinned. "Gretta made them. Papa told her to. Do you like them?"

She returned his grin. Ever since the rebel attack, Alex called Dragos "Papa." She reached for his hand. "Yes, I do. You are dressed like a disciple. Are you hungry? Let us go find something to eat."

She did not like Alex in the tower. There were no railings or barriers to keep him from falling out. Rolayna scolded him once already for climbing the steep steps. She would need to be more careful in the future, so he did not follow her again.

They walked into the courtyard as the black carriage came to a stop. The soldiers filed in on their mounts dressed for battle.

Rolayna swallowed her fear. Who came to visit with warriors?

Dragos stood on the front steps watching the new arrivals. Fury tightened his lips.

She took a quick step backward when she read the hatred in his expression as he gazed at the newcomer. Catching Alex to her, she whispered for him to keep still.

Dragos turned to her and motioned for them to stay where they were.

She nodded to let him know she understood.

Miles stepped out beside her husband, staring at the men on horseback while his hand caressed the hilt of his sword.

Dragos turned to the carriage. He pulled his sword from its scabbard in warning and advanced.

Chapter Fifteen

Rolayna watched in horror as the soldier on the lead horse gave a battle cry and charged at her husband. Metal hit metal as Dragos deflected the blow with his broadsword. The two men exchanged furious thrusts and parries until they broke apart, and the horseman rode toward the gate.

She thought for one tiny moment the soldier admitted defeat until he wheeled his horse around and charged toward her husband with his sword held high. They met with a clash of sword and shield.

In the flurry, the soldier's sword cut a wide swathe across Dragos' right arm as he rode away toward the gate.

Her husband roared and slapped a hand across the wound. Blood dripped between his fingers.

Rolayna cried out and rushed forward, but one of the guards blocked her path. "The master ordered us to keep everyone back."

She stomped her foot in frustration.

Dragos had his back to her as he dealt with his wound. When he heard her cry, he lifted his head to glance at her.

She had a quick impression of eyes dark as midnight and the veins in his face and neck black as coal. She shook her head and stared. When he turned again, his eyes and veins returned to their normal color.

Rolayna gaped at him, confused and shocked. Did anyone else notice the unusual color of his eyes, or had she imagined it? She gazed around the courtyard.

Every eye present focused on the two men. No one spoke or moved.

Dragos' men stood shoulder to shoulder in front of the portcullis, blocking any escape. They held their weapons ready, their faces expressionless. Even Miles remained motionless, his hand still resting on the hilt of his sword and his gaze on the battle.

Rolayna blinked. She must have lost her senses from too many sleepless nights and tension. With a shrug, she put the matter from her mind.

Ramiel appeared at her side.

He took Alex by the hand and motioned for her to follow. "Come, we will see you inside."

Rolayna shook her head. "Take Alex. I will stay here."

The disciple disappeared with Alex. Azazel appeared at her other side. "The master wants you inside where you are safe. This man is dangerous."

"Who is this warrior?"

The soldier gave a cry and made his third rush with a raised sword.

Her husband knocked the soldier from his horse and turned to face his adversary with his legs braced wide.

"The man challenging the master is his uncle, the Duke of Northernfell."

Rolayna felt faint. "His uncle?"

Azazel nodded. "He trained the master as a squire."

The soldier got to his feet and removed his helmet. The man possessed gray hair and silver eyes.

"The village where Dragos and I married is—"

"Aye. It belongs to the master's uncle." Azazel stood stiffly beside her.

"Why did he marry me *there*? Why not invite his uncle if he is Lord of Northernfell? What—" Rolayna's eyes widened as sword clashed with sword.

"It is best to ask the master your questions."

Dragos caught his uncle with a fist to the face and knocked him off his feet. Then, he strode over and put his boot on the older man's neck. He glanced at his uncle's men. "Bid your master farewell."

He raised his sword above the duke's chest when a woman screamed, "Stop."

Rolayna gazed at the carriage.

A woman covered in a black cloak stepped out onto the cobblestones. "You have your revenge. Let him up." She removed the hood from her head, and Rolayna gasped. The woman possessed stunning beauty with long golden hair and bright blue eyes. She stopped in front of Dragos. "Let him go. Killing him will not accomplish anything."

He ignored her and glared down at his uncle. "Why are you here?"

"I have news of the rebels." The duke had a deep, raspy voice.

Dragos stared long and hard into his uncle's eyes. "If this is a trick, I swear before all the gods I will skin you and feed you to the dogs. Tell me your news before I regret my decision to let you live." He removed his boot and stepped back.

The Duke of Northernfell rose to his feet. "I come by the king's command. Invite me in, and I will give you the message he sent me to deliver."

They stood eye to eye and glared at each other for several minutes. "Only for the king. One night and remember, Uncle, this is my castle. I am master here."

The duke shrugged and motioned for his men to dismount.

The lady smiled at Dragos. "Is this your bride?" She tilted her chin in Rolayna's direction. "How...flattering." She turned and studied Rolayna for several long uncomfortable minutes before her smile dropped. "Make ready a chamber for us." She snapped her fingers to emphasize her command.

Dragos' eyes turned to mercury. "You will address my wife with respect, or you can sleep in the courtyard." He strode toward Rolayna and took her arm. "Walk with me, my sweet."

Her chin rose, not understanding the undercurrents passing between her husband and the newcomers but determined to hold her own in any event.

The blonde woman stepped into their path as laughter erupted from her throat. "I wondered why we were not invited to your wedding, Dragos. The villagers told us you came to visit. Now, I see why." She threw her head back and laughed again. "You could not have me, so you found a wife close enough to be my twin. Is she the reason you hung your soiled linen from the inn? You wanted me to see you found someone else?"

"I left the message for another and gave no thought to you whatever." Dragos removed the woman from his path and took Rolayna's hand. "Come."

She hurried to keep up with him. Once they were far enough away they would not be overheard, she asked her questions. "What does she mean? Who is she? Were you engaged to her at one time—"

"She is nothing." His clipped voice said he did not wish to discuss the matter further.

"But who is she?" Her curiosity dared her to continue.

Dragos stopped. A deep sigh escaped him as he ran a hand through his hair and gazed down at her. "Her name is Lady Dahlia. She is my uncle's wife and the spawn of Satan. A more conniving, deceitful woman cannot be found. For once, do as I ask and stay away from her."

She nodded.

He left her in the long hall and stalked away, saying he would see to the guests' chambers. His voice echoed in the corridor as he called for Ivan and disappeared.

Rolayna's hands trembled. *Lady Dahlia.* Someone at court called her Lady Dahlia, and the young lord who escorted her laughed.

"Lady Rolayna is a pale imitation of Lady Dahlia."

She wondered what he meant, but now she understood. The other woman possessed a sensual self-confidence she did not. Shaken, she walked toward the fire and held trembling hands to the blaze.

"You have nothing to fear from Lady Dahlia." Miles Emberly approached from the courtyard and stopped beside her. He, too, held out his hands toward the fire.

She assessed his dark brown hair and emerald eyes. Muscular and handsome, she would have been well off with him, for they made a good match. She never would have loved him, though. Her heart yearned for something different, someone different. Dragos, with his black hair and onyx eyes, flashed through her mind.

Her knees grew weak, and her breath hitched. She craved, wanted, and loved Dragos. She loved him! Frowning over the realization, Rolayna put a hand to her head to stay the dizziness.

"Is it so bad?" the duke asked, watching her expression.

She glanced up in surprise. "Is what so bad?"

Miles gazed at her for a minute. "I admit it is awkward being here together like this." He turned back to the fire. "But there is no reason why we cannot be friends." Several minutes of silence followed before he cleared his throat and continued. "I have not gotten a chance to thank you."

"Thank me? For what?" Confusion wrinkled her brow.

The duke turned to face her. "I wanted to thank you for breaking our engagement. I never would have found Christina without you." His gaze wandered over her face. "Dragos is a good man and has been my best friend for as long as I can remember. Do not be angry with him for speaking with me about his troubles. We have shared everything for so many years I do not believe he considered how you would feel when you discovered him confiding in me. He does not trust easily, and rightfully so. He nearly lost his life the last time he listened to his heart. He loved a lady and believed she loved him in return. Later, he discovered the woman used him to make her husband jealous, and he has not been the same man since. I see how he stares at you. He loves you. He may not admit it, but he does. He would give his life for you. Do not hurt him. I do not think he would recover this time."

She wanted to ask him more, but Christina entered

from the kitchens. "There you are, Rolayna. I have been searching everywhere for you."

"Have you?" She had not seen Christina since the day she betrayed her. Rolayna turned toward the duchess and asked what she wanted to ask for two long years. "Why seek me out now when you could have anytime over the last two years?

Christina blushed bright red and glanced at Miles. "What would you have me say? I am happy with my station in life."

"I should think an apology would be a start." She rubbed the knot in her stomach. "The least you could do is release me from my vow or tell them the truth. My husband does not trust me, and I cannot explain what happened."

The duchess paled before glancing at Miles and shaking her head. "Nay, Rolayna. I cannot—"

"Tell me what?" Miles gazed from one to the other.

"There you are, duchess."

Rolayna whirled toward the door.

Lady Dahlia strolled into the long hall, followed by her husband, the Duke of Northernfell. "I am ready for my dinner. How long before it is ready?" She dismissed Rolayna with a wave of her hand and seated herself in the chair facing the fire before turning to her husband. "I find this fortress dismal and the hospitality lacking, Gregory. How long must we stay here?"

Rolayna faced them. "You are welcome to leave at any time. You were not invited, and my husband is a reluctant host. In my father's castle, guests waited to be invited to dine. They did not show up unannounced and make demands. Perhaps good manners are not observed so far to the north. Or is it only the people of

Northernfell who are lacking?"

Lady Dahlia's mouth gaped. "Did you hear her, Gregory?"

"This is my home, and I am mistress here. We shall dine when I say it is time. If you find us so lacking, perhaps you should continue your journey and stay elsewhere. I will not tolerate rudeness." Rolayna glanced at Christina. "I am not the shy, awkward girl I used to be, and I do not bow easily, not to anyone, not anymore." She walked out, leaving an awkward silence behind her.

Ivan served dinner an hour later. It proved to be a tense affair. Dragos and Rolayna sat side by side in the center. The Duke and Duchess of Emberly sat on Dragos' left-hand side. The Duke and Duchess of Northernfell sat on Rolayna's right. The disciples sat along either side of the long table.

Dragos simmered with rage the whole time. He answered with a grunt or not at all.

Rolayna swirled the food around on her trencher. Alex ate in the kitchen with Ivan. His childish laughter floated toward her, and she smiled in response. The boy created a ray of happiness in her dark world. She wished she were in the kitchen sharing her meal with him instead of enduring the heavy awkwardness of the long hall.

"Tell me this message you have for me, Uncle. I am impatient to hear what is so important you journey to Dragonthorne to relay." Dragos took a sip of his ale.

Gregory cleared his throat. "Always impatient. Let me eat my dinner, and I will tell you the news."

Dragos set his ale down on the table and leaned forward until he met his uncle's gaze. "Do not play games with me, Uncle. I am no longer a boy. Speak your piece, or I will throw you from the turret, and Dahlia will follow. You know you are not welcome here."

The duke put his mutton leg down on his trencher and licked his fingers. "I heard Baron Oliveander entered Dragonthorne through the tunnel while you were not here."

Dragos grunted.

"I heard he disappeared, and you cannot find him." The duke took a sip of his ale and wiped his mouth with the back of his hand.

Her husband grunted again. "Do you have a message for me, or do you come to gossip like a woman?"

The Duke of Northernfell slammed his mug on the table. "Be careful, Boy. I thrashed you once, I can do it again."

"Nay, Uncle. You are no longer the warrior you were, and I am no longer a youth. You live because of my leniency. I could have killed you today, and I did not. Do not make me regret my decision."

The duke stared at Dragos for long minutes. "Oliveander attacked Graystone. He gutted the castle and burned it to the ground. He took the priest, Father Bernard, captive and holds him for ransom. The king is furious. He sent me to help you kill the baron and stop the rebellion."

Rolayna dropped her head. "Graystone is my father's vassal, overlord of a vast area of my father's holdings. Father Bernard serviced Graystone as well as Seville. Rauf killed my father. He killed my people and threatened my life. Now he has my priest, Father

Bernard."

She gazed into Dragos' beautiful dark eyes. "Why will he not leave me alone?" She got up from the table and left the room.

****

No one moved or spoke for several minutes.

"Whatever you need of me, I will give," Miles said, breaking the silence. "My sword and my men are at your command."

Dragos nodded. "We must rescue the priest. Rolayna cannot take too much more. Already she lies awake at night and cries for her people and her father. She thinks I do not know, but I hear her. I cannot bear her sadness and yearn for the return of her smile. Without Alex, she would have been lost. He is the only person who anchors her emotions. We ride at dawn."

Miles nodded his head. "I will take Christina home and meet you at Graystone."

The Duke of Northernfell watched Dragos with narrowed eyes. "I ride with you."

Dragos shook his head. "I said you may stay one night, no more. Take your wife home. She is not welcome." Dragos set his goblet on the table and leaned back. "I am prepared to accept your pledge of fealty." His dark gaze challenged his uncle.

The Duke of Northernfell rose to his feet. "I do not offer fealty."

"Then I have no use for you. I am the king's second. You must pledge your loyalty to me by his command. You are stubborn, Uncle, and place too much trust in the word of a woman. Go home, old man, and take your whore with you."

Dahlia gasped and rose to her feet. "How dare

you!"

Dragos smiled thinly. "I dare because it is truth. I am overlord, and this is my castle. I did not invite you. Be gone before the sun rises."

He motioned for his disciples. They rose and followed him from the great hall leaving his guests to their musings.

Chapter Sixteen

Rolayna sat alone in the garden, contemplating the future. Once freedom filled her hopes and dreams. Now Dragos occupied their place. Life would not be possible without him in it. She wrapped her arms around her waist and breathed in the sweet scent of the flowers around her. Her oath to the *Thorns of the Rose* would not allow her to explain what happened, and she could not remedy what he thought of her. She shivered. The breeze turned chilly, and she did not have a shawl.

Suddenly, Dragos appeared beside her, wrapping his arm around her and drawing her into his heat. "I will find Father Bernard and bring him home. You have my word, wife."

She allowed herself the pleasure of his touch. "Why would Rauf take Father Bernard? Why would he burn Graystone? He could have burned Seville the night my father rescued Alex, but he did not. What does he gain by razing Graystone now? What does he want?"

"I do not know. I thought he would turn away after I married you in Northernfell. You are mine in every sense of the word. Everything you have belongs to me. I control your armies and own your lands. It is my castle he burns to the ground, and my priest he holds against his will. It makes no sense. This is a personal attack against me, and I cannot allow this to happen. I protect what is mine."

Rolayna shivered in his arms.

"Tell me true. What are your feelings for the baron?" Dragos stroked her arm as he spoke, sending tingles of awareness through her.

"I care not for him. He is nothing to me. I hope you find him and kill him before he comes back to—"

"What, Rolayna? Before he comes back to…what?" He tensed beside her as he waited for her answer.

"He told me he would come for me when I least expect it, and he would give me all I deserve." She shivered despite the warmth of his arm around her.

Dragos' gaze sharpened. "Did he say this to you the night he cowered in my keep?"

At her nod, he asked, "Why did you not tell me sooner? Do you think me incapable of protecting you?"

Her head came up, and she met his gaze for the first time. "He entered Dragonthorne. The thought scares me, so I do not sleep at night. If he can infiltrate this fortress, he can go anywhere."

Dragos' eyes darkened. "You belong to me, Rolayna, and are the heart of my dominion. Oliveander will never get close to you again. You must trust me." Dragos drew her against his chest and rubbed the tension from her shoulders. God's teeth, the bastard would pay for the insult he gave. They were yet to figure out who reopened the tunnel and let the enemy in. They pondered the extent of Josa's involvement and the identity of the man she met in the tunnel. Josa was not capable of digging out the opening alone, and they wanted the name of her accomplice. The disciples searched for her to question her but were unable to locate her.

Originally made as an escape for the resident priest should the enemy come, the tunnel was sealed by his father years ago. No one knew of its existence but those intimately connected to the family. Dragos frowned. The information he received from Alex did not make sense. Who or what is a black man? And what did they say about the air? Why did Josa have the wrong one, and what did it mean?

Miles and Christina emerged from the shadows. "Forgive us for interrupting. Christina has something of import to say."

Rolayna straightened.

Miles glanced from Rolayna to Dragos. "Hear her out, Dragos. What Christina has to say is for us both. I, for one, am intrigued."

"What are you doing?" Rolayna asked Christina in surprise.

"Allow me to explain." Her gaze searched Rolayna's. "Please. You were right to say what you did earlier, and I should have told the truth years ago. I owe you both that much."

"What about the pact? You held me to it. We swore to each other and sealed it with our blood." Rolayna held her wrist toward Christina, where a jagged white scar marred her smooth flesh.

"I started it, and I shall end it." Christina took a deep breath. "I cannot bear to see you suffer because of me. If I am honest, I will admit I cannot find happiness with Miles until he knows the truth." She included Dragos. "Until you both do."

****

Rolayna gazed into Christina's warm brown eyes and realized she meant what she said. For two years,

187

she'd waited for Christina to face the truth of what she did, but to no avail.

"I owe Rolayna an apology, and I owe both of you an explanation." The duchess twisted her hands together. "What I have to say is not easy for me. I wish I spoke up sooner." Christina glanced at her. "Please forgive me, Rolayna. I did not realize the extent of the damage done by my actions until this. When I listened to the duke earlier today, I realized how wrong I have been to hold you to our pact." She dropped her head and took another deep breath.

Rolayna studied Christina. The truth must come from her. So, she sat stiffly and waited.

"There were four of us, me, Rolayna, Elizabeth Cromwell, daughter of the High Chancellor, and Mary Statton, daughter of the Duke of Statton, keeper of the Royal Guard. We all met at court. We came from wealthy, privileged families and were rich, spoiled, and bored. We met at a ball at the palace and immediately formed a friendship of sorts. We were tired of conforming to society's rules where we were not allowed to make decisions for ourselves. We considered ourselves intelligent, yet we were told what to wear, how to sit, how to eat, how to walk, how to talk, who to talk to, who to avoid, the styles of our gowns, who our friends were, and who we must marry. From there, it would get worse. Our husbands would decide what we ate, where we slept, what our duties were, if we bore children or not, where we went, or if we went at all, etc. We hated the idea of it all and formed a protest group. I came up with the idea. We would thumb our noses at society, show them what we thought of their rules, and make rules of our own."

Dragos' eyebrow rose, but he said nothing.

Miles studied his wife's expressive face and waited.

"Men could form groups and have secret meetings. Why not us, as well?" Christina's chin rose.

"Why indeed," Miles murmured and nodded for her to continue.

"We called ourselves the *Thorns of the Rose* and deemed it an apt name. We were likened to roses, but we wanted everyone to realize we grew thorns as well. We formed our group and swore to never reveal its existence or anything about it to anyone, ever, on pain of death. We sliced our wrists and mingled our blood to seal our pact." She held her own wrist up so the men could see her identical one.

"Your wrist, darling?" Miles chuckled. "Surely you could think of a better place. A wrist is not the best choice for such a dramatic oath."

Christina smiled at him. "We thought it appropriate at the time." She glanced at Rolayna, who said nothing.

The duchess' smile faded. "We were tired of having our whole lives planned out and wanted excitement and experiences. We took turns daring each other to do scandalous things no girl in her right mind would do. I went first. For my dare, I drank a glass of port in front of the king." She smiled at the memory. "My father whisked me away from Evania and sentenced me to spend the rest of the season at our country estate for the embarrassment it caused."

"I know of this." Miles laughed aloud. "I wondered why a girl would do such a foolish thing. Once I got to know you, I realized it is part of your charm."

"Thank you, darling." Christina smiled at him.

"Delighted with our success, we dared Elizabeth Cromwell to wear a pair of men's breeches to the first ball of the next season. She did it in style, complete with a top hat and men's boots. Her father promptly married her off to Baron Toliver, a poor lovesick young man who courted her unsuccessfully until the day after her scandalous appearance." She stopped. "Rolayna came next. She just became engaged to you, my darling." Christina glanced anxiously at Miles. "I met you for the first time at her engagement party and fell in love with you in an instant. I wanted you for myself."

The duchess gazed from Miles to Rolayna and then at Dragos. "This is not easy for me to admit, but I cannot watch Rolayna suffer anymore because of me and my foolishness." She twisted her fingers together as she spoke. "We originally dared her to puff on a cigar in front of you, my darling. We wanted to see what your reaction would be. Instead, I changed it. I dared her to break her engagement with no apology and no explanation and gave her no choice. Either she accepted the dare or lose her only friends and be cast from the *Thorns of the Rose* forever. She swore a blood oath to follow our rules and never reveal our secrets. We reminded her of the consequences.

"Rolayna rose to the challenge and broke it off with a terse letter the next day. It caused a scandal bigger than either of the other two." Christina's voice dropped to a whisper. "I changed the dare because I wanted you for myself." Her gaze begged for Miles to understand. "I made sure I knew every event on your schedule and arranged mine to be wherever you were, darling. I wanted you more than anything in the world. Two weeks later, you proposed."

Rolayna glanced at Dragos. Did he believe the duchess? His expression gave nothing away.

"Can you forgive me for daring you to break your engagement?" Christina's soft brown eyes searched her face. "I have been mean and selfish. I accept I hurt you and did not consider how much until Dragos told Miles he could not trust your word after what happened. It is my fault you broke the engagement, not yours. I know the position I put you in. You could not back out of the dare. I knew what people said about you, and I told myself I did not care. They said you could not be trusted to keep your word. No one wanted to court you until Baron Oliveander offered for your hand. For two years, nobility whispered about you, and I knew what society thought. I enjoy a happy life, and I told myself it could not be as bad for you as it seemed. I ruined your life, Rolayna, and I am sorry."

****

Dragos' mind whirled with the information. Rolayna kept her word. She did not break her oath, even in her own defense. Society turned its back on her, and she lost the confidence of her father and all her friends. She did it for the oath she took with three foolish girls. He misjudged her. Despite the pressure, she never gave in. Damn if she did not impress him with her grit. Admiration filled him, and Dragos grinned as a new thought occurred. She did not spurn Miles after all.

He gazed at her sitting quietly beside him. "Will you answer the duchess, Rolayna? She asked if you forgive her."

His wife glanced up and smiled. "Thank you for telling Dragos and Miles the truth. I forgave you ages ago."

Christina nodded, relief and joy lighting her face. "I leave early in the morning. I hope they catch the baron and rescue your priest. I am sorry, Rolayna, for not coming forward before this."

The girls hugged, and Miles drew Christina away, leaving Dragos and Rolayna alone.

Dragos ran his thumbs along the dark smudges beneath her eyes. He knew of a solution for her restlessness. With a grin, he scooped her up in his arms and headed for the keep.

"Where are you taking me? Put me down, Dragos."

"You are cold, and I will warm you." He took the stairs of the keep two at a time until he reached the master chamber. Kicking the door shut with his heel, he turned to lock it.

Rolayna's eyes widened. "What are you doing?"

He kissed the side of her white neck and carried her to the massive bed. "I am going to put my wife to bed. She needs rest." His hands busied with her laces. How long had it been since he got lost in her softness? It seemed forever. He growled low in his throat and tugged at her strings.

"What about our guests? We cannot disappear." Her voice faded into a groan as his hands found her breasts.

"Our guests are probably busy working things out between them much the same way we are." He shed his clothing and slid into bed next to her.

"But…" She never finished her sentence.

Dragos swept her away into a sea of pleasure and guided her with expert hands along the river of ecstasy only he could navigate. She rode the waves of sensual delight until she fell headlong into the abyss of bliss Dragos created with his heat and his wicked, knowing lips. He tied her hands together with a strip of silk at the head of the bed while he plundered her body. The tying began after the first time he bedded her, and she touched the scars on his back. He could not bear to have her touch them, not again. Miles and the disciples were the only ones who knew the truth. With Lady Dahlia and his uncle in the castle, too many memories rose to the surface. His lovemaking became ferocious, intense, and deeply satisfying. When at last they fell apart, Dragos wiped the sweat from his brow and loosed her hands.

"Do you trust me?" he asked as he snuggled her against him.

She did not answer, for she slept in the crook of his arm. Her lashes curved darkly against the satin blush of her cheek. She looked as innocent as a cherub. She gave herself so freely, it humbled him, and his heart filled with wonder. He could never want another as he wanted her. Perfect in every way, she was his woman and his duchess. He took care of his dominion and would never let her go.

Dragos kissed her head and turned his mind to the task of rescuing her priest.

Chapter Seventeen

Rolayna awoke with a start. The rustle of paper sliding under their chamber door made her sit up. Footsteps retreated, and silence returned. She glanced at Dragos sleeping beside her and slipped from the high bed. Padding to the door, she retrieved the missive.

Once she reached the bed, she lit a candle and read Dragos' name on the outside.

"What is it?" He leaned over her and kissed the side of her neck.

"Someone slipped a note for you under the door just now." Rolayna held the paper toward him. She caught a whiff of hyacinths and knew who had sent the note.

He leaned forward and held the note beneath the candle. With a snort of disgust, he tossed it on the floor without opening it.

"Are you not curious about her note?" She tilted her head and studied his face.

"Not at all. Dahlia holds no interest for me. Read it if you want, but come back to bed so I can warm you."

Rolayna laughed and picked up the note, placing it on the chest beside the candle before sliding in bed beside him.

"It is a trick to get me alone. My uncle gave his information at dinner. Dahlia is an evil, conniving woman. Someday, Uncle will see her true form, and then may the gods have mercy on her, for he will not."

"Were you in love with her?"

Dragos sighed. "Nay. When this is over, sweet lady, ask me about the scars on my back. Ask me about Dahlia and my uncle. I have not the time now to answer your questions as I wish to." With those cryptic words, he pulled her into his arms and kissed her.

She allowed his caress, musing over his words.

He fell asleep a few minutes later, his snores filling the chamber.

Stroking the side of his face with her finger, she sighed. There were many questions she would ask when the rebellion ended.

Rolayna awoke alone. Rolling to her side, she slipped from the bed. Dragos would find Rauf, and all would be well. She and Alex were safe at Dragonthorne.

Dressing quickly, she brushed and plaited her hair. As she left the chamber, her gaze fell on the note, and she opened it.

Have important information about Oliveander. Come quickly to the chamber down the corridor. No one must know of this meeting. Lives depend upon it. Northernfell.

Rolayna smiled. Dragos knew of Dahlia's trickery and did not fall for it. She tucked the note deep into the pocket of her gown and forgot about it.

She walked into the keep some time later, searching for something to eat.

Lady Dahlia sat at the high table, picking at the food on her trencher.

Rolayna's gaze narrowed on the woman. Lady Dahlia sat in her seat.

"There you are at last. My mother taught me the hostess should rise early and tend to her guests' needs. I can see you were not properly trained. We in the north follow specific rules on what is acceptable and what is not. Perhaps you were not aware, or perhaps it is the people of Seville who are lacking." Lady Dahlia used her words against her.

One point for her, Rolayna thought.

The lady snapped her fingers and Ivan hurried into the room. "Aye, my lady?"

"Get her something to eat." She inclined her head in Rolayna's direction, challenged her. "I am sure anything is good enough."

When Ivan bowed to his mistress and remained at attention, Lady Dahlia stared down her nose at him. "Hurry up, man. Do as you are told!"

Ivan ignored her. "Good morning, your grace. What can I get for you?"

One point for Rolayna. "I would like a cup of tea, some fruit, and the Duke of Northernfell. Although not necessarily in the order listed."

The disciple grinned. "The master left Ramiel here to watch over you. Would you like him, too?"

"Aye." Rolayna advanced toward Lady Dahlia. "Remove yourself from my seat before I remove you from my home."

The lady laughed but made no effort to rise. "It is time you understood where you stand. Perhaps you are aware of the scars on Dragos' back? He received those fighting for me. Or has he never told you the tale?"

"I know everything I need to know about the scars he bears. I also know about you. Do you leave on your own, or do I throw you out?"

196

The woman's smile dropped, and her gaze turned calculating. "We met last night in the chamber next to yours after you fell asleep and relived our past. It is me Dragos wants, only me. I am to tell you the news and get rid of you. He wants you gone before he returns."

Rolayna did not turn her head, nor did she bother to answer, for she sensed the men enter the long hall. "Ramiel, escort Lady Dahlia from Dragonthorne and tell the guards to shut the gates behind her. She is not allowed entrance again."

Ramiel walked toward Lady Dahlia, grinning with anticipation. "With pleasure, Mistress."

The lady in question rose to her feet. "Dragos shall hear of this!"

"Aye, he certainly will," Rolayna agreed. Lady Dahlia hoped to cause discontent between them for Dragos' refusal to comply with her note.

Ivan entered the hall and hurried toward Rolayna. "The Duke of Northernfell left, my lady."

Lady Dahlia's smile fell. "What nonsense. The duke is in our chamber, asleep."

The disciple shook his head. "He and his soldiers are gone."

"What?" The duchess marched around the table. "This cannot be. He would never leave me behind without a word."

"Perhaps your husband is aware of your infidelity and left you for good. Will he cast you out, I wonder?" Rolayna folded her arms across her chest and smiled at her adversary.

"He would do no such thing. Gregory knows about Dragos and me. 'Tis he who gave Dragos the scars on his back." Lady Dahlia wrinkled her brow in perplexity.

"Gregory blames him for what happened. He would never raise a hand against me." Her chin rose. "I shall get to the bottom of this, and when I return, I expect you gone." She strode past with her nose in the air.

"You shall be disappointed, for here I will stay." Rolayna resisted the urge to trip her as she sailed past.

Ramiel took Lady Dahlia's arm and led her out of the hall. "Your horse waits for you beyond the gate."

She stared after them. So the Duke of Northernfell gave Dragos the massive scars which nearly ended his life, thrashing him over Lady Dahlia and her lies. Rolayna walked to her chamber to think the situation over.

"Hello." Alex walked through the door sometime later with his wooden sword tucked in his breeches.

"Hello. Where have you been?" She inspected him from head to toe. The wind outside ruffled his dark hair, and his cheeks were pink. He smelled like the outdoors. "Were you training with the soldiers?"

The boy shook his head. "I played hide and seek with Father Nikolas! He knows some good places to hide."

Rolayna smiled. "I am glad, dearest. Did you get something to eat?"

"I ate with Father Nikolas. He said to ask you if I can go on a picnic with him. He wants to show me something."

"You cannot go outside the wall and will have to have your picnic with the priest inside the gates."

Alex dropped his head. "Father Nikolas said he knows a hiding place he wants to show me."

She hugged the boy. "I am glad you and Father Nikolas get along so well, but we must do as Dragos asks. I am going to sit in the tower after I eat. Do you want to come with me?" She figured it would be easier to take the boy with her where she could watch him than to let him climb up there alone. Sooner or later, his curious wandering feet would go where she told him not to.

Alex shook his head. "Father Nikolas says we have a 'venture to take."

"A 'venture? You mean an adventure, do you not?"

The lad nodded his head. He hugged Rolayna and ran toward the keep.

She shook her head. She loved the boy and shuddered to think of what would have happened if her father had not gone to rescue him. Rauf would not have shown him mercy.

Chapter Eighteen

Father Nikolas paused at the top of the spiral steps. His huffs and puffs were audible several minutes before he appeared.

Rolayna turned from her position in front of the tower window. "Father Nikolas, what brings you up here?" She smiled at the rotund little priest and slid from her seat. "Come, sit and rest. When you catch your breath, you can tell me why you climbed those steep steps to find me."

Father Nikolas nodded his head and took Rolayna's seat on the low stone ledge. Several minutes passed before the priest could speak. "My lady, I have disturbing news. The guards found a soldier wandering in the forest. We allowed him in, and he informs us Dragos, and the disciples, are riding into an ambush." The priest fanned his face with his hand while he fought to control his breathing. "Oliveander is not at Graystone but waits in the narrow part of the pass with his army. Once Dragos is in the pass, he has nowhere to turn. He and the disciples will be cut down." Father Nikolas got to his feet. "We must do something, mistress. We cannot let the master die!"

Rolayna froze, her heart beating rapidly in her chest. "Come, we will find Ramiel and see what must be done." She hurried to the stairs. She must warn Dragos while she still had time. Running into the long hall several minutes later, she found Ramiel and Ivan speaking quietly together.

"Ramiel, what should we do? Dragos needs our help!"

The disciple straightened and shook his head. "The best thing to do is remain here. Hound will sense an ambush, and Azazel will see to the master's back. The master will not enter the pass unless it is safe. He always has an alternate plan."

Ivan nodded his agreement.

Rolayna's mouth gaped open. "We have to do something!"

"Nay, lady. Sometimes the best thing to do is nothing." Ramiel studied her face. "Trust the master. He has lived a long time and knows Oliveander is a coward. He will expect him to act the part."

She gazed from one to the other. They were serious. Neither one would do anything to help. Rolayna took a deep breath, her mind humming with plans. If they would not go, she would. She could not lose Dragos now, not when he meant so much to her. She smiled and nodded her head to keep them from guessing her thoughts.

"If you think it best to do nothing, we shall stay here and do nothing." She smiled at both men and wandered out the door. Once outside, Rolayna hurried around to the kitchen. She gathered bread and cheese, telling cook she planned to join Alex and Father Nikolas on their picnic. From there, she stole along the path to the stables and ditched the satchel of food. She found Father Nikolas sitting on the grass beside the church with Alex.

"Hello, Father. It is kind of you to keep an eye on

Alex. He enjoys the games you play with him and the adventures you take him on." She sat down beside Alex and gave him a hug.

"He is a good boy. I do not mind watching him. In truth, he keeps me entertained with his questions. He views the world with such joy and gives me such happiness." The priest took a bite of his bread. "Are the disciples going to leave soon to warn the master about the ambush?"

Rolayna shook her head. "Ramiel thinks Dragos will be on the lookout and does not plan to leave the fortress. Therefore, I come to speak with you, Father." She gazed around to make sure no one listened. "I plan to warn Dragos and have a horse and food prepared. I cannot rest until I know he is safe. The only difficulty I see is thinking of a way to get the guards to lower the drawbridge."

Father Nikolas nodded his head. "Tell them I took the boy on a picnic, and you are coming to find us. The guards changed an hour ago. The ones at the tower will not know if Alex and I are in the fortress or not."

Rolayna smiled. "Of course. It is a good plan. I have one other thing to ask. Will you watch Alex for me while I am away? If I ask Liska or Gretta, Ramiel will hear of my plan."

"Of course," the priest murmured. "I would be pleased to keep the boy safe."

"I want to come with you." The child threw his arms around her neck. "Please let me come."

She hugged him tight. "It is too dangerous, Alex. I can reach Dragos faster if I go alone. Be a good boy and stay with Father Nikolas."

The boy's lower lip stuck out. "Come back fast. I

cannot sleep unless you tell me a story."

She nodded in agreement. "I cannot sleep unless I read you one, either. I promise to come back as soon as I can." She kissed the top of his head, then got up and walked toward the keep to change. Gretta made her two gowns with split skirts for practicing fighting techniques with Scimitar.

Dragos inspected her from every angle the first time she wore one of them in his presence. "This skirt allows movement. Such a gown would have been welcome the first few weeks of our acquaintance. Tell Gretta I approve."

Rolayna smiled, unable to believe her ears. "Thank you, Gabriel Michael."

He paused and gave her a playful pat on her backside for using the hated name.

Who knew the Duke of Dragonthorne could be so accepting of her unladylike nature?

And now he had need of her. She gathered her cloak and saddled her favorite mare before trotting toward the towers. She told the guards she went to find Father Nikolas and Alex to join them on their picnic.

They let her cross without question.

Once she disappeared from the view of the tower, she nudged her horse into a gallop. She turned south and ran as fast as she could. Dragos left in the early hours and had nearly a full day's journey on her. She reasoned she could catch him sometime tomorrow if she kept up the pace.

Darkness fell, and the forest came alive with sound. She shivered with fright over every snap of a branch and rustle of the leaves. At midnight, she stopped at a small stream and allowed her mare to drink.

A twig snapped, and Rolayna jumped. She gazed around at the trees and shrubbery. Crickets chirped, and an owl hooted overhead. The silence of the night pressed down on her. Nothing out of the ordinary caught her attention. After a minute, her heart rate returned to normal.

Her horse whinnied and sidestepped. Rolayna patted the mare and spoke in soothing tones to calm her. Once the mare settled, she climbed into the saddle and nudged the horse into a gallop. She tried not to think about the blackness of the forest around her and gave the mare her head, trusting her horse to feel her way through the forest. Once she warned Dragos, she would return to Dragonthorne, and everything would be fine. An anxious feeling filled the pit of her stomach. Alex. She had not been without him since the moment she gave her word to her father. Tonight she had no choice but to leave him with Father Nikolas. Dragos needed her.

A wolf howled in the trees, not twenty feet to her right. Her mare whinnied and leaned into her stride. They flew through the forest. Trees blurred past, and twigs snapped, as branches caught at her cloak. She gasped for air and tugged on her reins to get her horse to slow down.

She would not. The mare reared and threw Rolayna over her head before racing away into the darkness. Landing on her back with a thud and the breath knocked out of her lungs, she lay there gathering her senses.

A snarl sounded in front of her.

She gazed around her. Bulky black shadows

prowled beneath the trees, as she struggled to her feet. Unblinking, yellow eyes stared at her from every direction, surrounding her. Terrified, she crept backward until her back came up against a tree. Keeping her gaze on the snarling figures slinking toward her, Rolayna caught the branch beside her and climbed as quickly as she could without glancing down. She knew if she did, she would stumble. Only when she braced herself high in the tree did she dare drop her gaze to the ground. Terror clawed at her chest. There were eight massive beasts beneath her, growling and snarling as they jumped at the tree trunk. Rolayna closed her eyes and thanked the gods she'd learned how to climb trees. Ripping a long strip from her underskirt which boasted a seam up the middle also, she tied herself to the tree. If she fell asleep, she might lose her balance and fall.

Rolayna took a deep breath. She was safe for now. As she leaned back against the tree, reaction set in. Her teeth chattered so hard she worried they would fall out, and her whole body trembled. Wrapping her cloak tight around her, she closed her eyes, wondering how far Dragos traveled and if she would she get to him in time.

She woke sometime later to a rock hitting the tree by her feet. Rolayna shook her head to clear the remnants of sleep from her mind.

Another rock hit the tree.

She glanced down at a tall woman standing beneath her. The wolves were gone. Sunlight lit the grass and filtered through the leaves of the forest. Removing her hood, she leaned forward. "Who are you? What do you want?"

"The wolves are gone. There is no danger."

Rolayna frowned down at the familiar voice. "Josa?"

The woman pushed her hood back as well. "Aye. Come down, my lady. You must hurry."

She untied herself from the tree and climbed to the ground. "What are you doing here? How did you find me?"

Josa pulled a face. "My family once owned this forest, so I know it well, and you were not hard to find. Your mare ran into my barns in the night, frightened and searching for grain. I recognized the mark on her flank and came to search for the rider from Dragonthorne. I followed the howls of the wolves, and I spotted you in the tree. After, I returned home. You were safe until morning."

"Thank you for coming back." She surveyed Josa carefully.

"This way. We must go before the wolves return." The woman walked away into the forest.

Rolayna shrugged and followed her. The weight of her dagger in her pocket comforted her, should the woman prove to be an enemy.

They walked into a small clearing with a little hut an hour later. No wonder the disciples were unable to find Josa. This hut lay deep in the forest, well hidden in the trees.

"My father's overseer built it as a young man," Josa said when they approached. "He knew how to pack the logs with mud to keep the weather and the animals out. I played here as a child."

A stable stood behind the house. Her mare rested in one of the stalls. So, the woman told the truth. Her mare did come here after throwing Rolayna to the ground.

Josa entered the little house and held the door open in invitation. "It is not Dragonthorne, but it is warm."

Rolayna stepped inside, her senses alert for danger.

"Sit," the womana invited. She poured a cup of hot coffee and served her visitor a slice of bread and cheese.

"Thank you, Josa." Rolayna ate the bread while she studied the woman. "Why did you come for me? After the way we parted, I would suppose our meeting to be different."

The woman's face twisted. "I came for you because, despite what you think, I am loyal to Dragos and the people of Dragonthorne."

Rolayna bit into her bread. "Dragos knows you spoke with a man in the tunnel. He knows you were involved in the attack on Dragonthorne. I do not call this loyalty, and neither will he."

The woman stared at her. "You do not understand. I did not tell anyone about the tunnel. I did not allow anyone to enter, nor did I take part in the attack. I attempted to stop it from happening!"

"How?" Rolayna asked. "Alex saw you in the tunnel with a man. You spoke with him about the air, and you said something about being the wrong one. If you were trying to stop it, why were you there?"

The woman groaned out loud. "I hoped you would understand. After our disagreement, when you ordered me to leave, the soldiers allowed me time to gather my things, and I went to the tunnel to be alone. Dragonthorne is the only home I know. All the family I have in the world is there. I walked in the dark to think of a way to stay. I did not want to leave the safety of the fortress."

Rolayna nodded her head.

"When I discovered the tunnel open and the makeshift bridge across the moat, I knew we were all in danger. Dragonthorne would fall if attacked. I wanted to use the information to convince Dragos to let me stay." Josa stared at her.

"Why did you not tell him? Baron Oliveander used the tunnel to breach Dragonthorne. He could have killed us all if Dragos did not return when he did."

"I tried, but before I made it more than three feet, I ran into Father Nikolas." Josa picked up the poker and roused the fire. "He came down from the kitchens and surprised me. I did not expect the priest to be there. When I asked him his purpose for being there, he told me to mind my own affairs. I asked how he knew of the tunnel, and he said the first Duke of Dragonthorne built it for the resident priest, and he had every right to be there." Josa turned toward her with a serious gaze. "I told the priest, Dragos would be furious. With the tunnel open, the rebels could sneak in and kill you in the night or take you hostage. Father Nikolas laughed and said you were the wrong heir. They were not after you."

Rolayna frowned. "What do you mean he is not after me. Who is he after then? Are you sure Father Nikolas is the man you spoke with? He is such a kind man. He loves playing with Alex, and he is always there when I need a friend to talk to. I have a hard time believing he is part of this."

Josa brushed her hair to the side, revealing her neck. A jagged red line marked the side of her throat. "Does this appear kind? He ordered rebel soldiers to kill me. There were several with him that day. They all came up through the tunnel. Father Nikolas made them tie me up, gag me, and take me into the forest. He told them to kill me and dump my body."

Rolayna fought to breathe around the panic. If Josa spoke the truth, Alex was in danger. "Why did the soldiers of Dragonthorne not report you missing? They were to escort you outside the wall. How is it you are alive?"

"Father Nikolas told the soldiers he escorted me out, and they believed him. As for how I escaped?" Josa shrugged. "I watched the men train often enough. I knocked one soldier down with my shoulder, kicked the other one in the privates, and ran. I rubbed my binding on a rock until my hands were free. When I came to a stream, I ducked below the water and let it carry me away. I only lifted my head long enough to breathe. I do not care what you think of me because I do not do this for you. I do it for Dragos and the others. I do not want them to believe I am a traitor. So, you must find Dragos and warn him about Father Nikolas."

Rolayna shook her head. "I cannot believe the priest did this."

Josa put a hand on her shoulder. "Think, my lady. Who told Dragos about the burning village?"

"Father Nikolas."

"Right, who told you the rebels planned to ambush Dragos?"

She stared at the woman. "How do you know about the ambush?"

"They spoke of it when they carried me into the woods. It is all part of the plan to get you away from Dragonthorne."

Rolayna frowned again. "Why would they want me

away from Dragonthorne?" And then she knew. *Alex.* Alex is the one they wanted. She kept the child in sight, checked on him regularly, and knew his whereabouts every minute of every day. They could not abduct him with her close by. Without her in the fortress, he became an easy target.

"Alex!" She screamed his name and ran for the stables and her mare.

Chapter Nineteen

Rolayna raced through the trees, furious with herself for leaving Alex alone. Dragos told her to trust him, but she had not. She should have trusted Ivan and Ramiel as well, and now the boy was in danger because of her. Alex's black man must be Father Nikolas, for he wore black with a white collar. The child must not have seen the priest's face to call him such, and now, it all made sense. Thank the gods the boy left the tunnel when he did, or he may have been discovered and killed. Rolayna swallowed tightly. Her hands shook, and she kicked the mare to go faster. Her tears dried on her cheeks as she ran through the forest. She prayed Josa's accusations against the priest were wrong, and she would find Alex safe inside Dragonthorne.

Oh Alex, please be there. The boy said Father Nikolas wanted to take him on an adventure and show him something when they played hide and seek. *Dear God! What have I done?* Fear swept through her, urging her to go faster and faster. She gazed up at the pillars of Dragonthorne through the trees, and terror tightened her chest. *Alex, I am coming*! She waved at the guards in the tower, and they lowered the drawbridge. Frantically, she raced across the wooden structure into the courtyard and slipped from the mare's back. "Alex!" Her screams filled the silence.

Ivan and Ramiel appeared with their swords drawn.

"My lady, you are back. Where have you been? The master will be angry with me for allowing you outside the fortress in his absence."

Rolayna grabbed Ivan. "Where is Alex?" She licked her dry lips and shook his tunic. "Tell me where he is!"

Ramiel pried her fingers from Ivan. "The guards in the tower said you went to find the priest and the boy. When you did not return last night, we sent soldiers to search for you. We found the wagon several miles up the road, but no sign of you, the priest, or the boy."

Her heart squeezed tight in her chest. "Get me a fresh horse. I must find Alex and rescue him."

The disciple patted her shoulder. "If he is with Father Nikolas, he is safe. The priest will take care of him."

"Nay!" Rolayna yelled. "Please, listen to me. The man in the tunnel, the one Alex told Dragos about, is Father Nikolas. He is the black man and the traitor. He let the rebel army in, *and he has Alex!*"

Both men glanced at each other.

She stamped her foot in frustration. "Can you not see? Father Nikolas delivered news of the burning village, and no one questioned his word. He created a ruse to get Dragos and the disciples out of the fortress so the rebels could attack." Rolayna grew frantic. "Father Nikolas also delivered news of the ambush because he knew I would warn Dragos." She dropped her head. "Without me in the castle, no one would think twice about the priest taking Alex with him. I even lied to the guards and told them I left the castle grounds to go on the picnic, too. But I did not. I went to warn Dragos, like they knew I would. The priest had hours before anyone realized they did not return."

Her gaze lifted to his face. "The priest took Alex after distracting me with Dragos. The rebels wanted the boy all this time, not me."

Ramiel nodded his head. "It makes sense, but why do they want the child?"

"I do not know!" Rolayna cried out and stomped her foot again. "But I have to find him. He needs me. They will kill him, and I cannot let it happen."

The disciple shook his head. "Think, Mistress. This may be another trick. We will send a rider to the master with news of the situation and wait for his answer. This could be another ruse to get you alone. Oliveander has not been able to get to you. He could have taken you the night he hid in the keep were it not for his wound, but he knew he would never make it out with you alive. What better way to get you to come to them than to take the boy?"

Rolayna's shoulders drooped.

The disciple put a hand on her arm. "The master will be upset if anything happens to you. Go inside and rest, my lady. As soon as the rider returns with the master's instructions, I will send for you."

She nodded and walked toward the keep. Ramiel spoke the truth. She went over the situation in her mind and climbed the stairs until she reached Alex's chamber. With a trembling hand, she opened the door and stepped inside. The boy's windblown hair and trusting eyes danced before her as she thought of the last time she gazed upon him, sitting in the grass eating his lunch. Regret twisted a knot in her stomach. She should have listened when Dragos warned her about Rauf, and she never should have left the boy alone.

Rolayna walked over to Alex's chest and ran her fingers over the carving on the lid. Tears ran down her cheeks and dripped onto the wood. Sinking onto his bed, she buried her head in his pillow. How could she be so stupid? Her father made her swear to protect Alex, and she handed him over to the enemy without a thought.

If they killed him, she would not be able to live knowing she caused his death. She sat up and set the pillow back on the bed. Such a thing must not be allowed to happen. A glimmer of metal on the floor beside the chest caught her gaze. Bending, she picked up a little locket, and a sense of foreboding stole over her. With trembling fingers, she flicked it open. One side held the likeness of a woman. The other side contained the likeness of *her father*. The artist portrayed him just as she remembered. Rolayna peered at the image of the woman, and recognition dawned. The image depicted Lady Dorset, her mother's best friend. She gasped as the truth hit her. Alex turned five summers this year. Her mother died six years ago. Widowed and lonely, Lady Dorset often came to their townhouse in Evania and stayed with her mother while she was ill. The Duke of Seville spent countless months in Evania following her mother's death. *Alex was her half-brother!*

Rolayna trembled with fear. If Oliveander found out, Alex *would* be killed. She froze as the truth hit her. Rauf already knew! Somehow, he knew Alex was the son and heir of Seville!

The priest told Josa they sought the wrong heir. They knew.

Burying her head in her hands, she rocked back

and forth. Why did her father keep Alex's birth and identity a secret? She remembered the day he brought Alex home and introduced him as an orphan and his ward. Rolayna shook her head. Why deceive her about the child? Then, she stopped. Her father was still in mourning when Lady Dorset conceived Alex. He must have turned to the lady in his loneliness and grief, and this is the reason he did not tell her the truth. Her father would do anything to avoid a scandal.

Rolayna wrinkled her brow, remembering. Lady Dorset died about the same time Alex came to Seville to live. She sucked in a breath. *Papa brought Alex to Seville because he no longer had a mother to care for him.* Jumping to her feet, she tucked her hands behind her back and paced. So much made sense, like why her father left her with Dragos and went after Alex. He knew the danger if the rebels discovered the boy, even if she did not. Somehow, she must rescue Alex and stop Rauf from succeeding.

Picking up the locket, Rolayna went in search of Ramiel. She found him in the courtyard speaking to a soldier and waited until he finished his conversation before handing him the locket. "I understand why Rauf wants Alex. It has nothing to do with me." She indicated the locket. "Open it. It is the locket Alex held when he said goodbye to my father."

Ramiel opened the locket and glanced sharply at Rolayna.

"The woman is Lady Dorset, one of my mother's friends, widowed years ago and never remarried."

"Alex is your brother." His gaze searched hers in concern.

She nodded her head. "He is the reason Rauf

continues to attack, the reason the baron is at Graystone, and the reason he followed us to Dragonthorne. The rebels want my brother, not me." Rolayna put a shaking hand to her head. "And now they have him. I left Father Nikolas in charge of him and trusted him to keep Alex safe." She swayed as the gravity of the situation hit her anew.

Ramiel caught her elbow. "We must wait for the master." His voice dropped. "Please, Mistress. Do not do anything foolish until the master learns of this. He will find Alex and bring him home."

Rolayna shook her head. "There is no time. Rauf will take Alex to Seville and force the lords to deliver their men. Then, he will kill my brother. Everything Dragos has done to stop the rebellion will be for naught. Alex's only chance—" She swallowed hard. "—is me."

The disciple shook his head. "You cannot leave the fortress. The master gave orders to keep you here, and I cannot disobey. I will send another rider to the master. Trust him, my lady."

She met Ramiel's gaze and held it for several seconds. They both knew she was right, but Rolayna nodded acquiessence and walked back to the keep. She lay on her bed until midnight, making plans. Once she sorted it out, she set the locket in the middle of the large bed and scribbled a quick note to Dragos. Gathering her black cloak from the wardrobe, she slipped down the stairs to the courtyard and walked in the shadows to the stables. Reaching for the door, she froze.

A man stood beside the door holding the reins of a young black stallion, saddled and ready to ride. "I knew you would go after him, Mistress." Ivan stepped forward. "I packed the saddlebags with food for your journey. The flask is full of water." He lifted a flintlock toward her. "Do you know how to shoot one of these?"

Rolayna nodded. "I practiced at Seville with Papa and later with Captain Jameson." She took the gun and put it into the saddlebag. "Thank you, Ivan."

He helped her mount. "Do not take any chances, Mistress. The master will come for you. Trust in him. I do not agree with you going, but I understand the reason. Do what you can for young Alex."

She nodded and turned the horse around.

"One other thing." Ivan took hold of her bridle, gazing up at Rolayna in the light of the moon. "Come back to us, Mistress."

She swallowed the lump in her throat and nodded again before trotting toward the portcullis.

Ivan stepped from the shadows and waved at the soldiers to let her through.

Rolayna waited while the heavy metal gate lifted and the guards lowered the drawbridge before riding across and gazing back at Dragonthorne.

She could see the towers and spires outlined against the midnight sky. Where once she thought the fortress dark and gloomy, now it provided warmth and security. Dragos would come for her. She knew he would. Her trust in him gave her courage.

Turning her stallion south, she nudged him into a gallop. Alex needed her, and she would rather be with him than anywhere else on earth.

Chapter Twenty

Rolayna caught up to the rebel army five days later. Or, rather, they caught her.

She spotted a squadron of soldiers through the trees wearing the blue and red uniforms of the rebel army and maneuvered her horse away from them. She wanted to follow them to their camp without being seen. So she reined her horse in and hid in the trees. The squadron rode past without glancing in her direction, and Rolayna sighed with relief. She kept off the road and followed the soldiers from higher ground. After an hour, the squadron drew to a halt. Curious about why they stopped, she stopped too, failing to see the small patrol coming up behind her.

A twig snapped behind her, and Rolayna whirled toward the sound with the flintlock in her hand. She caught a blur out of the corner of her eye before something knocked her off her horse and threw her to the ground.

A beefy soldier in red and blue jerked the hood from her head. "We got her!" He crowed in delight as he pried the flintlock from her death grip.

She lay on the ground gasping for breath. The weight of the buffoon on top of her made breathing difficult. Spitting leaves and dirt from her mouth, she thought hard about what to do next.

The soldier jerked her to her feet and threw her

against a tree, standing inches from her with a wide grin on his face.

Rolayna grunted with pain and wrapped her arms around her middle, glancing around for a way to escape.

"Tell the captain we caught the woman." The beefy soldier stuffed her gun down the front of his breeches and tied her hands in front of her. His gaze roamed her up and down while he leered in her face. "If the captain lets us have ye, I'm going first." He scratched his privates and leaned against her. His breath smelled like fish and stale cigars.

Rolayna's stomach rolled.

The soldier rubbed his hands over her body and squeezed her breasts.

She caught another whiff of his foul stench and emptied her stomach all over the front of him.

"God damn whore." The soldier hit her across the face, splitting her lip.

Wiping the blood from her mouth, she lifted her chin to meet the soldier's gaze comforted by the weight of her dagger in her pocket.

An officer rode up on a white gelding a moment later and stopped. "Good work, soldier. Hand the woman to me. The baron will decide what to do with her."

Rolayna's head whirled. She did not have time to respond before strong hands picked her up and sat her on the captain's horse. Slumping forward, she spat more blood from her mouth. A strange tingle vibrated on her split lip. Frowning. she touched her mouth with the tip of her fingers and discovered the bleeding had stopped.

The captain wrapped an arm around her and pulled her against his chest. His big arm rested under her bosom as he tightened his grip. "I can see why the men wanted to catch you. You are a beauty." He laughed. "We have been traveling for weeks with only the camp followers to strum. Now we have you, the men will all want a turn. Someone new, you understand. We are ready for a romp and a bit of ale. But do not worry about McKenzie. He will not have a turn until all the officers do. By then, you will hardly notice who rides you." He squeezed her hard and nudged his horse into a trot.

Rolayna leaned over and threw up all over his side.

"What the hell? You made a mess all over my breeches, you God damn whore. What is the matter with you?" He swore profusely as they rode through the trees into camp, where he dropped her on the ground outside a large, heavily guarded tent and ordered the soldiers to take her to the baron. Then, he rode off muttering under his breath.

Before she could catch a breath, a soldier pulled her to her feet and marched her into the tent.

Rauf sat in a richly carved chair in the center of the tent, sipping a glass of port. He glanced up at Rolayna's entrance and smiled an evil smile. "Hello, my dear. Nice of you to…stop by."

She assessed her surroundings, allowing her eyes time to adjust to the darkness inside the tent. A small sound caught her attention, and she turned toward it.

Alex lay inside a wooden cage against the far wall, tied and gagged. His eyes widened when he spotted Rolayna, and their gazes met. Terrified eyes stared into hers, and a whimper escaped.

With her heart in her throat, she studied him. Tears stained his face, and a bruise marked his cheek. Rage fired her blood. By all the gods, someone would pay for hurting him.

Fisting her hands, she stalked forward, staring at Rauf with contempt. "What have you done to Alex? I can see bruises on him. What kind of courage does it take to strike a child? I thought you a man at one time. Apparently, I am mistaken."

The baron laughed. "So, you doubt I am a man?" Rising to his feet, he advanced toward her. "Those are the first words you say to me? You promised to be my wife, giving me your maidenhead and your men. Instead, you gave them to the devil you call husband. Perhaps I should show you what you are missing, show you how much of a man I am."

Rolayna swallowed hard. She did not care for the gleam in his eye and took a hasty step back.

He caught her with one quick motion and wound a hand in her hair, pinning her in place

"Do not touch me." She glared with all the hostility she could muster.

The baron laughed again. "Does the devil satisfy your desires, Rolayna? Does he fill you until you cry out in ecstasy? Maybe you came here to find out what a real man is, how a real man can make you feel."

"I came for Alex." She stared into his cold, dead soul and shivered.

"Do I excite you?" Rauf asked. "I admit I wanted to wait to take you until your devil husband is here. He took what belonged to me, and I want him to watch me take it back. I want him to see your face as I ride you hard and fast and then cut your heart out before cutting out his. I will feed you both to the wolves a piece at a time. It will be an evening to remember."

She threw a glance at Alex.

His eyes were wide and frightened as he clawed at the bars of his cage and yelled around the gag. Somehow, he must be spared the vileness of the baron's intentions.

Rauf tossed her toward his desk on the opposite side of the tent, following close behind.

Pinning her face down over the wooden structure, he ground his pelvis into her backside and laughed.

Rolayna screamed while she bucked and twisted to loosen his hold on her, but to no avail. If only her hands were free, she would plunge her dagger into his evil little heart.

Her captor leaned over and whispered in her ear. "Maybe we will have a practice session before your husband arrives." His breath came fast against the side of her face.

She stilled and slumped against the desk as if in defeat while she closed her eyes and analyzed the situation. Her only chance would be to take him by surprise. Her split skirt would help deter his assault, at least for a few minutes.

The baron tugged at her skirt and swore as he fumbled with the front of his breeches. "You wore these damn things?"

Now! Rolayna bunted her head back, bloodying Rauf's nose and sending him stumbling backward. Turning quickly, she brought her knee up hard, sending him crumbling to the floor, holding his nose, and gasping in pain. She followed with a good kick to the groin for good measure. When she thought about what he intended to do, nausea rose in her throat, and she retched all over him. When she finished, she fumbled with her kerchief and wiped her face. She did not anticipate meeting Rauf face to face. Her plans were to find the rebels and sneak the boy out in the night.

Alex kicked the side of his cage and yelled.

Rolayna jumped at the sound and glanced toward him.

The boy's eyes were wild with fright as he kicked the door again and rocked back and forth. He stared at her and opened his mouth to speak, but no sound came out.

Hurrying over, she worked on the ropes holding the cage door closed frantic to release the boy from his prison.

Before the first knot came undone, an officer stepped inside the tent and let the flap drop behind him. Glancing from the baron to her and back to Rauf, a chuckle rose to his lips. "I thought you said the girl would be no trouble, sir."

Rolayna worked the ropes faster, keeping her gaze on Rauf. Somehow, she must get Alex free. Her gaze swiveled to his sword lying on his desk.

The officer stood at attention, waiting for orders and blocking Rolayna's only escape.

The baron rose painfully to his feet and shook vomit from his arms and face. Fury darkened his features. "Get the woman and the boy out of my sight before I kill them with my bare hands. I want the ransom demand sent to Dragonthorne tonight. I do not care what my brother says. I will wait no longer to give the devil his due." His face went red as he glared at Rolayna. "You will pay for this. It would have been better for you to submit. Now, I shall not be gentle at all."

She shivered. "Would you before?"

"I would have taken you slow. Now, I shall bury my rod in you without mercy."

He turned to the officer. "Take them to an empty tent and guard them. Do not let anyone near. I want them unspoiled for the surprise I have in mind. We travel for Seville at first light. Send me a courier. I have a message for the devil."

Rolayna narrowed her gaze as the soldier walked toward her.

"I will return as soon as I clean up. I expect the paper and ink on my desk when I get back."

Rauf's dark gaze rested on Rolayna. "I once considered making you my queen and envisioned many nights riding you in my bed before I slit your throat." He shook his head. "But now, I will have to settle for what pleasure I find in your pain as your husband looks on."

Rolayna shook with relief. They were spared for now, and Alex would be with her in the tent. She must keep her wits about her. Another day alive meant another opportunity to escape.

The soldier walked to the cage and unlocked the door, pulling Alex out and shoving him toward Rolayna.

She caught him against her and walked outside, anxious to comfort the child.

Alex trembled as his blue eyes gazed up at her.

"It is all right. I am here." She held him tight against her side as she walked.

They followed the soldier to a small tent, where he

opened the flap and shoved her inside.

Alex tumbled after her.

Rolayna knelt on the ground and tugged him toward her, looping her arms over him and drawing him onto her lap, where he shook in her embrace. Hugging him to her, she angled her hands to remove his gag.

"Do not attempt to escape. We will be right outside, all night." The soldier's gaze pinned her to the ground.

His companion stepped into the tent and gazed up and down Rolayna's body. "I will take the first watch." He leered at her chest and licked his lips. "I will be coming to check on you as soon as camp gets quiet, so get ready."

They left the tent.

The first guard's voice spoke outside. "The baron wants them undisturbed. He says he has a special surprise for them."

Dragos would come for them.

She focused on a terrified Alex as she pulled her dagger from her pocket. "Hold still, and I will cut you free."

She worked the knife until his binding fell to the ground.

The boy threw his little body at her and wrapped his arms around her neck. Hot tears ran down his face and soaked her shoulder.

"Hush, Alex. I am here. I am here, and you are safe. I will not let them hurt you, anymore. We will figure a way out. Dragos will come and rescue us. We have to trust him." She could not hold him. Her own hands were still bound tight in front of her.

Her little half-brother stopped after a bit and stared

at her. "I am scared." His eyes were wide and wet with tears.

"I am scared, too." She smiled at him. "Alex, can you cut my binding?"

The boy picked up her dagger and worked the blade until her twine broke.

With a cry, Rolayna caught him and rocked him back and forth in her arms. "I am so sorry, dearest. I did not know the black man and Father Nikolas were the same, or I would not have let you go with him. I did not know he let the soldiers into Dragonthorne, either. Forgive me. I shall never forgive myself for putting you in danger."

He held her in a death grip. "Father Nikolas hit me."

Rolayna groaned out loud. "I am so sorry, Alex. This is all my fault. I should have kept you close, and I never should have trusted the priest. The baron is evil, and I did not keep you safe as I promised to do. When this is over, I shall never let you out of my sight again."

The boy buried his head in her shoulder. "The bad man wants me to say, 'Bring me your men,' but I do not want to. I want Papa."

"I want him, too, but you must be brave, Alex. He will come for us. But first, we must escape and make our way back to Dragonthorne. Papa will find us along the way."

Alex nodded his head.

She waited until midnight before waking the child. The moon shone bright on the outside of the tent. When silence filled the camp, Rolayna clutched her dagger and took Alex's hand.

With careful motion, she slit the tent wall and

slipped outside before helping the boy through the opening. With a finger to her lips, she turned and walked into an ambush.

Rauf stood with twenty soldiers waiting for them in the dark.

Father Nikolas gave a crow of delight. "See! I told you she had a knife and would try to escape. She showed it to me the day Ramiel made it and cried on my shoulder because the demon kept from her bed."

Rolayna brought her knife up, tucking Alex behind her as she eyed the soldiers. "You shall not touch him. I will kill anyone who dares."

"And me?" The voice came from behind her.

She swung around.

Rauf's second held her half-brother with a knife to his throat.

With a groan of pain, Rolayna dropped her dagger in defeat and fell to her knees. She could not fight with Alex's life on the line. "Please let him go. He is but a boy!"

The baron chuckled. "He shall not die tonight, and neither shall you. Although this attempt to flee deserves punishment." He motioned for the men to lock them in a cage mounted on the bed of a wagon and with an evil laugh, he walked away.

They had no blankets, just each other for warmth. The night grew long, dark, and cold. Rolayna lay in the silence, holding the sleeping child and praying for the devil to find them. Her husband would come. He had to.

****

Dragos emerged from the dark forest midday. Tired and sickened by the smell of burning flesh, he

227

shook his head to clear it. Oliveander should burn in the fires of hell for the cruelty he dealt to the innocent. Graystone lay in ashes, set ablaze with all her people trapped inside. Scenes of the destruction and suffering the castle's inhabitants endured played across his mind as he halted outside Dragonthorne.

Gazing up at the watchtower, he saluted. The drawbridge lowered, and the portcullis rose. He thundered across the wooden bridge and into the courtyard.

The disciples followed behind.

Ramiel emerged from the long hall. "Master, I must speak with you."

"Meet me in the hall in twenty minutes. I will listen to your report then."

Dragos ran lightly up the stairs, anxious to see Rolayna. God, how he missed her. Her smile would chase away the memory of the last week, and her husky laugh would erase the screams from his mind. He wanted to drown in her softness and ease the ache in his heart for the helpless victims he could not save. It amazed him how much he looked forward to holding her.

Opening the door to the master chamber, he expected to see her fussing about but found it empty. The air smelled as if no one had entered for several days, and he frowned as he gazed around, noting the silence. A glimmer of gold on his bed and the note beside it caught his gaze. Trepidation gripped his chest as he flipped the missive open and read.

I trust you, Dragos, with all my heart and soul. I know you will come for me. We need you, please hurry!
Rolayna

His long fingers picked up the locket, recognizing it as the one Alex kept close when something or someone frightened him. Dragos flicked it open, and his mind worked furiously on the images before him. Understanding blazed with a flash of fire. Alex was Rolayna's brother. Then, he understood Rolayna's note. She went to protect Alex, and they were both in grave danger. Seville and all her bounty belonged to the boy, not his wife. Oliveander chased them to Dragonthorne for Alex, and his persistence meant he knew who the boy was. Dragos' roar of displeasure shook the fortress to the base of Devil's Backbone.

The disciples gathered in the courtyard and readied their weapons as they waited for instructions.

When their master emerged from the keep and strode toward them, black fury rolled off him in a palpable wave of heat.

"Where are Rolayna and Alex?" His chest tightened. The nightmare of his parents' death haunted him, making it difficult to breathe. It could not be happening again, for he would not let it. By the gods, he would find his wife and son, and they better be alive, or Oliveander's entrance to hell would be merciless.

Ramiel stepped forward to make his report, but Dragos stopped him.

The soldiers stationed in the tower signaled that a rider approached.

Azazel waved to allow entrance while Dragos folded his arms and waited, glaring at the gate and contemplating how many ways the baron would die.

A rebel courier crossed the drawbridge waving a white flag of peace. "I have a message for the devil."

Dragos stared at the man. "Deliver it if you dare."

He drawled the words and narrowed his gaze as the soldier trotted toward them. Only a fool rode into the devil's lair with nothing but a white flag for protection.

Azazel took the missive and read it. "Oliveander has Lady Rolayna and Alex and journeys for Seville. You are to meet him there in two weeks' time, alone carrying no weapons. If you do not, he will cut them to pieces and throw them from the tower for the wolves to feed on. He will spare the mistress and the boy upon your surrender." Azazel swallowed and glanced at Dragos.

"So begins the end of the rebellion," Dragos replied as he pulled his broadsword. "I have a message for your master." Dragos swung his sword and the courier fell in two.

He stalked toward the long hall, and the disciples hurried after him, grinning, knowing this time it would be a battle to the death. They would destroy the rebels and rid the kingdom of their foul stench.

"Ramiel, give us your report," Dragos commanded as he turned his back to the mantel and faced them.

The disciple told them everything.

"Who ordered the drawbridge lowered?" the master asked and paced in front of the massive hearth, his mind whirring.

"I did," Ivan entered the hall and walked forward. "Oliveander took Alex. The mistress would have gone after him whether I helped or not. She would not stay here in idleness with the boy captive any more than she did when she thought your life in danger, Master. I made sure she went properly armed and supplied. Her life is in your hands. She said if she failed to help the boy escape, she would stall for time."

Dragos stared into the fire for a long time. When he lifted his head, the disciples took a step back. They understood the expression on their master's face, for he would unleash a storm on Oliveander which rivaled the fire and brimstone of hell. Their master flexed his broad shoulders in anticipation as he strode out the door and called for his warhorse. The devil protected his dominion, and God help anyone who stood in his way.

****

They rode for days, bound and gagged in the rolling cage. Rolayna kept Alex by her side and did her best to shield him from the crudeness and cruelty of the soldiers, who poked them with sticks and threw things at them for entertainment. They let them leave the cage once a day to relieve themselves. She thought of Dragos every moment and prayed he would come for them. He had to.

Father Nikolas approached the cage on the second day and snickered at her through the bars. "The great mistress of Dragonthorne rides in a cage. I will wager you were surprised by my participation in the rebellion."

Rolayna glanced up. Alex slept by her side, and she drew him closer as she eyed the priest. He needed to brag about his involvement. When Dragos found out the extent of his treachery, he would die and dwell in eternal fire and torment. She stared at the evil little man as he strutted beside their cage.

"I fooled you. I played my part, and you never suspected me of being the traitor. All those times you came to me and cried your heart out, I gathered information for the baron." He smiled. "Aye, I dug the tunnel out a little at a time. It took the soldiers and me several weeks, working at night, so no one noticed my absence. Oliveander paid me a great deal of gold to fashion the bridge against the side of Devil's Backbone. I had to put serious thought into a way to cross the damn moat." He laughed. "But I figured it out and did it right under Dragos' nose." He stared at Rolayna. "Of course, the night presented the best time to work, because the master spent his time pleasuring you. The noise you made drowned out any sound I made while I prepared the way for the rebel army to make their attack."

Rolayna refused to allow the priest to rattle her composure. "When Dragos finds you, he will kill you. Then what good will your gold do? Coin has no value in hell." She stared at the priest without blinking, unafraid of him and his threats. He could do nothing to her, now.

Father Nikolas stiffened. "Dragos will be dead soon. Oliveander has a plan, and I shall enjoy watching the bastard die." The priest shook the bars of her prison. "When he is dead, I shall visit you and purge the devil from your soul. All those nights of lying in his arms while he plundered you will be cleansed when I cut out your womb and feed it to the crows." He laughed a high-pitched shriek, plucking her dagger from the folds of his robe and holding it high in the air. "And I shall do it with the knife the demon made just for you." The stones set in the handle of her blade gleamed in the light of the sun as if promising her freedom.

Rolayna shivered at the demented gleam in his eyes. Father Nikolas had gone mad.

He wandered off, muttering and screeching.

She glanced down at Alex and thanked the gods he

slept through the priest's conversation.

Two weeks after the rebels captured her, they turned into the gates of Seville. Rolayna sat up and stared with wonder at her former home. The towers sparkled in the light of the sun, and a cool breeze blew against her face as they rolled forward. Nothing moved, and an eerie silence hung over the courtyard and empty castle like a desolate cloud. Tears slid down her cheeks. Seville would never be the same again. Rauf made sure of it. No soldiers stood on the wall. Nobody hurried to greet them. The stillness echoed in her head and in her heart. *Oh Papa, at last I understand. Help me get through this. Help me keep Alex safe. And help Dragos reach us in time.*

Chapter Twenty-One

Rolayna did not know her father's castle contained a dungeon until the rebel soldiers shoved her roughly down the stone steps and locked her inside one of the cells. She knew most castles did, but her father never mentioned it. No one else did either. Cold and damp, the dungeon stones were black with mold, and the locks on the doors rusted with age. Rats and mice scurried about in great numbers, unafraid of their human companions, and dirty straw littered the floor.

Rolayna had not slept for over a week, not since they arrived at Seville. Gazing up at the barred little window high on the cold stone wall, she wished she could see the sky. How wonderful it would be to feel the warmth of the sun. Birds chirped, and every so often a breeze touched her face. Alex lay asleep on the narrow cot covered with a threadbare blanket. Rolayna brushed a hand at her hair and grimaced at her dirty palms. She needed a bath, and so did Alex. The soldiers brought little food, and she gave most of her portion to Alex. Her stomach could not hold more than a little food since their capture. Every night she lay awake and wondered if it were her last night on earth. Every day she stared at the bars and wondered if today Dragos would come for them.

How odd life was. Once, she thought of Dragos as a devil and wished for Rauf to find her, rescue her, and take her away. Now, she wished for the devil to rescue her from Rauf, for he was not a gentleman or any of the things she believed. She lay imprisoned in her own castle by the man she thought she loved. She thanked the gods above she did not make it to Whitehall Abbey that day, or she would have married a fiend. Perhaps, she would even be dead and buried beside her father.

Dropping to her knees, Rolayna prayed the gods to speed Dragos' journey to her.

A guard holding a tray with two bowls clattered down the stone stairs, interrupting her.

More watery soup, she supposed, and a little bit of bread. Alex would be hungry. She would not wake him until the guard left. The little boy grew weaker by the day, and the soldiers frightened him. He stuttered now and could hardly get a sentence out. Anything Rolayna could do to help him feel safe and take his mind off the situation, she did.

"'Ere's yer food." The soldier opened the door and set the tray on the ground. He straightened. "It will not be long now afore ye are food for the crows."

She glanced at the boy's face, grateful he slept. "What do you mean?"

The soldier chuckled. "Dragos is coming to surrender. The guards reported he topped the hill earlier today and should be 'ere by nightfall." The soldier licked his lips. "Once he does, the baron has a surprise."

Rolayna's heart jumped in her throat, and she rose to her feet. "Dragos is here?" Her words were whispered. Her mouth and throat were too dry to make much sound.

"Aye. The baron wants 'im dead. He 'as to come

alone with no weapons or ye both die." The soldier chuckled and rubbed his hands together. "It were gettin' a mite boring 'ere waitin' all this time. I 'spect there will be plenty of excitement tomorrow!" He grinned at her. "Enjoy yer evenin'."

Rolayna trembled. She barely had the strength to stand until the soldier walked out of sight. Shaking, she sank to the ground, sobbing into her hands. How could it go so wrong? Rauf must have threatened to kill them if Dragos did not come alone. He would surrender to Rauf and the rebel army, trading his life for theirs. She knew it, and the pain became more than she could bear. Rauf would kill them all, whether Dragos submitted or not. He would never let them leave or live.

Rolayna curled up in a ball and wrapped her arms around her stomach. She cared nothing for the stench of the rotting straw. Alex was too small and innocent to die at the hands of a lunatic. She cared not for herself, but for her half-brother. There must be a way to create a diversion and give the boy a chance for freedom. She must help him escape.

Noise came from the stone steps, and Rolayna roused herself. Warily she sat up and faced the sound.

Father Nikolas came into view, followed by two soldiers.

She stiffened. The demented priest delighted in tormenting her. She rose to her feet with trembling legs and turned toward him. Dread filled the hollow space in her stomach.

"Lady Rolayna, Duchess of Dragonthorne, whore of the devil, prepare yourself for what is to come." His eerie voice echoed inside the cold dungeon.

Rolayna shivered despite her resolution to hide her

reaction. Father Nikolas thrived on fear, and she resolved to show no emotion.

"I did not send for a priest. Take him away." She addressed the soldiers, ignoring the evil little man.

The priest screeched with laughter. "I came to administer the last rites. Soon you shall be dead, and the animals will chew on your bones. I thought you would be happy to see me. I do you a service by coming here."

Rolayna stiffened her spine to keep her shaking frame from giving away her distress. "You do me no service, and we do not require the last rites. Dragos will come for us and kill you all." She turned to the guard. "Take him away."

The priest dropped his smile and stalked to the cell door. "The devil cannot save you from the baron. I grow weary of your belief he has more power than I. Thus, sayeth God, I am the way and the light. Trust in me, and you shall be delivered. I alone have the power to save you! I am God unto you, and thou shalt worship me."

Rolayna stared into the priest's bloodshot eyes. "I worship no one, least of all you. You took Alex from the safety of Dragonthorne and delivered him to the rebels. I trusted you. You gave your word to keep him safe, and you betrayed us both. I shall never forgive you. Alex is a child and should be protected from war and death, not used as a pawn in a bid for the throne. My husband will find you and kill you for what you have done."

Father Nikolas spat at her. "The boy is the spawn of Satan and must be destroyed." His black beady eyes roamed her up and down. "They both shall die. I will see they are removed from the living and cast into hell.

I shall cut out their hearts myself. You have my promise."

Rolayna took a step back, horrified. "Alex is but a boy."

The priest stared at her for several minutes. Then, he turned toward Alex chanting a low guttural litany while he stared at the boy's sleeping form, holding his hands together and rocking back and forth on his heels as if in a trance.

"Get out. Get out now!" Rolayna took a deep breath and screamed as loud as she could. Soldiers ran down the stone steps and filled the doorway.

Rauf's second appeared a few seconds later. "What goes on here?"

"The priest wants to take Alex away from me. He told me he will help the child escape but will not allow me to come with them. He thought to open the cell door and take the boy. I cannot be separated from him. Please do not let him take the boy from me." Rolayna lied to get the soldiers to remove Father Nikolas for she could not listen to his threats anymore. She screamed again, hoping the agony in her voice would convince them all.

Rauf's second turned to Father Nikolas. "Is this true?"

The priest laughed. "She lies." He glanced back at her. "You shall not escape me, Lady Rolayna. I will come for all of you in the black of night, and none can rescue you from my righteous wrath. I shall triumph over evil and stamp your spawn from existence. You shall burn in eternal fire, and none can deliver." After this dark promise, Father Nikolas turned and hurried from the dungeon.

The others followed suit.

Rolayna sank to the floor as soon as the soldiers left. Her whole body shook from the effort to stand. She lay in the straw for some time, too weak to get up.

Rodents emerged from the shadows and sniffed their way to the food tray.

She roused enough to shoo them away. Alex must eat to keep his strength up. She gazed at the cot.

His wide blue eyes gazed at her. "My...papa is here."

His words were the first whole sentence the boy said for days. Rolayna turned toward him. "You listened to the soldier. I thought you were asleep."

"I-I-I...tried-tried...to-to...sleep." His face drooped. "He...said...my papa."

She rose to her feet and went to the cot, sitting on the edge. "He did. Dragos is here. He is coming to the castle tomorrow." She stroked the black hair. "I did not want you to hear because the baron plans to...hurt Dragos."

"He...said...surr-surrender."

Rolayna sighed. "He is going to surrender to the baron so you can go free. He wants you to live. When we get you out of here, you must go to the forest where the duke played with you. I will send someone to take you to the disciples. We must be quick, and you must be brave."

Her father took Alex to a woodcutter's hut in the forest. She knew not what they did there, but it lay close enough for Alex to run to. Afterward, she would figure out how to get word to the disciples. The boy must get away before Rauf realized what happened.

Alex stared at her. "You...not...come?"

239

"I will if I can. I may have to help Dragos." Rolayna fought the urge to be sick.

"I…help…papa."

"You can help Dragos by running when it is time to run. Can you do that?" She searched his pale face.

Alex nodded, his gaze solemn. "I want to go home."

Rolayna held him in her arms. "I do, too, Alex. I do, too."

They were taken from the dungeon before the sun rose. Baron Oliveander had them escorted to the tower wall on the north where they were bound back-to-back and placed on the edge of the overlook, high above the ground. They teetered on the narrow ledge.

"I'm…cold," Alex chattered as the breeze whipped their clothing.

Rolayna grabbed his hand in hers, where they were bound behind his back. "I know, dearest. Soon it will be over, and we will be warm."

Tears pricked her eyes. If only she could lie in Dragos' arms one more time before she died. She squeezed them shut and prayed for the demon to carry them away with every ounce of strength she possessed.

The sun rose on her right and warmed her face. Rolayna shivered as the warm rays spread over her freezing body. Soldiers leaned against the wall on either side of them where they were perched on the highest part of the wall, their feet level with the soldiers' shoulders.

Baron Oliveander stood in the center of the wall. He set his arms on the edge where Rolayna and Alex stood and held an eyeglass to his face as he surveyed the area to the north.

"Today is the day I have waited on for months. I must confess I am giddy with excitement." He handed the glass to his second in command. "Today, I collect the men I need to make my army complete. Tomorrow I ride for Evania and challenge the king. By the end of the week, all of Kingsland will be mine."

"My lord, riders appear." The captain of the guard walked to the baron's side and pointed at the road to the south.

A line of men on horses appeared, holding banners and marching in procession.

"Ah, the under lords. Allow them entrance and take their weapons. Assemble them in the great hall." Rauf peered through his looking glass once more.

The captain pounded his chest. "As you command."

The baron put his glass away and turned to Alex. "They come to hear you speak. You will tell them to gather their armies and serve me."

The boy stiffened.

Rolayna squeezed his hand and whispered, "Dragos is coming."

Rauf laughed. "Aye, the great devil of Dragonthorne is coming. He will kneel before me and pledge his allegiance. Then, after he has been properly humbled, I shall cut off his head and feed him to the crows." He walked several paces and stopped. "Actually, he will kneel before me and witness the 'surprises' I have planned. The surprises involve the two of you. When I am finished, he will watch me cut off your heads. When he appreciates the moment to the fullest, I shall cut off his head and feed you all to the crows."

"My papa will stop you."

Rolayna stiffened in surprise, for Alex spoke the words with surprising clarity. Something he had not done since leaving Dragonthorne.

Rauf whirled around and faced the child. "Is that so? Well, my little captive, he will not get a chance to do anything. You see, he is coming alone and without any weapon. Unless he truly is the devil and can command legions to rise from the pits of hell, he will die as soon as I get my men. It is important he watch me take everything from him, for his dominion will be at an end. The devil shall receive his due. Today I am transformed from baron to king, and I get to kill the devil in the process."

The captain walked to the baron's side and whispered in his ear.

Rauf turned to Rolayna and Alex. "As much as I enjoy watching you balance there on the ledge, I must go inside and greet my…guests." He walked away without a backward glance. "Do not let the wind cause you to sway. I should hate for you to fall from this height." His laughter followed him into the castle.

Rolayna teetered. Weak from lack of food and sleep, she stiffened her legs to keep them upright and swayed again. Dear lord, if she swooned, they would topple from the wall to their deaths, and there would be nothing left of either of them.

A swoosh whipped past her, and she toppled backward off the wall. The force of the fall knocked the breath from her. Alex lay beside her on the stone walkway. Rolayna groaned and caught his hand when he whimpered. She took a minute to get control of herself, trembling from head to toe.

"What in the hell?" A soldier bent over them and picked up an arrow, tied to another arrow with a piece of twine tied between them. The arrows flew on either side of her and Alex. The twine tied between the arrows knocked them backward, saving them before they fell from the edge.

Malphas.

Rolayna said the word in her mind. Only he possessed the skill to do such a thing. *Dragos.* She felt his presence, and relief spilled onto her cheeks. He must hurry before their time ran out.

"Yer comin' with me." The soldier pulled them to their feet. He cut their binding and shoved them along the wall toward the stairs.

She lost consciousness halfway across the walkway.

When she came to, she recognized the walls and ceiling of the long hall. Her father's under lords and barons filled the room, and she lay on the floor beside the great hearth.

Alex stood in front of her as protector while Rauf yelled something at him. The boy stood shaking his head with his arms folded in front of him.

Rauf advanced stiff with anger. His gaze focused on Alex; a muscle worked along his jaw.

Rolayna sat up. "What in God's name is going on?"

"Tell these men to obey me." The baron ignored her and reached for the sword on his side.

She scrambled to her feet. "Nay, wait." She put a hand to her head to slow the dizziness and give herself time to focus. "What is happening? Rauf, stop! Let me talk to Alex. He is a boy, only a boy. I will help him understand. Give me a minute to speak with him."

Rauf stopped. "There is nothing to understand, Rolayna. Alex will not say what I tell him to say. He knows what I want and refuses to obey." The rebel's sword lifted as he prepared to strike the boy down.

"Nay!" She lunged for a nearby soldier and relieved him of his sword, bringing it up in one quick motion to deflect the blow.

Rauf roared with anger. "Get out of my way! How can a woman know the use of a sword?"

He brought the blade around, and her dagger flashed in his other hand.

Rolayna was momentarily blinded by the stones in the handle, and his sword caught her in the side. She hit the floor with a thud as blood poured from the wound. Rolayna glanced down and covered her side with both hands, pressing down to slow the bleeding.

"Damn you!" Rauf lifted his sword again.

"Dragos is here!" The captain of the guard burst into the long hall, shoving a disheveled and bound prisoner in front of him.

Her husband stumbled and hit the floor with his knees. Turning his head, his gaze met hers across the length of the great hall where she lay in a puddle of her own blood.

She smiled at him.

His gaze sharpened on the blood around her, and he nodded his head.

Rolayna understood. He came for her. She nodded back.

Chapter Twenty-Two

His gaze searched the great hall for Rolayna as the soldier shoved him to his knees. He spotted her on the floor beside the hearth. Her long golden hair lay matted and dirty against the cold stone floor. Her stained gown and pale face infuriated him. He gazed into her beautiful blue eyes and read her pain. Dragos searched her face and body and then caught sight of the cause. She lay in a puddle of blood created by a fearsome wound in her side. He nodded his head to let her know it would be all right because he came to rescue her.

She nodded back.

Her trust settled over him like a golden shield, and Dragos rose to his feet. Little Alex faced Oliveander with a frown. He stood with his little legs braced wide apart and stared at the man. His gaze sharpened on the bruises covering the boy's face and arms. Rolayna had them, too. White-hot anger pumped through his body, and he tested the twine binding him. He could break it with one twist of his wrists. He turned to face Oliveander, caring not whether the disciples were ready, for rage roared through his veins. Rolling his shoulders in preparation, he caught the movement of the disciples as they sifted through the shadows. The room filled with his men, and their numbers increased by the second. No one noticed as they stole into the long hall on silent feet.

The Duke of Seville's under lords stood silent. Every eye rested on him and Baron Oliveander.

Dragos gazed into Oliveander's blackened soul and envisioned all the things he planned to do to the bastard.

The rebel smiled. "So, here you are. The greatest warrior of all time bound with a simple piece of twine and completely at my mercy." He strolled closer, lifting his sword as he did so. Rolayna's dagger flashed in his other hand.

Dragos narrowed his gaze.

"I have dreamed of this day and all the things I intend to do to make you suffer. Now you are here, I hardly know where to begin." The rebel sliced downward, and the tip of his sword cut the length of Dragos' arm. Blood dripped onto the stone floor.

He did not flinch, keeping his gaze trained on the enemy. Another second or two, and he would tear the bastard apart. He waited only for Azazel.

Baron Oliveander frowned and glanced around at his audience. "The great warrior refuses to show pain. How predictable. He thinks he is invincible." He laughed aloud. "We shall soon see what he is made of for all men have a breaking point, and we shall find his. The demon will cry like a newborn babe before I am through." He wiped the tip of his sword on Dragos' other arm. "Sometimes a man's breaking point is connected to someone else." He glanced at Alex.

"Take the boy, for example. How much of *his* pain can you take? Since you are so uncooperative, I think I shall begin with him. He is most disagreeable, refusing to say the simple words I instructed. I drew my sword because I tire of the boy's insolence, but Rolayna threw herself in front of my sword, so I cut her down. I would have liked to watch your face when it happened. I am sorry you missed it. I had a few things in mind when it came to your wife. I want to watch your face as I perform them. Women are meant to be...enjoyed. Don't you agree?" He walked over to Rolayna, picked her up, and kissed her long and hard. One hand fondled her breast before he dropped her to the floor.

She groaned and curled up. Her eyes closed, and Dragos fought the panic rising in his chest. She could not die. Not with him so close to rescuing them. He growled low in his throat, wanting to tear Oliveander's heart out with his bare hands.

The baron smiled when he heard the growl. "So, you do make noise. I thought you might. You are not as strong when it comes to your wife, are you? I could have my men stand her up so I can begin with her. Or should I have them strip her and bend her over for me? I cannot decide which." He stared down at Rolayna. "I do hope my blow was not fatal. I wanted to stare into your eyes as I cut her heart out with her own dagger. Now, I shall have to content myself with watching your reaction as I cut the boy to ribbons, piece by piece."

Dragos' rage knew no limit, surging through his veins like liquid fire. His gaze followed Oliveander's every move through narrow slits in his eyes like a predator studying his prey. When he glimpsed Azazel signal him out of the corner of his eye, he grinned. It was about damned time, for he could wait no longer.

Oliveander lifted his sword above Alex's head.

Dragos snapped the twine binding his wrists and grasped the hilt of his broadsword behind his neck hidden inside his tunic. He leaped forward and met the baron's strike, shoving the bastard back.

Regaining his balance, the rebel swung his sword up and turned to Alex again. Dragos whistled, and Azazel whisked the boy out of Oliveander's reach.

The baron roared with rage. "You bastard!" His face turned purple as he lunged with his sword extended.

Dragos grinned and parried Oliveander's blow. "I, too, have waited for this moment. I shall enjoy introducing you to the fires of hell." He caught sight of Wolfbane lifting Rolayna up into his arms. Wolfbane nodded at him, and the distraction proved fatal.

The rebel screamed in fury and rushed at Dragos. "You are ruining everything! Rolayna must be punished and sacrificed for her betrayal! The boy must be laid upon the altar. My brother saw it in vision." He threw the knife at Alex while his broadsword swung around and sliced his opponent across the middle.

Disbelief flashed across Dragos' face before he fell face-first to the floor. Blood pooled out beneath him

"Nay!" Rolayna's scream filled the great hall. Her limp form came to life in Wolfbane's arms. "Nay! Let me go to him! Let me go!"

The disciple refused. "Wait."

Oliveander crowed in victory, circling his victim's prone figure. "How the mighty warrior falls! Bind him, so I may tear his insides out before killing his whore and child."

Dragos sucked in a breath. He never meant to reveal his true nature in this manner and hoped to God Rolayna possessed the fortitude to withstand it. Transforming to demon form, he placed his black-veined hand over his injury, and focused his energy on the laceration.

Several rebel soldiers and Seville's lords faced him. When they caught sight of him, they cried out and rushed toward the door.

Dragos nodded as his men killed the rebels and herded the lords back into the hall, holding them there at swordpoint. The middle of his stomach tingled as the injury healed. When the bleeding stopped, he transformed back and rose to his feet to the consternation of all. He did not glance at Rolayna but focused on Oliveander and his wicked sword.

"How are you standing?" Rauf's voice trailed off as they crossed swords again and again.

Rebel soldiers stood frozen, gaping from their positions around the room.

The disciples drew their swords, and all hell broke loose.

Dragos smiled and lunged. "They speak of me as a demon for a reason."

Oliveander's eyes widened as realization struck.

Wolfbane left the hall with Rolayna.

Oliveander screamed in fury and ran at Dragos, swinging his sword from side to side.

The demon deflected the blows and cut a wide swathe across the baron's middle.

He howled with pain. "Damn you to hell! I will not allow you to win. The throne is mine. The kingdom is mine. All of it is mine. I am ordained of heaven to be king, shown to me in vision. As a demon, you are damned and cannot hope to find victory over me!"

Dragos snorted. "You will not live to see the sunset."

Their combined armies outnumbered the rebels ten

to one. The Duke of Northernfell held the northern gate. His army surrounded Seville on the north and the east. The Duke of Emberly held the southern gate. His army surrounded Seville to the south and to the west. The rebel army floundered and died by the hundreds.

Oliveander stumbled, his eyes snapping with fury. "I will see you dead, and your whore hung from the highest turret." He lunged, hoping to catch his opponent off guard.

The demon swatted the baron's sword aside. "You were dead the minute you touched what is mine. I see the bruises on my son's face and the wound on my wife's side. You will soon see what happens when you dance with the devil." He swung his sword and cut the tendons in Oliveander's legs.

The baron fell to the ground.

Dragos caught him by his tunic and tossed him through the door of the long hall into the corridor.

Soldiers lay dead all around them. The disciples cut through the rebels inside Seville as a pack of wolves tearing through a flock of lambs. The fight lasted mere minutes.

Oliveander screamed and rolled to his side. "I will win. The throne belongs to me. Kingsland belongs to me! You cannot hope to defeat me and my army. We are too great. We will find you and exact our revenge when you least expect it—"

"You threatened Rolayna with the same promise when you attacked my fortress. There is no rebel army, and you will never be king. Look around you. All your soldiers are dead. The rebellion is over, as are you." He kicked the rebel out into the courtyard. Grabbing the front of his tunic, Dragos dragged him up the stairs to the tower where Oliveander displayed Rolayna and Alex earlier.

"You stood my weakened wife upon this wall, tied to the beaten body of my son. She swayed for lack of food and water. If she swooned, they would have fallen to their deaths. How does it feel to see the ground from this level and realize you shall meet the fate you prepared for them?"

Rauf's gaze widened at the scene before him.

Dragos smiled as realization spread across the traitor's face. Death and destruction lay all around. His soldiers were dead, and the wall stood deserted. Only the devil and his disciples stood before him. Beyond the gates, armies stood in perfect formation, waiting for the demon's command.

Oliveander panicked. "Even if you kill me, you cannot win. My brother will succeed where I failed. It is prophesied I shall be king. Let me go. Once I am king, I will reward you for sparing my life. You have my word. I can make you more powerful than any man in the kingdom, just let me go."

Dragos shook his head. "It is too late. Your word is worth nothing. I came as you asked and walked into the castle alone. My hands held no weapon. You never planned to keep your end of the bargain. I found Rolayna wounded on the floor, Alex covered in bruises, and you were brandishing your sword over his head." He gazed at the baron. "When you make a deal with the devil—" Drawing his sword, he held the tip against Oleander's throat. "—you should keep it."

"Go to hell." The baron spat at the ground as his blue eyes flashed fire in the sun.

"You first." Dragos removed his wife's dagger

from the rebel's hand before he cut off his head with one swift blow of his broadsword. He threw both pieces from the wall and turned away. He did this for Rolayna and Alex. The gods only knew what horrors they endured at the bastard's hands.

Hurrying across the courtyard and into the keep, images of Wolfbane carrying Rolayna flashed through him. His disciple's quick nod told him she would be all right, and he hoped to God Wolfbane was right.

He ran up the stairs where Brawn and Malphas stood guard outside a chamber on the first floor and walked inside.

Rolayna lay on her side on the bed in the center of the room, covered with a fine woven blanket. Only a nasty wound along her left side remained visible.

Wolfbane bent over her stitching the flesh together while Ramiel held a lantern high to give him the light he needed.

Dragos stepped to her side and studied her.

Her lashes fanned dark against her pale skin, and her breathing though barely visible was even.

"It is a flesh wound and healing fast." Wolfbane knotted the thread and snapped it off. "She is weak from lack of food and sleep. See the bruising beneath her eyes?"

He did, and his chest tightened. "Are there any other wounds?" His fingers caressed her cheek, tracing over the black and blue marks staining her skin.

His disciple glanced up. "None I can see, but I did not do a thorough search. I focused on the bleeding."

Dragos nodded. His wrath knew no boundaries. He turned as Scimitar entered. "How is the boy?"

Scimitar shook his head. "His speech is broken. He

is frightened and asks for you."

"Fetch him. He is afraid of what he cannot see. When he is with Rolayna, he will calm down."

A few minutes later, he held the boy in his arms. "Rolayna...she...did not...let...the...man...kill...me." Alex whispered the words against his chest and trembled in his arms.

The demon nodded. "You faced the enemy like a true warrior when I came into the hall. You are very brave, and I am proud of you for protecting your sister."

Alex frowned. "Sister?"

He studied the little tear-streaked face. "The duke is Rolayna's father, as well as your father. Rolayna is your sister. Do you understand?"

The boy nodded his head slowly. "My lord said to watch her. He said to keep her safe. He said to do my du...my du—"

"Your duty?"

"Aye." The child bent over and touched Rolayna's hand. Lifting his head, he gazed at Dragos. "I want to go home."

"As soon as Rolayna can travel, we will go home. The bad man is gone and will never come again." Dragos hugged the boy. "As soon as you are big enough, I will teach you how to use a sword. Then, no one will ever hurt you or Rolayna again. We will both keep her safe."

The boy turned Dragos' head toward him. "Father Nikolas...say die...to Rolayna." He sighed deeply and laying his head on Dragos' shoulder, fell asleep a few minutes later.

Dragos ordered a cot carried in so the boy could be close to Rolayna. They both slept like the dead.

"Find Father Nikolas, Ramiel. He and I have unfinished business."

The disciple left the chamber.

Scimitar and Malphas followed.

When they returned, they delivered unhappy news. No one saw the priest since they entered the great hall. Somehow during the fighting, the little man disappeared.

Dragos strode from the chamber and closed the door behind him. He did not want to be overheard.

"Father Nikolas has much to answer for and will pay for his betrayal. Rolayna and Alex must be kept safe."

"Are they in danger? The rebel army is defeated. Who threatens the mistress?" Brawn strolled toward Dragos, and the others, a heavy frown on his face. "If the little priest is behind this, I shall tear him apart. No one shall get close to the mistress. She needs rest and food. I canna abide lookin' at the poor mite. They must 'ave starved her nigh to death."

Dragos nodded his agreement. "Alex speaks of a threat the priest made, threatening my wife's life. The priest must be found."

****

Dragos updated Hound on the priest, and the disciples went to search the woods around Seville. His trail led them from the castle to the woods, where they followed him for days through the forest until he left Seville land and journeyed to the sea. His tracks ended at the seashore, and no boat could be seen in any direction.

Hound swore. The evil little man escaped, and the mistress was in danger if the priest lived. Lady Rolayna made the master happy and must be protected at all costs.

The disciples returned to Seville with the news. No one knew what became of the little priest.

Following the battle with the rebels, Dragos spoke with Seville's under lords, quieting their fear of him and introducing them to Alex in the great hall where they knelt and pledged their loyalty. They were instructed to send word to Dragonthorne if they needed any assistance. "Alex is my son and heir. With him comes the promise of my protection and interest in your welfare. You shall remain under my protection until the boy comes of age. Send me monthly reports on your holdings. I will come to your aid if needed, for I protect my dominion."

They agreed and returned to their holdings and duties.

****

Wolfbane stopped Dragos the next morning. "Lady Rolayna's side is healed. I took the stitiches out when I brought new bandages to clean her wound." He leaned closer. "There is no mark to indicate a sword cut her side."

The master paused with a curious expression. "None?"

The disciple shook his head. "Did your blood mix with hers??"

"No, I make sure it does not." He frowned. "She has not been turned. There must be another explanation." He paused for a minute. "Make sure your mistress has the rest she requires. She has been through much."

Wolbane nodded and offered Rolayna a sleeping

potion. She slept for a week, only waking long enough to sip the richly flavored broths Brawn handed her. By the end of the second week, the color returned to her cheeks and the shine to her hair.

Dragos hired servants to tend to the castle and land. Many of them came from neighboring castles Oliveander burned to the ground and were grateful for a place to work and call home.

Father Bernard, the priest of Seville, arrived a few days later. Dragos' soldiers rescued him from the prison Oliveander threw him in.

Rolayna wept when he entered her chamber and hurried to her side.

"My lady." He sat down beside her. "It is good to see you."

She clutched his hand. "It is good to see you as well, Father. For a time, I wondered if we should meet again. The soldiers reported you were captured by the rebels and held for ransom."

Father Bernard nodded. "Baron Oliveander caught me following the attack on Seville. I thought I would be safe, but he did not honor the code to protect men of the cloth. He ordered me bound and gagged." The priest sighed. "I fear I let you down, my lady." He shook his head and squeezed her hand.

"How? You are here, and all is right."

"I brought the records of the Duke of Seville's marriage to Lady Dorset and Alex's birth with me. I thought to take them to Graystone and hide them before the rebels attacked Seville, but they caught me first. 'Tis how they learned of Master Alex and his importance. I shall never forgive myself for putting the lad in danger."

"How could you know Rauf would capture you? How could you know the evil things he planned? 'Tis all right, father. You kept Papa's secret and did your best to keep Alex's identity hidden. I knew not the truth until the moment I opened the locket. Do not blame yourself. Dragos came, and all is well."

"You father worried you would not understand why he kept Alex's identity from you. He spoke of it with me on several occasions and worried you would think he dishonored your mother by wedding Lady Dorset while in mourning. The lad's birth came as a surprise to them both. They loved the boy and spoke of a time when they could tell you about him. Lady Dorset became ill and died before it could be arranged. Distraught and heartbroken the duke knew not what to do. We made the decision to bring Alex to Seville and present him as the duke's ward rather than his heir. He used to take Alex to the woodcutter's cabin here at Seville where he need not pretend to be anything but a man and his son. Your father wrestled a great deal with his conscience over the matter. He loved you, child. Never believe otherwise."

Rolayna nodded. Papa risked everything for them both. The ache of loss tightened her throat. "I loved him, too."

Father Bernard left the chamber soon after.

Dragos stopped him in the corridor. "I would like a word, Father."

"Of course. What can I do for you?" The priest tucked his hands in the ends of his large sleeves and waited.

"I would like you to come to Dragonthorne. We need a priest, and Rolayna and Alex trust you. I do not think they will trust another man of the cloth so easily, not after Father Nikolas's treachery. The position is open. Please consider it."

Father Bernard smiled. "No need to consider. I accept. Without Seville and Graystone, I have nowhere to go. Thank you for the offer."

"Thank you, Father," he murmured and turned to go.

Rolayna smiled. *Father Bernard is just what Dragonthorne needs.*

The Duke of Northernfell stopped Dragos before he walked away. "I leave for the north."

His nephew nodded. "I thank you for your help with the rebels. As your lord, I will be available to offer aid should you need it. Send word next time you have need of me, and we shall meet on neutral ground. Do not come to Dragonthorne again. Neither you nor Dahlia shall be allowed within her walls."

Rolayna straightened. She never intended to listen to the conversation but could not turn aside, either.

The Duke of Northernfell sighed. "I understand your reasoning and cannot say I blame you."

Dragos left the corridor, and she sent her maid to entreat the duke to come to her.

The Duke of Northernfell entered her chamber with care having no interest in a battle with Dragos or his disciples.

Rolayna read his hesitation and motioned him closer. "I need to speak with you."

The duke nodded, standing awkwardly inside the chamber door.

"I wondered if you were aware of Lady Dahlia's attempt to seduce my husband on your last visit to

Dragonthorne?"

He frowned ferociously. "Careful, lady, you do not know of what you speak."

Rolayna patted the bed next to her. "Come inside, Uncle. What I speak of is for your ears only."

He stepped to the bed but did not sit, proud and stubborn as Dragos.

She sighed and told him of waking in the night and the note slipped beneath their chamber door.

"I will kill him if he touched my wife!"

"He did not. 'Twas she who sought to entice him. Dragos spoke the truth all those years ago. Dahlia forced her attentions on him, not the other way around."

The duke turned to leave. "I shall not listen to this. Keep a better eye on your husband. If I see him near Dahlia again, I will kill him."

Rolayna slipped Dahlia's note from under her pillow. She forgot about it until the maid retrieved it from the pocket of her gown while helping her into a night rail. Somehow it survived all that happened to her. She held the note out to the duke. "This is for you. Perhaps you will see the truth once you read the note Dahlia sent to Dragos at Dragonthorne."

Gregory took the note and opened it. His scowl deepened.

"It is Dahlia's hand, is it not?" Rolayna persisted.

The duke glanced at her and nodded. "It is." He turned on his heel and left the castle, returning to Northernfell.

The Duke of Emberly left two days later and traveled back to his castle on the east coast of Kingsland. Lady Cristina was with child, and the duke could not bear to be parted from her for any length of time.

****

A fortnight after the fighting, Dragos carried Rolayna out of Seville Castle and placed her on the velvet seats of his carriage for their return to Dragonthorne.

Birds sang as they flew from tree to tree, and his wife smiled, telling him of the days she stared at the bars of the dungeon and yearned to feel the sun on her face. Awe and gratitude shone from her beautiful face as she watched the country go by.

Dragos smiled. She regained her strength, but still suffered from stomach complaints. Something he worried over as he studied her.

Alex rode beside her on the red velvet seat asking his usual questions, and Rolayna answered each one, never growing tired of his chatter.

When he slid between the furs beside her the first night, she turned from him. Wondering if what she learned of him at Seville frightened her, he made no attempt to touch her again. Night after night, she did the same, speaking only when spoken to and growing more and more withdrawn the closer they got to Dragonthorne.

Dragos grew resigned. He knew his true form would be a shock. She may decide she no longer wanted him, and a stone settled in his stomach. He knew not what he would do without her, but he would not force her to stay. He gave his word she could leave when the rebellion ended, and he would keep it.

As he studied her movements and noted her slowness, a new thought crossed his mind. Did she suffer from some abuse he knew nothing about?

Whatever ailed her, he would know of it once they reached the security of the fortress.

At last, they rumbled across the wooden drawbridge of Dragonthorne.

Rolayna's face paled. She excused herself and went to bed as soon as they arrived complaining of a headache.

Dragos frowned but said nothing. He took care of the affairs of the fortress which could not be put off, and two hours later he sent Alex with Azazel so he could be alone with Rolayna. Pacing back and forth in the great hall, he thought about her withdrawal from him and decided he must stay calm, no matter what she told him. If he found out the bastards touched her, he would pat her shoulder to let her know he did not blame her. Then he would breathe fire and brimstone on any who still lived and introduce them to the fires of hell as only he could. If she planned to leave because of his demonic nature, he would smile, let her know he understood, and nurse the fatal wound after she left. Whatever happened, he would be gracious, and she would never see the true nature of his thoughts.

Dragos walked up the stairs as soon as he made his decision. One way or another, things would be settled between them this night. He did not think he could wait much longer to end this silence between them.

Opening the door to their chamber, he stepped inside, stopping short.

Rolayna stood fully dressed beside the bed, and tears ran down her cheeks unheeded. A valise sat open before her, and clothing littered the coverlet. She folded garment after garment and stuffed them into the valise. The only sound in the room came from an occasional sob or hiccup.

"What in the hell are you doing?" Dragos roared. "You plan to leave, then?" His heart pounded in his chest, and fear clutched his belly.

She turned. Her eyes were red from crying and her face pale. "The rebellion is over, and Oliveander is defeated."

"And?" Seeing her pack her valise sent terror through his system. He closed the door, striving to regain his composure as he waited for her to continue. She called him "Oliveander" not "Rauf." He tucked the information away.

Rolayna rolled her eyes. "You told me you would take Alex as your son and heir if I agreed to marry you until the rebellion ended. I would have to leave once it did. You said I would be free." She gazed at him and shook her head. "Dragos, our agreement is complete, and I leave at first light. Please do not ask me to go sooner. I am too tired and hoped you would let me rest one night before I go."

He stared at her. His mind frozen. "You think I *want* you to go? I thought you were offended by my true form after what you witnessed at Seville."

"Because you are a demon? Nay. I have known for some time. Your…abilities make you who you are. My feelings toward you remain unchanged." Sadness spread across her face. "It is our agreement. You kept your word, and now I keep mine."

Chapter Twenty-Three

Rolayna searched Dragos' face. He said nothing, just stared at her, and she sighed. Leaving him was the hardest thing she would ever do. "May I see Alex in the morning before I go?"

His gaze darkened as he locked the door and walked toward her. "You know I am demon, and yet it is our agreement you cry over and leave me for?"

She swallowed. "I gave my word." If he touched her, she would be lost. "Please go, Dragos, I do not think I can bear anymore." Anguish squeezed her chest, and tears spilled from her eyes once more.

"I remember our arrangement a little different then you do. I did not ask you to leave when the rebellion ended. I told you I would allow it because you wanted Oliveander. So, I told you I would give you your freedom." He pulled her into his arms. "I changed my mind. I no longer keep my word to you in this instance." He kissed the top of her head and rubbed slow circles over her back.

Rolayna closed her eyes, too weary to consider his words. It felt so good to let him hold her.

"I can never let you go."

She frowned in confusion. "Have you changed our deal, then?"

Dragos shook his head, and his dark eyes flashed. "I did not change it. I told you what you needed to hear at the time. If I told you I intended to bed you so Oliveander would not pursue you any longer, you would have run away as fast as you could, and you would have been right to do so. I could think of no other solution. No matter what we did or how far north we rode, the rebel followed. I wondered for a time if he intended to chase you into the heart of Dragonthorne. I could think of no other way to stop him than to take what he wanted. I thought he would abandon his pursuit once you were married and no longer a virgin. The marriage could not be annulled at that point, and he would have to admit defeat."

He shook his head at her. "I have no intention of letting you go, Rolayna, not ever. I need you, I need your smile, and I need your laughter. Most of all I need your love. My heart stopped when you trembled on the edge of the tower wall at Seville. One misstep and I would lose you forever. I thank the gods for Malphas. He fitted two arrows to his bow and tied them together with twine. He turned his bow sideways, and it worked. You fell back, and my heart beat once more."

Dragos stroked the side of her face. "Never leave me again, my love. You do not know how I felt when I returned to Dragonthorne and found you missing."

Rolayna glanced up at him. "I had to go after Alex. I could not leave him alone with that monster. I knew you would come for us."

"I must ask a difficult question, and I want an honest answer. Even if you think it will make me angry. I must know." He kissed the top of her head. "Did the soldiers touch you?" He stroked her back and waited.

"One or two of them tried." She gazed up at him. "And Oliveander. I lost my food all over them, and they did not bother me after."

He stiffened. "Who are these men? Do you have names or a description?"

She gazed into his amazing metallic eyes. "Two dead rebel soldiers. I watched them die."

He stared at her. "And Oliveander?"

The violence in his expression gave her pause. "They are dead, Dragos, by your hand." She stroked his cheek with her fingers.

"I want the truth of it. What did the rebel do to you?"

"He did not force me. He tried, but I fought back before anything happened."

Dragos took a deep breath and stroked her back once more. "It is difficult to kill someone for the second time. Were he not in hell at this moment, I would send him there. No one will ever touch you again. I swear it."

Rolayna wrapped her arms around his waist and kissed him with all the yearning and passion she could muster.

He growled low in his throat and held her tight against him. Reaching for the laces behind her, he tugged, and her gown fell to the floor in a puddle of silk. Then his warm hands worked on the laces to her corset. It followed her gown.

She pulled away a few minutes later and glanced toward the door. "Alex. I must find Alex before I forget myself."

Dragos lifted his head. His dark eyes were slumberous with desire. "He is with Azazel. We have the whole night, alone." He tilted her mouth up to his for an open-mouth kiss. His large hands roamed her body.

She shuddered when he cupped her breasts and rubbed his thumb over her hardened nipples.

He groaned in response. "I want to lose myself in your softness. I want to plunge inside you again and again. Let me love you, Rolayna. Open yourself to me."

Rolayna could not speak. His assault on her senses drugged her into a state of euphoria. Incapable of thought, she whimpered when he scooped her up in his arms and set her on the high bed. His warm hands caressed her calf, and she shivered to the soles of her feet. This time he did not bind her hands.

Her breathing became erratic. He removed first one slipper, and then the other. His hands stroked up her legs and stopped at her thighs. She trembled in anticipation. His mouth settled on her neck while his hands roamed up the inside of her legs. She cried out when he rubbed his hand against her core through the silk of her pantalets. She gasped against him and lifted her hips for more.

He laughed softly against her neck. "I think you want me as much as I want you. It is good to know, angel."

He ripped her chemise and pantalets from her body and stared at her nakedness trembling before him.

"Dragos, please," Rolayna whispered, gazing into his glittering eyes.

He was naked and beside her before she finished asking. Rolling atop her, he spread her legs with his thighs. "It has been so long, my love. I may not be able to control my passion. Do not let me hurt you." His heated member pressed urgently into her belly.

She groaned and lifted her hips to meet him. She

grew wet for him, and if he did not enter her soon, she would die. Rolayna's head thrashed side to side. "Please, Dragos. I need you now."

He thrust inside with one powerful surge, and she screamed with ecstasy. He lifted her head up to his and thrust his tongue into her mouth in time with the thrusting of his body. His wicked, knowing hands and lips plundered every part of her as he showed her with his lips and tongue how much he missed her. He pleasured her as only a demon can.

She got lost in his white-hot heat and knew only the fires of passion he aroused. Rolayna rode his sensual wave of pleasure until it crashed over her and sent her spiraling in a sea of pure bliss, screaming as her release shook her to her core and left her splintered in a million pinpoints of blinding pleasure.

Soon after, Dragos shouted his own release, shaking with its intensity. When the last tremor faded away, he rolled to his side taking her with him. Their sweat-soaked bodies glistened in the light of the glowing fire as he stroked her hair and kissed the top of her head. Rolayna smiled and snuggled close, wrapping her arms around him and caressing his back. Her fingers traced over his scars, and Dragos stiffened. His breathing grew ragged.

She frowned. "Tell me about them, Dragos. Let me in. It is your turn to open yourself to me. I want to know how it happened."

He drew the coverlet over them both and stared at the plaster ceiling, saying nothing.

Rolayna smoothed a hand over the scars on his back once more.

"You know all of me. Why cannot I know all of

you? You told me when the rebellion ended to ask about the scars. I am asking."

Dragos turned to her, his eyes flashing in the light of the fire. "It is not a pretty tale."

She smiled up at him. "I would hear it all."

After a minute, Dragos spoke. "My father was a strong man and expected much of me at a young age, requiring me to rise before the sun to train with the men. He would say I must succeed where he failed. War tore the land apart. When my father turned fourteen summers, the enemy killed his parents in front of him. Untrained with a broadsword, he picked one up and did his best. The enemy left him mortally wounded and dying beside his parents. He lay there in anguish for hours, crying out for help. An old man dressed as a priest found him and offered life in exchange for his soul. He agreed, and the devil performed his blood ritual allowing him to posses my father. With the possession came unnatural abilities and eternal life. Once healed, my father sought out every soldier in the country with skill and paid them to teach him how to fight. He did so for retribution and became the master of war."

Rolayna nodded. She remembered the stories of Darius Dragos and the battles he fought.

"I trained as a page when I was five. At the age of ten I trained to be a squire. My father would not allow the same terror to happen to me. He made sure I knew the use of weapons and acquired the skill to defend those I love."

She glanced up. "A boy is usually seven before he begins to train as page and does not train to be a squire until the age of fourteen."

"This is true. A band of priests roamed the country during this time and called their group 'the saviors.' They were fanatics fueled with righteous indignation for those who would not follow their beliefs. They heard of a mortal woman married to a demon and feared what might come of their union."

She smiled. "Is this why your mother named you after angels?"

He chuckled. "She did it to calm my father's mind when he learned of her condition. My mother told him something born of love could never be evil and gave me the names of two angels as guardians over my soul." He cleared his throat and continued. "The priests came one night to my father's castle disguised as minstrels claiming they traveled to Evania to play for the king. They did not know of me until they arrived. My father made the mistake of allowing them to stay the night. I remember, they sat alone through dinner and spoke quietly together, never taking their eyes from me. My mother must have sensed something amiss for she sent me to sleep with the soldiers.

"The minstrels waited until the castle slept and attacked my parents. Silver is the only weakness my father possessed, and somehow they knew of it. They bound his hands and feet with silver chains and carried my mother and him to the woods. These priests killed my mother in front of him and then stabbed him with their devil knife. This knife is made of pure silver and boasts ancient spells cut into the bone handle. I found their bodies the next morning when I returned from my morning ride and followed the priests' trail into the forest. My parents bled to death from their wounds, and I arrived too late to save them. The devil knife lodged in my father's chest, preventing him from healing." Dragos stopped for a second. He stroked Rolayna's hair as he fought with the feelings his memories resurrected. "Uncle Gregory came to our holding following the death of my father and took me to Northernfell to begin my training. He blamed me for the death of my family and tolerated no weakness, not even in a lad of ten summers. He reminded me daily of my father's mistake in trusting the minstrels. He wanted me to be a better man, a better warrior.

"At the age of fifteen, I began my training as a knight. I learned all I could about weapons, battle techniques, and fighting skills. For three long years, I trained. Waking up before the sun and going to bed long after dark. I yearned to please my uncle, to hear his praise for my efforts, but it never happened.

"One day, around my eighteenth year, Dahlia caught me alone in the stables. I thought nothing of it because she claimed her saddle came loose during her ride. She stabled her mare in a stall on the far end. I went to inspect the saddle strap and found myself trapped between Dahlia and the stable wall. She removed her clothing one piece at a time, telling me of her love for me. I could not believe my eyes.

"My experience thus far was hurried couplings with the housemaids. I did not have the experience to withstand the onslaught of Dahlia's sensual nature."

Rolayna closed her eyes. She did not want to hear this, but at the same time, she must learn the truth behind the scars and his relationship with Dahlia.

"She urged me to lie with her. When I would not, she used her knowledge of men and her experience against me. She pleasured me with her lips and tongue.

I did not stop to consider the consequences. Once her lips were upon me, I froze." Dragos took a deep breath. "Afterward, I realized what I allowed her to do, and the guilt ate at me. I told Dahlia it must never happen again. I could not betray my uncle."

"But you lay with her. You did betray him." Rolayna held her stomach. The images in her head made her nauseous.

"Nay. I did not. She pleasured me with her lips, but I did not bed her." He studied Rolayna's face. "Would you have me stop? Listening to Dahlia was the biggest mistake of my life, and I have paid the price ever since."

"Nay, do not stop. It is difficult to hear, but I would know the truth of it."

Dragos nodded. "I avoided Dahlia after and volunteered for duties away from the castle. I spent as much time outside as I could away from her and any place she might be. For more than a year, I stayed far from the castle and Dahlia. Then, Gregory called me to his war room. The baron on the east fought a border battle, and my uncle went to help with the problem. He placed me in charge of his keep. I argued and begged to go with him, but he refused. Having not been knighted yet, I could not answer a call of fealty. So, I stayed."

Dragos stared into the flames for a good while.

"What happened? Did Dahlia approach you again?"

A deep sigh filled the silence. "Aye. Every day. She wore revealing gowns and removed her clothing in front of me. She touched me and urged me to touch her. She begged me to lie with her, but I would not and avoided her as much as possible. Everywhere I went,

Dahlia found me. She followed me as I attended to my duties and spoke of love and happiness. In my foolishness, I believed her. She swore she loved me and wanted only me. One night, she snuck into my chamber without my knowledge. When I slid into bed, I found her there, naked. She clung to me and sought to excite me with her hands and lips, as before. I got angry and ordered her from my bed and my chamber. When I did so, she became ill. She would not eat and grew pale and listless. When I inquired what I could do to help, she blamed her illness on me. She said she fevered with love for me, and if I took her to my bed, she would recover.

Rolayna rolled her eyes. "Did you believe her?"

"I told her nay. Gregory is my uncle, and I would not betray him. She grew worse day by day. On the morning Gregory came home, I received an urgent note saying Dahlia fell. I ran to her chamber and found her listless on the floor, naked. I picked her up, placed her on the bed, and sent the soldier outside her door for the healer. As soon as the soldier went, Dahlia came to life. She wrapped her arms around my neck and pulled me on top of her. She kissed me and murmured over and over how much she loved me.

"I thought I loved her too, but I did not know the difference between love and lust. She wanted me to run away with her and painted such a picture of the two of us together, I nearly gave in. I listened to her lies, thinking there might be a chance of happiness with her. Then, Gregory roared from the chamber door. He tore me from the bed and knocked me off my feet. Dahlia screamed and accused me of forcing myself on her. She told Gregory I came to her chamber nightly and had my way with her. She begged him to make me suffer."

Rolayna sat up. "How could she lie in such a manner? What did Gregory say? Surely he knew she lied."

Dragos sat up beside her and put an arm around her shoulders. "Gregory ordered me taken to the courtyard and stretched between two pillars. He took a whip to my back, demanding I admit my guilt. When I refused, he whipped me until he could no longer lift his arm. Then, his second in command took over."

She gave a cry of dismay. "How could they be so cruel? You were innocent."

Dragos shook his head. "Dahlia convinced him. She plays the part of a victim to perfection and is well versed in the art of deception."

"Then what happened?" Rolayna could not bear to hear more of his feelings for Dahlia. She did not want to hear of his injury either but yearned to know the truth.

"Gregory's second whipped me until no more skin covered my back. My uncle cursed me the whole time. He believed Dahlia's lies and left me to bleed to death between the posts. I lost consciousness for a time. When I came to, Dahlia stood before me in the dark, dressed in black to avoid detection. She told me if I agreed to bed her, she would tell Gregory she made a mistake. She would take me to her sister where I could heal, and we could be together. When I refused, she flew into a rage and attacked me with her nails and fists. A soldier making his rounds caught her and pulled her away from me. He took me to the dungeon and locked me in one of the cells to rot. I have no family except Gregory. No one would notice my absence. If it were not for the priest, I would have died."

Rolayna snuggled closer. "This priest, is he the same man who bartered with your father?"

Dragos sighed. "Yes. The priest offered me life, and I gave him my soul on one condition, the scars on my back remain to remind me of my foolishness. Once we agreed, he performed a ritual and mixed his blood with mine. The devil used herbs on my back, and the scars remain. My speed, hearing, sense of smell, and eyesight improved. They are far superior to any human."

"He mixed his blood with yours?" An image of Dragos' pale face as he ripped her gown the first day they met came to mind. She sat up. "You tore my gown after I stabbed you with my hat pin because you worried I received a wound and our blood would mix, turning me as you did."

He nodded. "I would have you as you are." A frown furrowed his brow. "You said you knew I was a demon for some time. How?"

Rolayna shrugged. "You knew what I planned as if privy to my thoughts, and you found me every time I ran away. The day I went to the stream and you saved me, there is no way a normal man would know what direction I went or make it in time to rescue me from the water. It took hours and hours to get back to the castle afterward, and I thought about your answer when I questioned you. How could you smell my essence from such a distance? Then there was the battle with your uncle at Dragonthorne. Your eyes and veins turned black, and when you came to me later, you bore no wound. There were too many unanswered questions. I considered all the stories I heard wherein they called you devil and demon and decided they were truth." A deep sigh escaped her. "I am sorry, Dragos, I did not know your life has been so difficult."

"Do not be sorry, Rolayna. If I died of my wounds in Northernfell and not become demon, I would not have come for you, and Olivander would have killed you. As for Dahlia, I thank the gods Gregory came home when he did and found us. If not, I would have given in to her and made the biggest mistake of my life. When Dahlia accused me, I realized her true character. The scars on my back remind me of her treachery."

Rolayna lay still beside him. "Dahlia is the reason you do not like me to touch your back."

Dragos gazed into her eyes. "My scars remind me of my weakness, not Dahlia."

"Most men would have given in to her pleading. The fact you did not makes you powerful. I think this is the reason she hates you. She has no power over you, and it makes her mad."

He gazed at her for a long time. "You may be right, but it does not matter what Dahlia thinks or believes. She will not be allowed inside Dragonthorne again." He kissed the top of her head. "I owe you an apology."

Rolayna glanced up in surprise. "Why?"

He sighed. "I treated you poorly those first weeks because of Dahlia. I assumed you were like her. Your scent drew me in, and I thought of nothing but tasting you. At the same time, I hated you for who I thought you were. When you fought for your freedom so fiercely, I realized you are nothing like Dahlia, and it pleases me greatly."

Now she understood. "You thought I would betray you because I resemble her. Is that why you kissed me and then accused me of being unfaithful to Rauf? You confused me, but I could not resist you when you took me in your arms. Afterward, you would say the most awful things to me. It is starting to make sense."

Dragos nodded. "You are so tender with Alex, and I realized my mistake. You have a kind heart and a gentle nature. You are sweet, honest, and loyal. I offer my apology and ask for your forgiveness."

Rolayna swallowed the lump in her throat. "Of course, but there is nothing to forgive. We both have much to apologize for." She smiled over his mention of the boy because Dragos' manner with Alex convinced her he was not the monster she thought him, either.

"What happened after the priest turned you? What did you do?" She wanted to hear the rest of Dragos' story.

"I left my uncle's castle and traveled by foot to Emberly. Miles and his father took me in. I received my knighthood while in the duke's service and fought with them and for them. I trained with the best swordsmen in the kingdom and made a name for myself. Soon after, the king sent for me. A spy from our enemy lurked in the capitol, and the king wanted him found and disposed of. I did what he asked and became the king's secret weapon. He sent me on many errands and missions no one knew anything about. In my travels, I acquired my disciples one by one, and we became what we are today. The king gave me the honor of being his second before sending me to end the rebellion. Few knew of it. My uncle sat in the council when the king commanded. I am the king's second. Gregory must give me his vow of fealty. He refuses to bow to me because of Dahlia and her lies. One day, I shall have his oath."

Rolayna lay quiet and hoped her note to Gregory would right this wrong.

Chapter Twenty-Four

Rolayna woke to find two wide blue eyes staring into hers. Dragos had gone, and Alex lay on his belly beside her, chin in his hands.

"You are awake." His speech improved daily.

"I am. How are you?" She did not wait for his answer. Her stomach rolled, and she barely reached the bedpan before emptying her stomach all over the polished wooden floor.

The boy disappeared.

Two minutes later, Dragos took her by the shoulders and laid her back. Concern worried his brow. "What is wrong? Does the food not agree with you?"

Rolayna shook her head. She did not know. She thought the sickness plaguing her during her captivity would leave once she returned home with good food and rest. It did not and afflicted her daily. She kept her sickness from him as best she could, but somehow, he knew all the same. The servants must tell him. For she made certain she did not lose her stomach in front of him.

Dragos sent for the healer, Agatha, an old woman who tended the women in the fortress. Wrinkled and gray with bright blue eyes which comprehended more than she let on, she hunched over her cane as she walked. She wore a faded black gown with an apron. She cared not for the apron but for the pockets it contained. Those pockets bulged with her herbs and tinctures.

Agatha came quickly when the master called. She closed the door to the master chamber and thoroughly examined Rolayna. After several questions about her menses and the nature of her illness, the old woman chuckled. "'Tis as I suspected. There is naught wrong with ye, Mistress."

Rolayna gazed at the old woman with concern. "Then why am I ill? I cannot keep anything in my stomach, and yet it grows. It is no longer flat as it used to be. See how it curves out. I know something is amiss; smells affect me. I walked into the kitchens yesterday, and whatever cook stirred in the big pot made my stomach roll. I lost my breakfast in the corridor. It is not natural to be so sensitive. There must be something you can give me. Perhaps you have a tea for my constitution?"

Agatha chuckled again. "Ain't no tea for what ye've got, but do not worry. Yer stomach will be back to normal in the spring."

Rolayna gasped. "It cannot be so bad. Tell me what ails me."

The old woman glanced up in surprise. "Surely ye guessed. After all the pleasurin' the master gives ye, and ye don't know? Ye carry his child."

Her mouth fell open. It could not be. Worry over Alex and recovering from their ordeal distracted her, and she just now realized she missed her last three menses. She stared at the healer. "When is the baby coming?"

"In the spring," Agatha answered as she picked up her cloak in preparation to leave.

Rolayna placed a hand on her stomach. A baby. A child she made with Dragos. She thought of all the times she lost her food, and a frown furrowed her brow. The child grew within her when the soldiers caught her and imprisoned her at Seville. "Agatha, wait."

The old woman stopped in the doorway and glanced back.

"The baron cut my side with his sword. How is it the child lived?" Rolayna thought of something else. "Does Azazel know?" He commented on the swiftness with which she healed. Her baby carried Dragos' blood and shared its special ability with her.

Agatha walked back to her. "Do not fret, Mistress. The child is strong like the master. A little cut from a rebel is nothing. Azazel did not notice because he is a man and unused to the ways of women." She shook her head. "Once he gets a wife, things will change."

The wound was more than a little cut, but Rolayna did not argue. Did everyone here read minds? "Thank you for your help."

The old woman nodded. "We will keep a close watch on ye. Now ye are with child the master will be even more protective of ye. He will take care of ye. Not to worry, Mistress. Everything will work out. Ye'll see." She left, closing the door behind her.

Rolayna sucked in a deep breath. How would she tell Dragos the news? Would he be happy about a babe?

The door to her chamber banged open, and she jumped at the sound.

Her husband stood there with a strange expression. His gaze went from her eyes to her stomach and back to her eyes. "You carry my child?"

Rolayna sat up. "I do." She placed both hands over

her stomach in a protective gesture. "She will be perfect."

His voice gentled. "How long does Agatha say you have been with child?"

"Since before Oliveander captured me. She explained the babe caused the sickness. The weakness and dizziness were all signs, as well. So is the constant loss of my food. I knew not carrying a child caused such things."

Dragos stood beside her in an instant and placed his hand over both of hers.

She glanced up.

His gaze rested on her belly. His large hand covered the entire area. He said nothing for several minutes.

"Are you angry?" she whispered.

Dragos' gaze jumped to hers. "Nay. My anger is not directed at you. I am furious with Oliveander for the things he did to you. To find you were carrying my child the entire time requires me to practice considerable self-control. The bastard hit you and did not feed you properly. He tied your hands and kept you in the dungeon. He *touched* you." Rage simmered in the metallic depths of his eyes. They flashed like lightning. "I should like to end his life again for the things he did to you and our child."

Rolayna slipped her hand from under his and stroked his cheek. "The babe lives, Agatha said. She is strong like her father. You were half-demon and half-human before you made your own bargain. Do not worry. Our babe shall be beautiful and gentle. She shall do much good."

"She?" One eyebrow rose at her suggestion.

"Of course. What else would the babe be? A daughter is a fine blessing. She will give you joy and happiness." Rolayna smiled. A daughter would be the perfect thing. Dragos must see that.

"A son will be a greater blessing. He will give me pride and honor." Her husband stood upright and stared at her. "You will give me a son."

"I gave you Alex. He is your son. He will give you all the pride and honor you need. I will bear you a daughter, and you will see I am right." She gazed up at him, checking to see if he accepted her challenge.

Dragos dropped his lids over his eyes. "We shall see." His hand caressed her belly one more time before he bent his head and placed a gentle kiss on the slight mound. He stroked her cheek and strode from the room without another word.

Rolayna stared after him. A smile tugged at her mouth. His gruff manner did not deceive her. News of the child pleased him. Rolayna ran her hands over her stomach. She had so much to plan and sighed with happiness. Nothing could mar her joy.

****

She awoke screaming in the dead of night. Rolayna sat up in bed and beat the hands grasping her. "Leave me alone! Let me go!" Her hair lay plastered to her forehead with perspiration. Her nightmare lingered, holding her in its deathly grip while she shook with terror.

Dragos pulled her into his arms. "Shhhh, love. It is I who holds you."

The second he spoke, she quit fighting and went limp. This made the third week in a row. Every night she woke screaming in fear.

"I am here, Rolayna. Did you dream of Father Nikolas, again?" He stroked her golden hair and cradled her body against him.

"Aye," she whispered. Tears filled her beautiful blue eyes. "I walked in the corridor by the kitchens, and he jumped out from behind the tapestry, holding a knife. He told me he came to kill Alex." Rolayna sobbed uncontrollably.

"So, it is the same dream? We sealed the tunnel entrance by the kitchens after Oliveander breached the castle. Father Nikolas cannot get inside Dragonthorne. You are safe."

She pressed her face into his chest. "In my dream, he threatened to kill the baby. He held the knife above my stomach." Rolayna shuddered against him.

Dragos growled. "We will send soldiers into the tunnel again tomorrow to check the entrance." He placed a warm hand on her rounded belly. "'Twas a dream, Rolayna. Father Nikolas does not know about the babe, and my son is safe. Nothing shall harm you or him. Alex is protected. Ramiel and Azazel take turns watching him through the night. Malphas and Scimitar patrol the grounds. Brawn and Ivan guard the keep. We are all here, beside you, keeping you safe."

She sobbed louder. "He knows, Dragos. He knows about the baby. The priest knows."

"How? No one spoke of this before we returned to Dragonthorne."

Rolayna lifted her head, her eyes wide with fear. "When he came to the dungeon and threatened me, he said he would kill them both. He said 'both,' Dragos. He knows. Somehow, he knows about the babe."

The fear in her eyes penetrated him to his core.

"We will find the priest, Rolayna. He will not get close to you or my children. You have nothing to fear." The terror in her gaze shook him. "Hush, sweet love. You must trust me. I will keep you safe."

Rolayna's nightmares remained.

Wolfbane mixed up a potion which would allow her to rest. Meticulous with his calculations, he measured twice, so the babe remained unharmed by his elixir while affording his mistress much needed rest.

One day Dragos returned from training with his men to find his wife sitting upright on their chamber floor. She sat upon a thick blanket wearing only his shirt. Her feet were each twisted up onto the opposite thigh and her eyes were closed. Her hands rested on her knees palm up, and her thumbs touched her first fingers.

"What are you doing?" The position could not be comfortable, especially for a mother-to-be. "It cannot be natural to sit so straight with your legs folded in such a manner."

"I am relaxing my mind," Rolayna murmured. "Ivan is showing me some of the skills he learned in India."

Dragos chuckled. "And you do this wearing nothing but my shirt? This is part of his skills?" Skilled in the art of fighting with his hands and feet, Ivan needed no weapon. His hands and feet were his weapons, quick and deadly. He learned the skills while staying at a monastery in India. "I have not seen Ivan practice this sitting position. Does it hurt?"

She opened one eye. "I am certain Ivan wears his own shirt when he trains. This position is quite comfortable when one practices it often." She opened the other eye. "Ivan is teaching me to fight."

Rolayna did not have the power or the speed to do much damage. But if it kept her mind off Father Nikolas and helped her feel safe, he would give his consent. "You have my permission."

Rolayna smiled. "I do not ask for permission. I tell you, so you do not get hurt should you surprise me."

Dragos chuckled and placed a kiss against her lips. "You may practice on me anytime you choose."

****

Rolayna's pregnancy progressed. Her stomach rounded out, and she had difficulty getting around. Her mood changed by the hour. The people of the fortress were gracious and kind and looked with anticipation for the blessed day.

Dragos grew fierce in his attention to her safety. He insisted on carrying her up and down the stairs so she would not fall. Brawn spent hours consulting with Cook on what to feed Rolayna, determined she eat the right foods, so the master's babe grew strong and healthy.

One day the disciples approached her where she sat in a rocker beside the hearth.

Dragos turned from his position in front of the fire. "What is this?"

They glanced at one another and then at him.

"We have a gift for the mistress," Azazel said.

Rolayna glanced up from her stitching and smiled. "What is this gift?"

Ramiel stepped forward and held out a bouquet of lavender wildflowers.

Brawn presented her with a cream cake.

"We know how worried you have been about…the

situation," Malphas said.

"And we remember how ye chanted about wildflowers and cake when ye were scared..." Brawn put in. "So, we gathered some for ye to ease yer mind about...things. I made the cake."

"Do not worry, Mistress. I will find this priest. Nothing will happen to you," Hound announced.

"We thought the flowers and cake would help," Scimitar added.

"We want you to be happy, Mistress," Azazel summed up.

Rolayna's smile lit the room. They were so thoughtful of her feelings. "Thank you all." She took the lavender wildflowers and held them to her nose. "They smell so sweet. This is kind of all of you, and I shall treasure the gifts."

Brawn placed the cream cake on the tea table beside her elbow. The men nodded and left.

Dragos bent and kissed her cheek. "You have won the hearts of my disciples. Well done, love."

Rolayna sighed with happiness. They accepted her as one of them.

The disciples took turns following her around during the day. Dragos put them on shifts, always keeping her in sight. At first, she thought it a novelty to have someone to talk to whenever she chose, but she soon grew tired of it. The constant admonishing to watch her step and be careful wore on her nerves. While she appreciated everyone's concern, they smothered her. She could not turn around without bumping into someone hovering behind her, anxious to keep her safe.

One day, Rolayna decided to go for a picnic and

asked to leave the fortress.

Dragos refused.

After a heated discussion, they compromised. She settled for the little space of grass behind the chapel, where Father Nikolas spent his time with Alex.

Dragos agreed to let her be alone for one hour.

She could see the men training from her perch on the grass and sighed with contentment.

She turned to Scimitar when he sat down beside her. "Tell Dragos no more guards. He promised me an hour by myself, and I shall have it." She smiled to ease the sting of her words. "This cannot be much fun for you, either."

Scimitar smiled. "It is more fun than dealing with the master should something befall you and the child."

Rolayna understood. "You may come back after an hour and check on me. I shall be right here. I have no other plans but to sit." One hour alone would be heavenly.

The disciple nodded and walked away.

Lifting her face to the sun, she took a deep breath. The air smelled of lilacs and fresh grass. She leaned back against the mountain of cushions Dragos placed there earlier and sighed. Her husband knew what she wanted almost before she did. She rubbed her hand over her swollen belly and wondered for the thousandth time what her daughter would look like. The babe could come at any moment. Agatha assured her all would be well, but Rolayna grew more anxious by the day about the birthing. She confided as much in Dragos one evening, and he turned his dark gaze to hers.

Placing a large hand on her stomach, he asked, "What is it you fear? I shall be there with you, and we will welcome our babe into the world together. Naught shall happen. I will not allow anything to hurt you or our child."

"I know." How could she explain her fear of the unknown? Having grown up without a mother or sister, she had little idea of what occurred.

The baby kicked, bringing Rolayna back to the present. Her daughter grew strong like her father. She placed a hand over her belly and waited for the child to move again. A strange metallic scraping came from behind her, but she did not turn her head. The people believed the old well to be possessed. Eerie noises often came from within it. Many of the people within the fortress avoided the patch of grass behind the church, saying strange things happened here, but she did not credit the stories. What could happen with the church nearby?

Suddenly, a hand closed around her throat and squeezed.

Rolayna choked on the scream rising to her lips and froze in terror.

A man stood behind her blocking the sun. "Hello, duchess. I have come for you and the spawn you carry."

Father Nikolas! How did he get inside the fortress? Icy fingers raced down her spine. She opened her mouth to yell for help, but he tightened his grip. She choked and gasped for air, clawing at the hand around her throat.

Bending forward, she sucked in a mouthful through the constricted space. "Let me go. Run while you can. When Dragos realizes you are here, he will kill you." The words were raspy and stung her throat.

Father Nikolas laughed. "The devil cannot hurt me,

for I am ordained of heaven. God and his holy angels shall protect me." He replaced the hand around her throat with a blade. "Do not scream, or it shall be the last thing you do." He walked around in front of her, trading hands with the knife. His gaze took in her enormous stomach, and a smile split his face. "I rejoice I am in time to stop Satan's spawn from spreading. I will kill the devil you bear and then find the boy. I shall destroy you all and purge the land of your evil."

Rolayna straightened and stared at him.

Thinner than he used to be, with ragged, filthy clothing, a crazed gleam shone in his eye as he glanced wildly from side to side. "Get up, or I shall kill you here."

She nodded and leaned forward. She put her dagger away when she grew too large for normal clothes and kept a knife in her boot since her nightmares began. Now when she needed it, she could not reach it because of her belly. Rolayna glanced at the field where the men trained, but no one turned toward her. With growing anxiety, she blew the hair from her eyes and wished Scimitar were nearby.

The priest chuckled. "The disciples are too far away. Even if you screamed, they would not get to you in time. The guards in the tower are doing their rounds. Dragos has gone on his ride with the boy, and Ivan is busy putting out a mysterious fire by the kitchens. There is no one to help you." His eerie laugh surrounded her. "I made sure we were alone."

Rolayna rose to her feet and gazed behind her to the well, remembering the metallic scraping. Is this how the priest got inside the fortress?

"So, you figured it out. I have worked on the tunnel

at the bottom of the well for over a year. No one knew because I kept it a secret. I knew one day I would use it for God's work." He grabbed her arm and shoved her toward the well. "I have a special place picked out for the sacrifice of your devil spawn. It is deep within the forest. Spirits keep it hidden from unwanted visitors."

Fear clutched her heart, and her hands trembled. She must alert Dragos to her predicament. Ivan's lessons filtered through her mind, and she knew what to do. Filled with determination, she turned to Father Nikolas. "Dragos will find you. The gods who watch over him are stronger than whatever spirit you worship."

The priest stopped. His shining black eyes stared at her. "They warned us of the devil in theology. The cardinal taught us the devil could tempt the angels of heaven to turn from God. I never believed him, but now I see he is right. You have fallen from grace, my lady, and soon you shall meet the great deceiver." He grabbed the front of her gown with both hands to throw her into the well.

She made a quick kick to both of his shins and brought her fist to her chest with her arm horizontal to the ground. Using the flat bone of her forearm to knock the priest over, she hit hard and fast.

He landed on his back with a groan.

Rolayna turned and ran as fast as she could toward the keep, stopping in the courtyard to scream with all her strength.

Disciples came running from every direction.

Suddenly, Dragos stood in front of her catching her in his arms.

She fell forward and wrapped her arms around him

to keep upright. There was a gush, and wetness ran down the inside of both thighs. A sharp pain tore at her stomach. Rolayna gasped and caught his arms in a death grip. She dropped her chin and waited for the pain to subside.

"What is it, love?" Dragos picked her up in his arms. "Is it the babe?"

She could hardly breathe. She pointed toward the grass and the well. "Father…Nikolas…the…well." The disciples turned and ran toward the church.

Rolayna grasped Dragos by the tunic as another pain tore her apart. "She…is…coming."

Chapter Twenty-Five

Dragos strode toward the keep. "Ivan!" He held Rolayna close in his arms.

The little man appeared at his side.

"Send for Agatha. It is time." He took the steps two at a time. Soon, he laid her back against the cool sheets of their bed.

"Rolayna, talk to me. Tell me what happened." Dragos stroked the fine golden hair and held her hand in his larger one.

She related all which occurred. The sentences were broken as she fought for control over the pain gripping her. When it subsided, she wiped the perspiration from her brow with a trembling hand and squeezed Dragos' fingers. "I am frightened."

He kissed her forehead. "I am here, my love. We will have this babe together. I gave my word and shall not leave you again."

Another pain tore through her. She screamed and struggled to sit up. "I am too warm, Dragos. I need some air." She pushed him away and slid to the edge of the massive bed, tucking her chin to her chest. She rocked back and forth with her arms around her middle while her belly tightened. She could not decide what to do to make it better. Her breath came fast as she dealt with the pain. When it was over, Rolayna lay on her side, rubbing her swollen stomach with shaking hands.

He got up and paced back and forth. "How did you know how to deliver the blow to Father Nikolas? I should not think a tiny lady like you would have enough strength to knock a man down."

"Ivan taught me," Rolayna answered weakly. "He showed me what to do if I were attacked."

Dragos paused beside the bed. "Ivan taught you?"

"You gave permission," she teased. Another pain ripped her insides apart. "Dragos." Rolayna could hardly breathe. She sat up and rocked.

He stood beside her in a second. "Tell me what to do."

She shook her head. "I do not know. It hurts, and I cannot breathe."

Agatha knocked sharply and entered the chamber, followed by two of the soldiers' wives. "I hear the babe is wanting to meet his papa." She smiled at Rolayna. "Take a deep breath, Mistress, and blow it out through your mouth." She helped the mistress until the pain subsided.

Agatha motioned for Dragos to leave.

He shook his head and folded his arms. "I gave my word I would be by her side. I will stay."

"She has hours to go before the babe comes. Go tend to your men and give us a few minutes alone. I must help the mistress undress and get her comfortable.

He glanced at Rolayna.

She nodded her head. "Go, Dragos, but make sure you return before too long. I cannot do this without you here."

He strode from the room and went in search of Ivan and found him behind the church with the disciples investigating the priest's tunnel.

"It runs under the wall and into the forest. Hound crawled through the entire length and is tracking the priest now." Ivan nodded toward the forest. "Azazel and Scimitar are with him. They waited for his whistle so they could locate the tunnel exit."

Dragos peered into the well. "Rolayna tells me the priest dug it out over a year. He came to kill her, our unborn child, and then Alex."

Alex appeared at his side. "Where is Rolayna? I want to show her my new sword."

Dragos squatted beside him. "Your sister is in our chamber. You will have to show her your sword later. Right now, she is busy. Soon you will see the babe who kicked in her belly."

The boy gazed up at Dragos with a wide grin on his face. "Is my new niece coming?"

He chuckled. "I see you spend a lot of time talking with Rolayna." He hugged the boy. "We will be excited if it is a nephew, too. Now, go find Gretta and see if she needs help. Your sister and I will be busy for a few hours. We will come for you when the babe is here."

Alex nodded his head and skipped toward the keep.

Dragos stared after him.

"He is a fine lad," Ivan said.

"I do not want him to know of Father Nikolas and his appearance from the well. The boy has his speech back and sleeps through the night. I do not want him upset."

Ivan agreed. "I will speak with Gretta and Liska."

Dragos glanced back at Ivan. "Rolayna used one of your moves on Father Nikolas and threw him on his back. You must show me these skills sometime. I am interested in learning them."

The disciple chuckled. "At last, the master comes to the servant and asks to be taught." He bowed. "It will delight me to teach you all I know."

Dragos turned toward the keep. If the women were not ready, it would be too bad. He would wait no longer. "Inform me of any developments. I go to help my babe enter the world."

Ivan clapped him on the back. "Good luck. Birthing is not for the faint-hearted."

Dragos ignored his comments and did not think of it again until Rolayna entered her third hour of pushing. Weak and dizzy, she could no longer hold her own head up. Her long blonde hair stuck to her face. She gazed at him and begged for a sip of water, but he could not. Agatha ordered him from the birthing chamber the last time he gave her a drink. The water came right back up, and Rolayna gagged, her already weakened body convulsing.

Dragos smoothed her hair from her face. "I would do anything for you, angel, but I cannot give you that." He took a square of linen, dipped it in water, and held it against her lips.

She groaned and sucked the moisture from the cloth, gazing at him through pain-filled eyes as the midwife urged her to bear down.

"I see the babe's head," Agatha said. "Give us another push."

Rolayna shook her head. "I cannot...I have not the strength...I fear I shall swoon." Her voice grew faint. Tears spilled down her cheeks as her body shook and her legs trembled.

"Tell me what to do." Dragos gazed urgently at Agatha. He could not bear to watch anymore.

"Hold her up," the midwife commanded.

Dragos' boots hit the floor. He climbed onto the bed and sat with his back to the wall, his legs on either side of her. He pulled her back against his chest, wrapped his arms around her, and whispered, "Take my strength, my love. Lean against me and take from me what you need."

****

Rolayna closed her eyes. Dragos' words filled her soul. She relaxed against him and fell asleep from pure exhaustion. A minute later, the urge to push took control of her, and she gave every ounce of strength she could muster.

"You are doing good, mistress. Keep pushing. Keep pushing," Agatha chanted.

She gritted her teeth and pushed, not daring to take a breath. When the pain subsided, she fell back against Dragos shaking with fatigue.

"The babe has blonde hair," the healer chuckled.

Rolayna's eyes opened. "Can you see it?"

"Aye, one more good push, and you will be holding him in your arms."

She found a new source of energy, took a deep breath, and pushed until the room darkened around her. A few minutes later, the screams of the newborn baby filled the chamber.

Rolayna fell back against Dragos' shuddering with fatigue.

He held her gently as the midwife worked on the crying, wiggling baby in her arms.

"You have a girl, master. She is healthy and pink." Agatha chuckled as she held the babe up. "I thought 'twas a boy, but you have an angel to watch over you."

Dragos stroked his wife's face. "You honor me, love. Thank you." He kissed her cheek.

The old healer cut the cord and swaddled the babe. Then she placed her on her mother's chest.

Dragos picked the tiny infant up from his position behind Rolayna. He gazed into her beautiful metallic eyes. Blonde hair surrounded her heart-shaped face like a halo. She was a perfect blend of them both.

"Her name shall be Charmeine, for she is the bringer of harmony."

****

They held the christening a month later. Rolayna could stand for longer periods of time without tiring. They invited everyone. The Duke and Duchess of Emberly arrived a day early to show off their three-month-old son, Christopher. The events of the past were forgotten in the joy of the present moment. Christopher was a chubby, healthy boy with large brown eyes and brown hair.

Rolayna took him in her arms and held him close. "He is so handsome. What a delight he must be to you both."

Christina nodded. "He is a joy. I cannot believe he belongs to me. I am so happy. Sometimes I want to pinch myself to make sure it is real."

The Duke of Emberly cleared his throat. "I have a proposal I would like to present to you both." He nodded at Dragos and Rolayna. "I would like to propose the idea of affiancing our children. They will marry when they are the proper age. I suggest this as a token of our friendship and unity. This would ensure our loyalty, love, and forgiveness for each other. A bond between us, which shall last forever.

Dragos nodded. "A union of our children would heal all the wounds of the past. It is a good plan." He glanced at his wife. "But I have learned the heart cannot be forced. We shall make the plan but keep it wisely. If either of the children is not willing when the time comes, we shall reconsider. It is their happiness which matters most."

The Duke of Emberly nodded. "Agreed."

The castle filled with guests. Rolayna held her daughter close and smiled at everyone. The front door drew her attention as Josa entered the great hall.

Dragos frowned and motioned for Malphas to see her out.

Handing her daughter over to Gretta, Rolayna hurried over.

"Leave this place. You are not welcome here." Her husband stood before Josa with his arms folded over his chest, surveying her with hostility.

She stepped to his side and took Josa's arm in hers. "I invited her, Dragos. She saved my life in the woods and told me about Father Nikolas. I wanted her to come to the christening tonight. Josa is not a traitor and has apologized for her behavior. I would like to invite her back to the fortress if it pleases you."

He glanced from one to the other. "You want her to come back?"

Rolayna smiled at him. "Aye. She *is* your mother's younger sister, and we *do* have a responsibility toward her."

He nodded at Josa. "You may enter, but do not give me cause to regret it."

Josa curtsied. "Thank you, Dragos."

Rolayna led her inside and introduced her to the

baby.

Josa crooned and cuddled the infant in her arms. Her eyes filled with tears as she smiled up at her. "Thank you, Mistress. It is good to be home."

Rolayna nodded and surveyed the room, worried over the disciples' absence. Hound must not have found Father Nikolas, or he would be here. She kept a close eye on Alex as she visited with their guests. She would rest easy, only when they found the priest.

Her husband stayed by her side, and the other disciples patrolled the grounds. No one wanted a surprise.

Then, a commotion came from the drawbridge as the soldiers fired a warning and shouted for the master.

Dragos nodded at Malphas and Brawn. They took their places on either side of their mistress as he hurried outside. Shouting came from the courtyard before the oak door closed behind her husband.

Rolayna clasped her babe to her chest and kept her eye on the door. Dragos would stop any threat, but she could not help but be nervous.

The door to the great hall opened, and Ramiel motioned at her. "Come, the master would like you to join him."

Rolayna turned to Gretta, handed the babe to her, and took Malphas's arm. "Let no one near her."

"I shall keep our lass in sight, Mistress. No one shall touch her until ye return." Brawn took his place beside Gretta and braced his legs. He folded his massive arms and stared out over the crowd.

Rolayna hurried outside.

Malphas escorted her to Dragos where a crowd gathered at the drawbridge. They parted to let her through.

Her blood fell to her feet at the sight.

The Duke of Northernfell stood facing Dragos. His expression remained solemn. Father Nikolas knelt on the ground before them, tied with heavy rope. The duke held the end of the rope in his large hand.

Hound, Scimitar, and Azazel stood beside her husband, scowling.

He motioned for Rolayna to come to him, and she stepped to his side.

Malphas took his position on her other side.

Dragos stared at his uncle. "Repeat what you said to me so my wife can hear it, too."

The duke glanced at Rolayna. "I found this filth running through my fields. Dragos' men were hot on his heels. They were almost upon him, but he ran into me first." He pulled the rope taut. "I came to offer the priest as a token of peace."

He stared at his nephew. "I owe you an apology, Dragos. I accused you of betraying me with Dahlia." He glanced at Rolayna. "I considered what you said to me at Seville and questioned Dahlia's maid. Once I did, I discovered my wife had been unfaithful to me for years. I have searched out each of her lovers and exacted my revenge. Dragos is the only man among them who remained true to me. I have dealt with Dahlia and her betrayal, and she is now an outcast. I removed her from my lands, and she is no longer welcome in the north. No one will invite her in." He took a step toward them.

The disciples stopped him.

Malphas stepped in front of Rolayna with his hand on his sword.

"I came to apologize to you, nephew. I judged you harshly." Gregory dropped his head "I punished you because of Dahlia and her lies." His head came up. "I would ask for your forgiveness. I know an apology does not undo the torment and pain of the past. So, I captured the priest. I could have killed him, but I gift him to you as a peace offering." He held the rope out to Dragos.

"Take the priest to the dungeon. I shall deal with him later," Dragos commanded. His gaze never left his uncle's face.

Hound and Azazel left with a screeching Father Nikolas.

Gregory watched them go. Then, he turned to Rolayna, leaning to the side to see around Malphas. "I hear I have a new relative."

Dragos stiffened. "Thank you for delivering the priest. You may go." He waved his uncle away with his hand.

The duke stared at his nephew for several seconds and then drew his sword.

Dragos stood carved in stone, his expression impassive.

Gregory walked toward Dragos until he stood two paces away and placed the sword on the ground. He got down on his knees and took Dragos' hand. "I promise to be faithful to my lord, never to cause you harm, and to observe my homage to you against all persons in good faith and without deceit."

Dragos' eyebrow lifted. "You swear fealty to me at last. What caused you to change your mind?"

His uncle grinned. "Your wife and discovering Dahlia's lies." He chuckled. "I have been told I have a niece. Now, may I come in and see the babe?"

His nephew stared at him for several seconds.

Rolayna stepped around Malphas. She patted his arm to let him know she no longer needed his protection. "Come with me, Uncle. The child is inside." She tucked her hand in Gregory's arm and led him away, smiling at Dragos as she did so.

He watched them go. Nothing would be the same again. Charmeine proved an apt name. Christened after the angel who was the bringer of harmony, his daughter elicited it into his life. In the short amount of time since her birth, the babe reunited him with his uncle and forged a bond of alliance with the Duke and Duchess of Emberly.

Dragos followed his wife into the great hall and surveyed the scene. The Duke and Duchess of Emberly spoke with Rolayna and Gregory. His uncle sat stiffly in an armchair close to the fire holding Charmeine and grinning like a fool. Alex stood beside Azazel, listening to the men tell tales of their search for the missing priest. Father Bernard stood in the corner speaking with a smiling Josa. The disciples gathered with friends and family. The great hall filled with laughter, joy, peace, and love. His gaze met Rolayna's. She smiled at him, and it took his breath away. The christening proved successful. His family glowed with happiness, and he nodded with satisfaction.

There remained one matter needing his attention. Dragos nodded at Azazel and went to the dungeon to deal with Father Nikolas.

The priest sat on the narrow cot in his cell with a Bible in his hands. He glanced up at Dragos' approach. "Depart from me, Satan. Return to the depths of hell and remain there. I rebuke thee."

Dragos unlocked his cell door. "It is a strange religion which requires the sacrifice of women and children. I think you worship someone other than a god. Who is it, priest?"

Father Nikolas laughed hysterically. "I worship a god you will never know. Death, hell, and destruction are at your gates. You cannot escape it. Even now, the tempest gathers. Repent, lest ye be dragged to hell for all eternity."

His captor opened the cell door and stepped inside. "If the fires of hell are the ragged bits of the rebellion I found outside my gate earlier today, they are dead. The thousand soldiers wearing the rebel uniform are no more. The fires of hell are quenched." He walked toward Father Nikolas. "What now, priest? I contacted the bishop at Whitehall Abbey. He did not know who you were and had no recollection of your name."

The little man paused. "He lies. He trained me.'

"A bishop would know his student. I suspect you would be one not easily forgotten." He snapped his fingers, and a manservant appeared behind him. "In my search for you, I did find someone who knew quite a bit about you. This man served as Baron Oliveander's valet, Franklin. He gave me some interesting information."

Father Nikolas gazed at the man and took a step back.

"Franklin informs me your real name is Nikolas *Oliveander*, younger brother of Rauf Oliveander. You are no priest at all." Dragos drew his sword. "Franklin also spoke of several meetings you attended in the rebels' camp where you plotted Rolayna and Alex's death." Dragos walked toward the quaking priest, flexing his shoulders.

"Stop. It is forbidden to kill a man of the cloth. The manservant lies. If you kill me, you will be breaking a cardinal law."

Dragos nodded his head. "And I would be…if I killed a priest. But you are not." He lifted Rolyana's dagger. "A demon forged this knife and worked his magic into the blade. When I plunge it into your heart, your soul will no longer be yours. It shall belong to the devil for all eternity. Ramiel made this for my wife's enemies, so they understand who they deal with. It is justice your soul is the first to go, for you betrayed her more than anyone." The stones in the handle glowed when Dragos struck his heart. It was the last thing Father Nikolas gazed upon before he joined his brother in hell.

Epilogue

Rolayna stood inside the door of the great hall and gazed with wonder at the two sitting at the high table. Dragos, fifth Duke of Dragonthorne, Earl of Whitewater, keeper of the north, and her husband sat across the table from their five-year-old daughter, Charmeine, having tea. The fiercest warrior in the kingdom wore a sparkly crown on his dark head and a string of pearls around his neck. He held the delicate teacup with two fingers.

"Not like that, Papa. Like this." Charmeine picked up her teacup and extended her littlest finger, taking a delicate sip. "You have to sip the tea, not drink it, or you do it wrong." She brushed her golden hair from her face and sighed. "Again, Papa, again."

Dragos fumbled with his instructions. His fingers were too large to hold the handle the right way, and he drained the cup with one sip. He flushed in irritation. "I am trying, Daughter." He caught sight of Rolayna and smiled with relief. "Perhaps Mama can sip with you." He motioned for her to come to him.

Charmeine pouted. Her soft pink lip stuck out a half-inch. "You said you would have tea with me and Mr. Muffy." She indicated the wooden doll sitting on the chair beside her.

Dragos frowned. "Papa cannot do it the right way, Angel." He glanced around for an escape. "Maybe we could do something else with Mr. Muffy."

Rolayna laughed as she approached. "Darling, Papa has to go train with Alex now. You must let him attend to his duties."

The child's pout grew. "What about Mr. Muffy? He wanted tea."

She scooped the crown from Dragos' head and lifted the pearls from around his neck. "I think Mr. Muffy would like to be a knight. What if Papa knighted him for being such a good visitor for tea?"

The child's eyes grew wide. "Papa would make Mr. Muffy a knight?"

Dragos murmured a quiet "thank you" to his wife and faced his daughter. "I would."

Rolayna chuckled. Charmeine could get Dragos to do the most amazing things.

Alex entered the hall and strutted toward them. "Is Papa coming? I have been waiting for most of an hour."

She held her hand toward him. "He is. First, he must knight Mr. Muffy, and then he will come."

"Again?" The boy rolled his eyes and leaned against the table. He trained as a page and grew anxious for Dragos to show him how to clean and sharpen the many weapons he used. Alex had grown tall and lanky in the last five years.

"Shhh," Rolayna whispered. "Do not tease her, or Papa will not be able to come for some time. You know he is the only one who can calm her down when she gets upset."

Alex nodded and rested his chin in his hand. He said no more.

Dragos pulled the chair containing Mr. Muffy around to face him. He drew his sword and tapped the wooden doll on both shoulders. "I hereby knight you, Sir Muffy, knight of the realm and defender of the innocent."

Charmeine squealed and clutched the doll to her chest. Her dark eyes gleamed with adoration at her papa. "Thank you," she breathed.

Dragos nodded his head. He sheathed his sword and turned toward Alex. "Come along, Son. Let us see to the weapons."

He caught Rolayna in his arms when he rounded the table. "Do not breathe a word of this to the disciples. I will not hear the end of it."

She did laugh then and pointed toward the door. "They already know."

Dragos turned his head in time to see the backsides of his disciples as they scattered. Loud male laughter echoed from the entry hall.

"Dammit to hell," Dragos muttered.

"Nay," Rolayna answered. "Bless our home, for this is what it is." She smiled up at him.

And he had to agree. Dragonthorne was home, at last. The torment, enmity, and turmoil of the past disappeared along with the pain and hatred. All that remained was beautiful. His relationship with Gregory improved greatly over the last five years. His uncle now served as his trusted second. The Duke and Duchess of Emberly were frequent visitors. They shared an unbreakable bond of friendship between the four of them. The children, Christopher and Charmeine were suited to each other and played well together. His people flourished. No longer did he dwell in eternal darkness and torment. No longer did he dwell in hell. He lived in the sunshine of love and laughter. He had a son and two golden-haired guardian angels who made his life complete. It was as Rolayna said, a true home, and he could not be more pleased.

A word about the author...

I enjoy knitting, crocheting, and quilting. I love roses and the smell of gardenias. I have two large dogs who like to keep me company while I write. Beethoven is an Aussie/Great Pyrenees mix, and Mozart is a Mastiff/Collie mix.

I occasionally bake when the mood strikes me. Mostly I consider cooking and baking necessary evils.

My husband of forty years is my greatest fan/critic, and I don't know what I would do without him. My family is my greatest support, and I love every minute I spend with them. Life is a journey, and I can't wait to see where it leads me next!

Thank you for purchasing
this publication of The Wild Rose Press, Inc.

For questions or more information
contact us at
info@thewildrosepress.com.

The Wild Rose Press, Inc.
www.thewildrosepress.com

www.ingramcontent.com/pod-product-compliance
Lightning Source LLC
Chambersburg PA
CBHW070048030726
4750*6CB00002B/400

* 9 7 8 1 5 0 9 2 4 4 4 8 5 *